Freedom Rides
R. D. Gregory

Freedom Rides
R. D. Gregory

This book is a work of fiction. Names, characters, places and incidents are either products of the author's imagination or are used fictitiously. Any resemblance to actual events or locales or persons, living or dead, is entirely coincidental.

ISBN (pbk) 978-1-64467-797-1

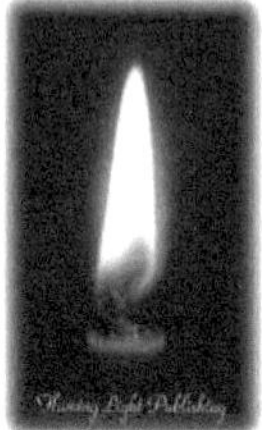

Flaming Light Publishing - A Division of Wonderment Records.

Freedom Rides
R. D. Gregory

Prelude

Deacon Reeves, works for the Balancer Detective Agency and is under contract with the government. He can get his contract released and have his freedom to ride. All he has do is find a missing senator's daughter and bring her back alive. His search for the girl lands him in the middle of a child slavery organization which leads him to Mexico. In his travels he crosses path with Rat Dobbs, a notorious outlaw, the man responsible for the death of the woman he loved.

Freedom Rides
R. D. Gregory

About the Author

R. D. Gregory grew up on a small ranch in Western Kentucky, where he started riding horses before he learned to walk. He was breaking and training horses as a teenager and started a multitude of colts through the years. He served his country in the United States Army and is a veteran of the Vietnam War where he served with the First Calvary Division.

Over the past ten years it became apparent his work with horses was not his only talent. When given the opportunity to work in film he excelled. He has shot several Country Western videos and received an award for his camera work in the award winning musical, "Dixie Burns." The film aired several times on DISH Network as well as Comcast.

His first published novel "Deacon Makes Four" was awarded Best Western Novel by the Pro Cowboy Country Artist Association in 2017. "Freedom Rides" is the second novel in the "Deacon series."

Freedom Rides
R. D. Gregory

Chapter 1

Deacon Reeves walked into the Balancer Detective Agency office in Denver, Colorado. He had been back from Texas less than a week; his report had been turned in and now he was to speak with Mister Howard Balancer concerning his conduct.

As he walked into the waiting room area Edith Smith, the secretary, looked up from her work at her desk. She was an attractive lady with auburn hair in her mid-forties. She smiled. "Good morning Deacon. Would you like some coffee, or maybe something stronger?"

He removed his hat. "Good morning, Edith. Coffee will do, make it black."

She walked to the coffee pot and poured him a cup, turning, she handed him the cup of steaming coffee. "Here you are. It's fresh."

He smiled. "Thanks. Is the boss in?"

"Yes, I'll inform him that you are here. Please take a seat."

He slouched down into a chair and sipped his coffee waiting for her return. The coffee was good.

Edith came back to her desk. "He will see you in a few minutes; he is reviewing your report."

Deacon frowned. "What kind of mood is he in?"

She shuffled some papers and looked up at him. "Sour."

Deacon grunted. "I was afraid of that." He drank the rest of his coffee while he waited. After finishing the cup, he stood and walked over to the table where the pot was and sat the cup down.

She looked up from her work. "You want more?"

"No thanks."

The door opened, and Mister Balancer stepped out. "Deacon, come into my office."

Deacon shifted his weight and moved his hat from his right hand to his left in expectations of shaking hands with his boss. Instead, he got a cold shoulder as the chief of the agency turned his back on him and walked back to his desk and sat down. "Shut the door and sit down."

Deacon did as he was instructed.

Mister Balancer looked at him for a moment before speaking. "Do the four of you think I'm a fool, or maybe a demented old man who can't find his way home?"

"No sir, why would you ask that?"

He held up a stack of papers. "These reports. If I was a betting man and I'm not. But if I was, I would bet that the four of you sat together and wrote these. Damn, they are almost word for word. Now tell me the truth, did you?"

Deacon shifted in his seat. "Sir, you must understand..." he was interrupted.

"A simple yes or no will do for now."

"Yes, but sir..."

"That is what I thought. Deacon, we can't have this. If for some reason any of our, and when I say our, I am referring to the agency. If any of our dealings go to court and these reports are called in question, they should not read alike. Each of you is to put down in your own words what transpired. Do you understand?"

"Yes sir, I understand. Sir, you've read my reports before and as you know I'm not real good at putting things down on paper. I, or should I say we, were only trying to make sure that our reports were accurate."

Mister Balancer held his hand up to stop him. "Deacon, you had no authority to call in Luke and the rest. Explain to me why you did this without clearing it through me first."

Deacon squirmed in his seat like he was sitting on hot coals. "Sir, I didn't have much time to waste. Things were heating up in Greenbrier and all hell was about to break loose. It won't happen again."

"It best not. Fortunate for you they weren't needed on another case at the time or your ass would be back in prison. I can't have you running around fighting your own personal battles. You work for me."

"Yes sir."

"So, why did you get involved in a range war? You were sent to arrest and bring back McManus."

"Yes sir, and we did that. May I speak freely?"

"Please do."

"You sent me to Greenbrier knowing it was my home town. I think you wanted to see if I would come back. Well, I came back, and I will keep coming back each time you send me out. But don't expect me to turn a blind eye. Those people there in Greenbrier are my family and they were in trouble. The sheriff, as you probably know, is my brother. McManus and his cowboys almost killed my younger brother. I could not ride away from that."

"You could have informed me of what was going on and I could have gotten the army involved."

"Yes sir, and by the time the army decided to get there my family would have been dead. I didn't have time to wait."

Mister Balancer got up from his chair and walked around his desk and leaned against the edge of it in front of Deacon. "Okay, now tell me about Rat Dobbs." Deacon shifted in his chair. "Leroy Dobbs, better known as Rat is a murdering low life. Colonel McManus hired him to fight his battle for him, to run the sheepherders off the range so he could expand his operation. He had somewhere around a dozen men riding with him. They were killing the sheepherders and burning them out."

"And the four of you took it on yourselves to stop these murders?"

"That's right. We did have some help from the sheriff and other folks."

"Which resulted in a gun fight in town and cost a young woman her life."

Deacon looked at the floor. "Yes sir, and for that I am truly sorry." He looked back up at Mister Balancer. "We rode after them, but they gave us the slip. When we came back to town he had doubled back and had taken over the town. He was burning it down. Which is what I think was his plan all along. It's not the first time he has burnt a town and killed most everybody in it."

"But, you let him get away."

"Yes, I did."

Mister Balancer took a deep breath and looked out the window for a few seconds. He turned back to Deacon. "Why didn't you go after him?"

"I did for several miles. He shot a cowboy on the trail and took his horse. He had a fresh mount and was riding into Apache country. Plus, this cowboy was going to die if I didn't get him back to town to the doctor."

"If that had been your wife and child that Rat had killed you would have ridden into hell after him and let that poor cowboy bleed to death. Isn't that right?"

Deacon's face got red. He had no right to bring his wife and child into this. Deacon stood, when he did Mister Balancer stood to his full height of five feet and ten inches and looked up at Deacon. "Tell me I'm wrong if you can."

Deacon looked at the smaller man who was old enough to be his father. "Mister Balancer, you have no right bringing my family into this. That is past, it's gone. I'm not that man anymore."

Mister Balancer smiled. "I know you're not, I wanted to hear you say it. Now sit back down so we can get on with our conversation."

Deacon took a deep breath and sat down.

Mister Balancer went to his chair and sat down. He opened a drawer and pulled out a photograph and slid it across his desk to Deacon. "This is a photograph of a young lady who is missing."

Deacon eased up from his chair and took the photograph and looked at it as he sat back down. "Who is she?"

"Her name is Anita Bennet. She has been gone now a little over two weeks and the local authorities have gotten nowhere. Her parents want her found."

"Where does she live?"

"St. Louis."

Deacon shifted in his chair and gave his boss a questioning look. "Doesn't the Agency have people in St. Louis, why aren't you using them?"

"We do, and we are. But I need you on this one. Deacon you have certain skills of finding people. You have proved that in the past. I'm not sure what is going on, but I think you will be the person I need on this job."

Deacon looked at the photograph again. "How old is this girl?"

"Sixteen."

He looked up. "Maybe she doesn't want to be found. Maybe she ran off with her feller."

"That could be. I don't know, all I know is they want her back alive. Deacon, Mister Marcus Bennet is a Missouri senator, a very influential man. He will do whatever it takes to get his daughter back. If you can bring her back alive the contract with you and the State of Colorado will be fulfilled. You will be a free man to do and go wherever you please."

Deacon looked at Mister Balancer in surprise and disbelief. "How... how can that be?"

"I told you Senator Bennet knows people. He and I worked this deal up and the Governor of Colorado has agreed. Deacon, she has to be alive when you bring her back or there is no deal."

"I see. But why... why did you do this? You have me over a barrel. You know I don't want to go back to prison. So why did you make this deal?"

Mister Balancer walked to the window and looked out at the street. He turned and looked at Deacon. "I know what you did, and I understand why you did it. It wasn't right, but I don't blame you. You have been with me now, what, three years and you have changed. You're still withdrawn and a loner for most part, but I see something in you."

He took a deep breath and walked over to where Deacon was sitting. He stood beside his chair and looked down in to Deacon's eyes. "You have the coldest eyes I have ever looked into. But down there deep in your soul is a warm and caring person who wants to be let loose. I can't be responsible for keeping the real you from coming out. And I believe by my holding this contract over you the real you will not come out. I have done all I can do to get that contract released. Now it is up to you."

Deacon stood and extended his hand to Mister Balancer. "Thank you."

Mister Balancer took his hand and smiled. "Your train leaves at six tomorrow morning. Take the photograph with you. Go see the senator; he will have information for you. Good luck. I'll see you when you get back."

Deacon turned to leave.

"By the way Deacon, you will need traveling money; see Mrs. Smith, she will give you a bank draft. If you need more send a wire."

Deacon nodded. "Thanks."

Chapter 2

The train clattered to a stop and Deacon made his way to the door. His few belongings were tucked away in his saddle bags hanging across his right shoulder. His rifle was in his right hand leaving his left hand free in case, for some reason he would need to pull his Colt. He wasn't expecting trouble but in his line of work trouble could come from anywhere at any time. He stepped off the train and onto the platform; he paused and looked around.

St. Louis was hot this time of year and he was thirsty. He also wanted a bath and a good meal, not necessarily in that order. As he started to walk toward the street, he heard a woman scream and saw a young boy running toward him with what looked like a woman's purse. As the boy ran past him, he grabbed him by the shirt collar, stopping the boy in his tracks.

"Whoa up there, young man. What's the hurry?"

The boy was struggling to get away from his captor. He swung at Deacon with the purse. "Let me go, mister." He kicked Deacon in the shin. "I said let me go."

The pain from the blow to his shin caused Deacon to hop around a little, but he didn't turn the boy free. "Son, you do that again I will whip you as if you were mine. Now you settle down."

At that moment a middle-aged woman with a heavy-set man came running up. The man could hardly breathe and was sweating profusely. "Thanks, mister. That little brat stole my wife's purse."

Deacon looked at the boy. His clothes were ragged, and he needed a bath badly. Deacon frowned at the boy and shook his head, indicating for him to be quiet. "I think you are mistaken, sir. The boy didn't steal the purse; he found it and was on his way back to return it. Isn't that right, son?"

The boy looked at Deacon and then to the man and his wife. He held the purse out to the woman for her to take. "Yeah, that's right I was returning it."

The woman took the purse. "I saw him take my purse. He is a thief, and he should be punished."

Deacon smiled at the lady. "Now, madam." He looked down at the boy. "Do you really think that this boy would steal anything... I mean, look at that face."

She looked at the boy. He had a sheepish look on his face, then he smiled at her. She frowned at him and looked at Deacon. "I think he should be turned over to the authorities."

Deacon took a long breath. "You got your purse back; check it to make sure everything is there."

She checked her purse. "Yes, everything is here."

"Good. You have your belongings and I have the boy. You go your way, and I will go mine and everything will be okay. Let's not make a big deal out of this. Okay?"

The woman gasped and took a step back. Her husband started to say something and decided against it when he looked into Deacon's eyes. He took his wife by the arm as he turned away. "Let's go, dear."

The boy grinned at Deacon. "Thanks, now let me go. I got places to be."

"Not so fast. What's your name?"

"Tadpole, I'm called Tadpole. Now will you turn me loose?"

"I'm not turning you loose till you promise to help me. I've never been here before and I need somebody to show me around. I'll pay for your service."

"How much?"

"Fifty cents a day."

"Make it sixty and you got a deal."

Deacon turned the boy loose and held out his hand to shake on the deal. Tadpole spat in his hand and shook hands with Deacon. "You got a name, mister?"

Deacon smiled. "Yeah, I'm called Deacon." He handed the boy his rifle. "Now take me to the Court House, I need to speak to the sheriff or whoever is in charge over there."

"Are you going to turn me in?"

"No. I'm here on business and they have some information I need. So, lead off, Tadpole."

The streets of St. Louis were busy as they made their way to the court house. Tadpole looked up at Deacon when they were standing in front of the three-story building. "This is as far as I go. The police station is on the first floor. You need to talk to the Chief of Police, I'm guessing. His name is Aaron Atkins."

Deacon took his rifle from the boy. "Why aren't you going in with me?"

"Me and the cops don't get along real good. It would be best if I wait for you out here."

"If you say so. I may be a while; stay put and stay out of trouble. I still need your assistance." He ruffled the boy's hair and walked into the court house.

As he entered the building he took notice of the different office doors till he found the one that read Chief of Police. He opened the door and a policeman looked up from his desk. "Can I help you?"

Deacon removed his hat and walked to the desk. "Yes, my name is Deacon Reeves and I would like to speak to Chief Atkins."

"May I ask what it is retaining to?"

"Anita Bennet."

"I see. One moment." He got up from his desk and

went to a door to the left of the room. He knocked and opened the door. "Sir, there is a Deacon Reeves here who wishes to speak to you concerning Anita Bennet."

Chief Atkins came to the door. He looked Deacon over noticing the rifle and the Colt on his hip. "Mister Reeves, please come in."

The two men shook hands and Deacon sat in a chair across from the chief's desk. Chief Atkins went back to his chair; and as he sat, he looked at Deacon. "Mister Reeves, I am going to have to ask you to not wear your pistol or go around packing a rifle while you are in the city. As you may have noticed, this is not the Wild West anymore and the good citizens of St. Louis expect the police force to keep them safe. It makes our job easier if everyone is not packing firearms. You do understand, don't you?"

"Yes, I understand. But in my line of work, I would hope that you understand that I need my firearms to protect myself and possibly my client."

"And what kind of work is that, Mister Reeves?"

"I am employed by the Balancer Detective Agency. I am here by request of Senator Bennet to locate his daughter."

Chief Atkins folded his hands, on top of his desk. "I see."

"I came to see you as soon as I arrived in town in hopes of gaining as much information as I could before I went to see the senator. I understand that the police force looked into her disappearance."

"Yes, two of my best men made inquiries. The results of their findings were that she has left town with a young man who is also missing."

"So, you think she ran off with this young man to parts unknown?"

"We do. I explained that to the senator."

"So, as far as you are concerned the case is closed?"

"Yes, the case is closed. If his daughter wants to run off with her boyfriend, there is nothing I can do about it. There is close to a hundred thousand people in this city. People come and go. There is no way the police force can keep up with everybody. I'm sorry that the senator's daughter is missing, but when she left the city she became someone else's problem."

"Then, you will have no problem with me looking into her disappearance?"

"No, not as long as you don't break any laws." He looked at the rifle and then at Deacon's side arm. "Again, Mister Reeves, I must ask that you surrender your Colt and the rifle while you are in St. Louis."

"Chief, how about I take it to the hotel and place it in the safe there? I may need to leave town, and I wouldn't want to have to come back here to pick it up."

The Chief of the Police smiled. "I can live with that. But let me warn you, if you are caught wearing that side arm, you will be arrested and placed in jail."

Deacon opened his coat to reveal the gun in the shoulder holster. "What about this one?"

Chief Atkins laughed. "Mister Reeves, I like you and I am going to allow it. I trust you will be discrete?"

Deacon smiled. "Of course, always."

Chief Atkins took pencil and paper and wrote something down. When he finished, he stood and walked around the desk to where Deacon was now standing. He handed him the paper. "Keep this on you, if any of my police officers question you concerning the shoulder gun, show them this."

He took the paper and placed it in his pocket. "Thanks."

As the two men walked out into the hall there was a commotion taking place at the entrance of the building. A police officer was dragging a complaining Tadpole up the hall. When the officer saw the chief, he came to where he and Deacon were watching. "Look who I found lurking around across the street."

The chief frowned at Tadpole. "What are you up to, boy?"

Tadpole was flailing his arms trying to break the officer's hold on him. "I ain't done nothing, honest. Now turn me loose!"

Deacon cleared his throat. "He's with me."

Chief Atkins looked at Deacon in wonderment. "What is he doing with you?"

"I hired him when I got off the train to show me around town."

The chief shook his head. "Deacon, may I call you Deacon?"

"Yes."

"He is trouble, with a capital T. You'd be better off wandering the streets by yourself."

Deacon smiled at Tadpole. "I'll take my chances with him."

"Okay, but don't say I didn't warn you."

"Thanks again." He took Tadpole by the back of the shirt. "Come on Trouble." They walked out into the street.

Chapter 3

When the two of them arrived at the Green Palace Hotel Deacon stopped. "I'm going to get a room and freshen up. You go home, clean up, and change clothes. Put on the best you have and meet me back here in the lobby at five."

"Why do you want me to clean up?"

"We are going to get a bite to eat and then we're going to see Senator Bennet."

"What are we going to see him for?"

"Just do as I say. I'll explain later. Now go."

After the two of them had eaten at the restaurant in the hotel they walked out into the street. During the meal and the small talk, Deacon found out that Tadpole's real name was Theodore Zimmerman. His mother had died during child birth of his younger brother. His dad worked at the docks, when he wasn't drunk, which was most of the time.

Deacon hired a man with a buggy to take them to the senator's house, which was a large estate setting on a bluff overlooking the Mississippi River. As they got out of the buggy at the senator's house he looked at Tadpole. "Tuck your shirttail in."

He looked down the long trail back toward the business section of St. Louis. "Driver wait for us, I'll make it worth your time."

"My pleasure, boss. Take your time; as long as you're paying, I'm staying."

A doorman let them in and escorted them down a hall to a large study. Deacon pointed to a chair not far from the door of the study. "You sit there and wait for me."

Tadpole went to the chair and sat down with a frown

on his face. Deacon smiled at him.

Senator Bennet and his wife met him as he walked into the room. "Mister Deacon Reeves, I believe?"

"Yes sir." They shook hands.

"Mister Reeves, I appreciate you coming so quickly. I do believe that time is of the essence. You come highly recommended by your employer. Please be seated. Would you like something to drink?"

"Whatever you have will be fine."

"I have some of the finest Kentucky bourbon; or if you prefer, I can offer you a beer bottled right here in St. Louis by the Budweiser Brewing Corporation."

"Bourbon will be fine. What can you tell me about your daughter's disappearance?"

Mrs. Bennet spoke up as her husband was pouring drinks. "She and a friend of hers were going to the theater. She never came home. When we spoke to her friend, we found, that in reality Anita had slipped off with a male friend behind our backs. According to Rachel, Anita's friend, she had been seeing this boy for some time. They would go off to the park and take walks by the river."

Deacon took a sip from his drink. "You said park, where and what is a park?"

Senator Bennet smiled. "A park is an area set aside in this case by the city. It can't be sold or used by any business and the city maintains the grounds. There are fountains and seats and walkways where people can go to enjoy nature."

Deacon rubbed his jaw. "So, it's got no real purpose?"

Mrs. Bennet laughed. "Of course, it does. People work hard and sometimes they need a place where they can go to relax."

Deacon shook his head. "If you say so. Now tell me

about this boy your daughter was seeing. Chief Atkins seems to think that your daughter and this young man ran off together. Is this possible?"

Senator Bennet set his glass down on a large mahogany top desk. "Atkins is an idiot. He is taking the word of two of his officers. Okay, I'll admit I'm not real happy with the idea of my sixteen year old daughter slipping off to be with this boy. But, I do not believe she ran off with him."

"What is his name and where can I find him?"

The senator dropped his head and looked over his wire rim glasses at Deacon. "He is missing, also."

"I see." Deacon took a drink from his very good glass of bourbon. "Senator, Mrs. Bennet, from the information so far, I am inclined to agree with the police."

"I knew you would. But that's not all of it. None of her clothes are gone, except for what she was wearing. She had no money and we have not heard from her. I have talked with the boy's parents and it is the same with him. They just disappeared."

"Tell me about the boy."

"He comes from a well-respected family. His name is Richard Kelly. They own and operate Kelly's Hardware store here in town, nice people."

"You have no problem with the boy seeing your daughter then?"

"Hell yes, I have a problem with it. He's at least eighteen or nineteen years old. He's too old for my daughter to be keeping company with."

Deacon looked from the senator to his wife. "Mrs. Bennet give me your gut feelings on this. Do you think she and the boy ran off? Either way makes no difference to me. I only need to know which way to start looking if

I'm going to find her."

Mrs. Bennet walked toward Deacon. He stood as she approached. "Ma'am, tell me."

She placed a hand on his arm. "Mister Deacon do what you have to do to find my daughter. My gut feeling, as you called it, tells me she is still alive. I don't think she ran off with that boy; but if she did, find her and bring her home. I wasn't much older than her when I started keeping company with my now husband. Love can make a person do things that a rational person would not normally do. She is in danger. I can feel it."

"Yes ma'am. I'll do what I can." He turned to the senator. "Sir, how much, how can I put this? If I get in trouble with the police can you help me?"

"Anything short of murder. The judge and I are card playing buddies, and he owes me a few favors."

The three of them walked out into the hallway that led to the door. Tadpole stood, ready to leave. Deacon stopped and glanced around. He looked at Tadpole and frowned. "Put it back."

Tadpole looked into Deacon's eyes. He reached into his shirt and pulled out a small figurine. He looked at Mrs. Bennet who was now frowning at him and placed the figurine back on a table where he had taken it from. He turned and walked toward the door.

Deacon spoke to him. "Theodore, come back here, and apologize to Senator and Mrs. Bennet."

Tadpole stopped. Deacon had never called him Theodore. He turned and walked back in front of the senator and his wife. Looking at the floor and in a low voice he said. "I'm sorry."

Deacon placed his hand in the middle of Tadpole's back and nodded to the senator and his wife. You will be hearing from me. Let's go Theodore, we got work to do."

Chapter 4

On the way back into the city Deacon's thoughts were on the girl and the young man. Had the two of them run off together, or was there something else going on? He thought about all the steam boats he saw tied up along the banks of the river. Two young people with wild ideals could probably get a job on one of those passenger boats.

"Driver take me to the docks."

The driver turned around and looked at Deacon. "Are you sure you want to go down there? It's going to be dark before long and that's not a good place to be after dark."

"We'll be fine, won't we, Tadpole?"

Tadpole didn't answer. Deacon noticed a touch of fear on his face.

When they reached the docks, he paid the driver as he got out of the buggy.

"You want me to hang around?"

"No. I don't know how long I'll be."

Tadpole looked around. "Mister Deacon this ain't a good place to be. There are some mean sonofabitches that hang out here."

"You stop using that language."

"But there are."

"Tadpole, if I wanted to know what was going on around these docks, who would I need to talk to?"

"That would be Big Joe. There ain't nothing that goes on around these docks that he don't know about."

"Where can I find this, Big Joe?"

"My guess would be in that beer joint over there."

"Okay then. Let's go talk to Big Joe."

"Are you sure you want to do that? He's the meanest

sonofa… He's mean."

Deacon smiled at him. "I'm meaner."

As they walked into the bar everybody turned to look at the cowboy and the kid. "Point him out to me."

"That's him over there, the big one."

Deacon looked at the big baldheaded man sitting at a table in the corner. He was at least six-two in his early to mid-forties. He would weigh at least two hundred eighty pounds. He had a barrel chest and his bare arms were almost as large as Deacon's legs.

Deacon walked up to the table where Big Joe was sitting with two other men, the man never looked up. "I'd like to speak to Big Joe… Alone."

Big Joe nodded for the other two men to leave. As they stood, their chairs scraped across the wooden floor. They gave Deacon a hard look. He smiled back at them.

Deacon sat down across from Big Joe. "I understand that if I want to know anything about the docks that you are the man to talk to."

Big Joe took a drink from his beer. "Who are you and what do you want?"

He pulled the picture from his pocket and showed it to Big Joe. "My name is Deacon and I'm looking for this girl."

Big Joe glanced at the picture. "Never saw her before."

"Take a closer look. She is the daughter of Senator Bennet."

"Like I said, never saw her."

"Do you know anything about her disappearance?"

"Nope."

Deacon stood. "Thanks for your time." He and Tadpole walked out into the street. Tadpole looked up at Deacon. "What now?"

"We wait. He knows more than he wants to tell." They walked over and stood in the shadows where they could watch the entrance of the bar. After a few minutes Big Joe came out and walked toward the docks. Deacon walked up behind him, he pulled his gun and stuck it in Big Joe's back. "Don't turn around, just keep walking."

Big Joe slowed his step. "What do you want, mister? I ain't got much money, but you're welcome to it."

"I don't want your money. Just keep walking."

When they reached a blacksmith shop Deacon looked through the open door. An older gentleman was laboring over a forge and anvil.

He poked Big Joe in the back with the gun. "In here."

As they entered the shop the man looked up from his work. "We're closed. Come back tomorrow."

Deacon took five dollars from his pocket and handed it to the man. "I need to borrow your building for a few minutes."

The man looked at the money and then at Deacon and Big Joe. He took the money. "What's going on?"

 "Never mind what is going on. As far as you are concerned, we were never here."

There was a set of long handle hot metal tongs lying on the anvil. Deacon took them and swung them around striking Big Joe across side of his head. The blow hit Big Joe in the temple in front of his right ear. He fell to the ground unconscious.

The older man gasped. "My God man, you've killed him."

"He's not dead, yet. Come here and help me." The two of them dragged Big Joe over to a support post and sat him against it. Deacon then took rope and tied his hands behind him. He then took rope and made a loop around the post and Big Joe's neck. The rope was long enough to reach a nearby post and end up back in front of Big Joe. He then poured a bucket of water in Big Joe's face. He turned the bucket upside down and sat down on it in front of Big Joe.

Big Joe gasped for air and tried to move. When he realized he was tied to the post he started cussing at Deacon. "Mister, you have made the biggest mistake of your life. I'm going to kill you real slow."

Deacon pulled on the rope that was around Big Joe's neck. He started struggling to breath. Just before he passed out Deacon eased up on the rope.

"Do I have your attention now?"

Big Joe cleared his throat. "Yeah. What do you want?"

Deacon took the photo of the girl from his pocket. "Where is she?"

"Hell man, I done told you, I don't know."

Deacon pulled on the rope. "Wrong answer."

Big Joe started gasping for air and just before he passed out Deacon released the rope, so he could get a breath of air. Deacon knelt beside him. "Joe, where is the girl and the boy she was with?"

Big Joe looked up into Deacon eyes. "Man, I told you, I don't know, I really don't. You can choke me all night, and I'll keep telling you the same thing, because I don't know."

"What do you know?"

He looked away from Deacon. "Nothing."

"Joe, you are lying to me now." He stood and walked over and picked up a three-pound hammer. As he walked back, Big Joe was watching him.

"What are you going to do?"

"I'm going to bust your knee cap. You'll heal from it, but you will walk with a limp for the rest of your life." He raised the hammer.

"No please don't. I'll tell you what I know."

Big Joe took a deep breath. "If they find out I talked to you they will kill me."

"Who will kill you?"

"Stanley Crawford. He runs the docks, and he has some of the police force on his payroll."

"Is the chief on his payroll?"

"No, I don't think so, he's as straight as they come."

"Tell me about the girl."

"She was a mistake. But once she was grabbed, they couldn't turn her free."

"Who took her and for what reason?"

"Crawford's goons, she is to be taken to Mexico and sold to some big shot."

"Why do you say she was a mistake?"

"Those guys don't usually grab girls of a good family. It makes people ask too many questions. A couple of Crawford's cops covered it up. They made it look like she ran off with that boy."

"What happen to the boy?"

Big Joe shrugged his shoulders. "Not sure, but I figure he's floating in the river as fish food."

"Okay, back to the girl. How do they get the girls to Mexico?"

"By steamboat. They pick up girls all down the river from what I've been told. They drop them off somewhere down river. Then they load them on to wagons and take them across country into Mexico. Look man, I've told you all I know. I don't know all the details, and I don't want to know. As far as I'm concerned, what they're doing is as about as low as a man can get. I've done some pretty bad stuff in my days, but there is no way I would take part in grabbing these young girls and selling them to them damn Mexicans."

Deacon untied the rope from around his neck. "Big Joe, I'm going to turn you loose. But we're not finished talking. I'm sorry for having to be so rough, but I needed answers and I needed them fast."

"What makes you think I will talk to you after you turn me free?"

Deacon grinned. "Big Joe, I think you would like to see this taking of these girls stopped. I intend to do just that. And I think you will help me."

"You're one crazy sonofabitch. You almost killed me and now you want me to help you."

"You got the idea."

With Deacon's help, Big Joe stood after he was released. He walked over to a tub of water and stuck his head in it. He washed the blood from his head and face and turned toward Deacon. He grinned at Deacon. "Now what's going to keep me from ripping your arm off and beating you to death with the bloody end?"

Deacon laughed. "Me. I'll kill you, and you know I will."

Big Joe laughed. "You would to, wouldn't you?" He shook his head and smiled. "You're a crazy sonofabitch."

Chapter 5

Deacon gave Tadpole a dollar and sent him home with instructions to meet him the next day at the hotel cafe at seven. He and Big Joe left the blacksmith shop and walked down to the docks to a secluded spot where they could talk and not be seen or heard. Big Joe gave Deacon names and dates of things that had transpired in the past.

Deacon took a long breath and looked the big man in the eye. "Why haven't you gone to the police with this before now?"

"Hell man, don't you think I wanted to? I don't know who to trust. If I say something to the wrong person, I'll be floating down the river like a dead catfish. You don't mess around with these people."

"Big Joe, I'm in a bad spot here. I would like to stay and weed these bastards out, but I can't. I got to go after the girl. If they get her all the way to Mexico, I'll have hell finding her down there."

"How do you plan on finding her?"

"The only way is to get on the next boat going down river. They will have to go to ground at some point and when they do I'll be able to follow them to where they are holding these girls. And with a little luck I'll find the girl I'm looking for."

Big Joe nodded his head. "Okay, I can help you there. I got enough pull with the captains that I can get you on a boat. Give me a couple days."

"I don't have a couple of days. I need to be going down river as soon as possible."

"I know that, I'm trying to get you on just the right boat."

"I don't care what kind of boat it is, If there is a boat

leaving sometime tomorrow I need to be on it."

"Okay, okay, I'll see what I can do. Meet me at the bar tomorrow, say around nine."

"I'll be there."

Deacon left Big Joe and walked back to the street. As he neared the bar he decided to step in and get a drink before he went to his hotel. He entered the smoke-filled room and walked up to the bar.

"Barkeep give me a shot of rye."

The bartender set a glass on the bar and poured him his drink. Deacon picked it up and shot it down. He placed the glass on the bar. "Again."

As the bartender was pouring, Deacon heard someone walking up beside him. He turned to look at the man, he was drunk.

The man leaned against the bar and looked at Deacon. "Mister, where's Tadpole?"

Deacon picked up his drink and looked at the man. "Who are you and why are you asking about Tadpole?"

"I'm his father and he didn't come home. I was told that he was seen with a cowboy and you're the only one I see. So, what have you done with him?"

"I sent him home over two hours ago."

"Well mister, he didn't make it, and it's your fault."

Deacon took a deep breath and drank the rest of his drink. He slammed the glass on the bar; the place grew quiet and everybody was looking at him. He looked around the room at the rough looking crowd of dock workers.

"I've been in this town less than twenty-four hours and what I've found out disturbs me. There are things going on here on these docks that you men should have put a stop to long ago."

One of the men stood and walked up to him, sizing

him up as he got closer. "Who the hell are you?"

"The name is Deacon, and that's not important. The important thing is that young people are being taken and are never heard of again. Why haven't you men stopped it?"

"We're not the law."

"So, because you're not the law you turn a blind eye to what's going on around you?"

"It don't concern us. If we don't do as we are told, we don't work. We have to feed our families."

"That's well and good, but what about the families of these missing children, and what is happening to these kids?"

"Mister, I think it would be a good idea if you mind your own business."

"I'm making this my business as of right now. One of your own has been taken. Tadpole is missing and with the help of you men we can find him before he is harmed."

The men in the room started talking among themselves. At that moment Big Joe walked into the room and looked around the room. He stopped when he got to Deacon. "What's going on?"

Deacon walked up to him. "Tadpole is missing; we need to find him tonight, right now. These men know these docks better than anyone. They will know where to look. Get them to organize a search party and let's find this kid."

Big Joe nodded his head. "Okay men let's do this. I want every corner of these docks searched. Check the warehouses, allies, backstreets and houses. Let's go find this boy."

Deacon watched as the men filed out the door. He turned to Mister Zimmerman. "You go home in case

Tadpole shows up there and sober up."

Without a word the man staggered out the door.

Big Joe was watching two men standing in the street. "Deacon, you see those two out there?"

"Yeah."

"Let's me and you keep an eye on them. I may be wrong, but I think they may know something."

Deacon turned to the bartender. "Give us another drink."

After their drinks they walked out into the street and watched the two men as they rounded a corner into an alley. They followed at a distance and saw them enter a big warehouse down near the river.

Big Joe took hold of Deacon's arm to stop him. "That's one of Crawford's warehouses. He keeps them locked so nobody can get in."

While they were talking, a man came out of the ware house and walked up the street. He mounted a horse and rode out of town.

"Well, it looks like somebody had a key. I think we need to get in there and see just what Mister Crawford has in there that is so important that he has to keep it locked up."

"Yeah, me too. Let's go this way, come on."
Deacon looked back up the street; he could see men with lanterns going from building to building. He smiled. "I think with a little encouragement these men may shut Crawford's slave trading down."

"Yeah, but at what cost. Some of us may lose our jobs and maybe our lives."

"Life isn't worth living if you have to live in fear all the time."

"True. Come on cowboy; let's go kick some ass."

They sprinted across the alley and up to the warehouse door. Deacon eased the door open and the two slipped inside. They could here men talking in the distance but couldn't see anything. There were barrels and crates stacked everywhere and very little light.

"Joe, I can't see a damn thing."

"Me either, but there is a reflection from a lantern over there. Come on."

"Yeah, I see it. Lead the way."

They eased around a stack of crates and about thirty feet away could see two men. One of the men was holding what looked like Tadpole by the arm.

"Look kid, we ain't going to hurt you if you tell us what this Deacon feller knows, and how he found out about the operation."

Tadpole glared at the two men. "I ain't telling you fish shits nothing."

"You sure are a stubborn little brat."

Tadpole kicked the man in the shin. "Let me go you mule's ass."

The man slapped Tadpole across the face, knocking him down.

Deacon started out from behind the crates when Big Joe pulled him back. "Not yet."

Deacon glared at him. "I can't abide him hitting that kid."

Tadpole rolled over and wiped the blood from his lip. "Mister, you just made the biggest mistake of your life."

"Why's that kid?"

"Cause, when Mister Deacon finds out that you hit me, he is going to work you over good."

"Is that right?"

"Yep. He's the meanest man I ever knowed. And he can whip you with one hand tied behind his back."

The man laughed. "Problem is son, this Deacon ain't

here and you ain't going to be around long enough to tell him."

Tadpole stood up and grinned. "That's what you think, dumb ass."

The man drew his hand back to hit Tadpole again. It was stopped in midair; as he turned, he got a glimpse of Deacon before his eyes were closed by Deacon's right fist.

Deacon looked at Tadpole. "Theodore, what did I tell you about that cussing?"

"Sorry."

Big Joe had the other man by the throat and pushed up against a stack of crates. "Want me to kill this one?"

"No, we will turn them over to the police."

Chapter 6

Deacon squatted down so he could get a better look at Tadpole. "Are you okay?"

"I am now that you are here. They tried to get me to tell them what you know and who told you. But I didn't say nothing."

Deacon smiled. "You did real good; you are a brave young man and I am proud of you."

"Mister Deacon, I think they were going to kill me. I knew you would come for me, but I was scared that you wouldn't make it in time."

"Well, I did and now it is time to get you home. Your father is worried about you."

"Yeah, I bet he is. All he cares about is where he is going to get his next drink."

"Tadpole, no matter what you think, your father still loves you. I'm sure it's not easy raising a family without the help of a woman around. So, you need to help him all you can."

"Okay, Mister Deacon."

Deacon stood and turned to look at Big Joe. "We need to get these two to the police station, but first we got to get him home."

Big Joe pushed the man he was holding to a sitting position. "You sit right there. Deacon I'll go get a couple of men to escort master Tadpole home. Then the two of us will take these two to the police station."

"Are you sure you want to be seen with me at the police station?"

"You're right. It's time we did something about Crawford's operation." He turned and walked toward the door.

Tadpole looked at Deacon. "I can get home by myself.

I don't need nobody to hold my hand."

"Anybody… I don't need anybody to hold my hand."

"That's what I said."

"I would prefer someone went with you tonight. It's not safe."

A few moments later they heard someone come into the warehouse, and they watched Big Joe and two police officers walked around the corner of a stack of crates. When Tadpole saw who it was, he bolted and ran behind the crates and out the door before anyone could get hold of him.

Deacon was surprised to the point that he failed to notice the guns the police officers were pointing at him till he turned back to look at Big Joe.

"What's going on?"

Big Joe grinned as he walked toward him. "Mister, you got to learn not to be so trusting of folks you don't know."

In the dim light from the lantern, Deacon saw the big fist coming but he couldn't get out of the way of it. The blow hit him and knocked him back against the wall and to the floor where he lay unmoving. Big Joe leaned down close to Deacon's ear. "Stay down, and don't move."

Tadpole ran outside and hid in the alley till he was sure no one followed him. He then slipped back and looked through a crack in the wall where he saw Big Joe and the two police officers. They and the other two men were arguing over what to do with Deacon.

Big Joe walked over and picked Deacon up on to his shoulder like a sack of potatoes. "I'll take care of him. And don't worry about the boy. He ain't going to say anything; he's too scared."

The man that Deacon had hit rubbed his jaw. "Let me

kill him, I owe him anyway. He about broke my jaw."

Big Joe headed for the door. "I'll deal with him. The way that river is running right now he will be half way to New Orleans by day light."

Tadpole watched from a distance as Big Joe and the others left the warehouse. Something had to be done or Deacon was going to be fish bait.

He ran home as fast as he could. When he burst through the back door he could see his father slumped over the kitchen table. "Pa... Pa, wake up, Pa."

He shook him, but it was no use his father was passed out drunk. An empty bottle was laying on the table beside one of his hands. He picked the bottle up and threw it across the room. "Damn you, Pa. Why can't you be there for me just once?"

He ran out the door and back to the docks. He looked everywhere he could think of trying to find Big Joe and Deacon. As he came from an alley down by the river, he saw Big Joe pushing a big cart headed toward the river. He followed him down to the river and watched as Big Joe dumped the contents of the cart into the river. He then picked up a hat and threw it in the river.

Tadpole teared up and started running toward Big Joe. He paused long enough to pick up a piece of driftwood. Big Joe was still watching the river when Tadpole hit him in the back with the piece of driftwood. "What the..."

He turned to see Tadpole drawing back for another swing. "Hold up little buddy."

Tadpole in anger yelled. "You killed him. Why did you kill him?"

Big Joe took hold of the boy and dragged him back toward the docks and into an alley without a word. Tadpole was screaming the entire time. "Why did you kill him? Why? Why did you kill him? He was my friend."

Big Joe took him by both shoulders and squatted down in front of him. When he did, Tadpole kicked him in the shin.

Big Joe grimaced. "Would you be quiet for a second and stop kicking me; it hurts."

Tadpole snarled at him. "I aim for it to hurt. You killed Mister Deacon. I wish I could kill you."

"Now listen and stop fighting me. Deacon is not dead."

"But... but I saw you dump his body into the river."

"That's what I wanted anybody who might be watching to think." He grinned and stood up. "Now follow me and keep quiet."

They slipped through the back alleys and ended up down by the stockyards at the rear entrance of the slaughter house. Deacon was sitting against the back wall holding a piece of beef steak to his bruised eye.

Tadpole ran to him. "I thought you was dead."

Deacon smiled at the boy and rubbed his head. "I'll be okay." He looked up at Big Joe. "I will say this though; Big Joe does have a wicked right cross."

He started to get up, as he did Big Joe took him by the arm to help him. "If you are up to it, you need to go the hotel and get your stuff. Stay in the shadows as much as possible and come back here."

"Okay, where's my hat?"

"I threw it in the river, along with that side of beef. If anyone was watching, they had to think that you are now gone forever. Now slip in there, grab your stuff and get back here. Without being seen."

"Okay. I'll be back in about an hour. I'll meet you here."

He reached in his pocket and pulled out some money.

He squatted down in front of Tadpole and handed him two dollars. "Tadpole, thank you for your help. Now, I want you to go home. Stay away from the docks till this is over. You've seen faces that you shouldn't have seen. Those people are going to be looking for you. You have to stay hid. Will you do that for me?"

"But, Mister Deacon I can help."

"You can help by staying safe till these bad men are caught and behind bars."

"Okay, Mister Deacon. Are you coming back?"

"Yes, I will be back in a few days."

"Promise?"

"Yes, Tadpole, I promise."

He took the money and Deacon stood and patted him on the shoulder. "Now go home."

He turned and looked at Big Joe. "Here in an hour."

Big Joe nodded. "I'll be here."

Chapter 7

Deacon made his way to the hotel and was back with his stuff in a little over an hour. Big Joe was waiting for him.

"Come on; we've got to get moving. I've arranged a ride down river for you. It will be daylight soon and you need to get on the boat."

Deacon nodded. "Let's go."

The two of them eased through the back alleys and walked up the gangplank to the "*Betsy Ann*."

The captain of the boat was waiting for them as they boarded. He was a short man with a big barrel chest. His hair was gray as was his beard. His left arm was off at the elbow and he had two fingers missing on his right hand. He was dressed in a dark blue jacket with big brass buttons and a small cap that set to one side on his snow-white hair.

He greeted Big Joe with a toothy smile. "I see you made it. This the gentleman that needs a ride down river?"

Big Joe nodded his head. "Yep, but he ain't no gentleman. This is Deacon."

Deacon shook hands with the captain. "Pleased to meet you, Captain."

As the captain shook his hand. "Most folks call me Stumpy. Lost this arm in the war from a Yankee bullet. Welcome aboard, we will be shoving off in about thirty minutes."

Big Joe stepped up closer to Deacon. "You be on the lookout for a boat called "*Naomi*." I found out that she went down river with a questionable cargo. The girl you're looking for may be on that boat." Big Joe turned to leave. "See you in a few days, Deacon; and thanks,

Stumpy, I owe you."

The captain turned to walk toward the bow of the boat. "Follow me, let's get you settled in."

Deacon followed the man down some narrow and steep steps to a small room. There was a cot, a chair and a small table in the very small room. Hanging from the ceiling was an oil lantern for light. There were no windows in the room, and it smelled musty.

Stumpy lit the lantern. "It's not much, but it's the best I can do. I'll have the cook bring you something to eat after we get under way."

Deacon smiled at the man. "This will do fine. Right now, I just want some sleep."

Stumpy stepped out of the room. "I'll leave you to it then. I'll come back and check on you in a few hours." He closed the door as he left.

Deacon sat down on the cot. His mind was racing with thoughts of the day. He looked around the small room. "I sure hope I don't have to spend much time in here. I'd go crazy or smother to death."

He blew out the lantern and lay back on the cot. At least in the dark he didn't feel so cramped. He closed his eyes and drifted off to sleep.

He woke from the sound of someone knocking on the door. He could hear the sound of the engine humming, as it turned the big paddle wheel, and the waves hitting the sides of the boat. As he stood he bumped his head on the lantern that was hanging from the ceiling. He rubbed his head and made his way to the door in the dark.

Stumpy was standing at the door when he opened it. "Thought you might be hungry, so I brought you a sandwich from the galley. You can eat here or come up top."

"I think I'll go up top to eat. I'm feeling mighty cramped in this room."

Stumpy nodded his head and smiled. "I understand. Come on up. We'll go to the wheelhouse."

As they climbed out on to the deck of the boat Deacon had to squint his eyes from the sun. In the wheelhouse he sat down and looked out down river. "Sure is a mighty big river."

"Yes sir, she is. And dangerous too. They call her the Mighty Muddy Mississippi."

Deacon looked at the sun. It was high in the sky. "How long did I sleep?"

"Bout' five hours."

"How far have we come?"

"We'll be at Cairo before dark."

"Is that a fact? Lot faster than horseback."

"Yeah, going down river is pretty fast coming back up ain't so easy. Got a lot of current to fight going north."

The captain opened a cabinet door and took out a bottle and two tin cups. He held the bottle up toward Deacon. "Care for some Kentucky sour mash. Guaranteed to cure what ails you, ifn' it don't kill you first."

Deacon smiled. "Don't mind if I do." He walked over and took the cup.

The Captain poured the drinks and set the bottle down. "Down the hatch." He then drank the cup empty and made a face.

Deacon watched then took a sip. He had drunk better whiskey, and he had tasted worse. He sipped on the drink and made small talk with the captain as they made their way down river.

As they neared Cairo the boat started slowing. The

captain watched as the man at the wheel navigated the sharp turns in the river. He turned to Deacon. "The docks for Cairo are on the Ohio; it dumps into the Mississippi just up ahead. We will have to turn and go up river a little way before we dock. We have some cargo to off load and then we will be on our way again. Normally I would lay over here till morning, not wanting to travel at night. But due to the urgency of your needs, I will make an exception."

"I appreciate that."

The boat made its way up the Ohio River and eased up to the docks at Cairo, Illinois.

"If you're hungry, there is a nice little cafe down the street yonder. We should be ready to pull out in about two hours."

Deacon nodded to the man as he stood. "Thanks, I'll be back. Just don't leave without me."

"No sir, I won't."

Deacon walked down the gangplank and toward the street. The air was filled with a pungent order. He walked on toward the street and to May's Cafe. He stopped as he entered the small building and looked around. The place was crowed but not overly. He walked to an empty table and sat down. The aromas coming from the kitchen smelled delicious. The sandwich he had around noon was long gone and his stomach was starting to think his throat had been cut, he was so hungry.

A young black lady walked up. "What'cha want, mister?"

Deacon looked at her. "Well, I'm not sure. What do you have?"

She cocked her head to one side and took a long breath, patted her foot on the floor as she looked toward the ceiling. "We got beef roast, pork roast, steak, taters, fried chicken, okra, gumbo, corn on the cob, and all kinds of pies and cakes." She smiled.

Deacon smiled at her. "I'll have the pork roast and a slice of apple pie and a cup of coffee."

"Be right back."

Shortly she returned with a hot cup of coffee and set it on the table in front of him. "Here's yer' coffee, be back dreckly with yer' food."

"Thanks."

The coffee was strong, just what he needed.

His meal arrived, and the lady refilled his cup from a coffee pot that she held with the folds of her apron to keep the handle from burning her hand.

He finished his meal and drank the last of the coffee in his cup. As he set it down, there she was again with the pot. He placed his hand over the cup. "No more, I'm done, thank you very much."

She frowned at him. "Supposed to turn the cup upside down if'n you don't want no more. That way I don't make a trip to the table fer' nutin'. You got any idee' how many steps I make in a day toten' this pot around?"

Deacon smiled at her. "No ma'am, but I would think it would be several."

She nodded her head. "It shore nuff is." She turned and walked away.

He paid for his meal and left a tip on the table. As he walked out the door he looked back; the lady was picking up the tip. She smiled at him. He smiled at her and started down the street toward the docks.

As he passed a saloon, he decided to have a drink and pick up a bottle of rye to take with him. He walked to the bar and the barkeep looked him over. "What's your poison?"

"Give me a bottle of your best rye."

"I only got one kind. It's the best I got and the worst I got. So, you're getting two in one. Maybe I should charge double." He laughed.

"That will do fine."

The barkeep placed the bottle on the bar. "That'll be four dollars."

Deacon laid the money on the bar. "I think you just did." He turned and walked out and turned towards the docks.

Chapter 8

As Deacon walked up the gangplank of the *"Betsey Ann"* he noticed another boat had docked not far away. It wasn't the *"Naomi"*, so it didn't concern him. Captain Stumpy was leaned against the rail smoking a cigar and drinking some of his sour mash when Deacon boarded.

The captain nodded to Deacon. "You get your belly full?"

"I sure did. Good grub."

"I told you so."

Deacon held up the bottle of rye. "You care to join me?"

"Sure, but I can't just now. Go by the galley and grab some cups, meet me in the wheelhouse after we get under way."

Deacon nodded and walked off. He went by the galley and retrieved two tin cups and proceeded to the small room that were his quarters. He opened the door, allowing what little light there was to show him the way into the room. He set the cups and the bottle on the table and lit a match that he had taken from his vest pocket. With his other hand, he pushed the lever down to raise the globe, so he could light the wick.

As the lantern lit, he felt the muzzle of a gun barrel press hard into his back. At the same time the door closed to the room.

"You stand real still, mister."

Deacon held his position as the man took his pistols and placed them in his belt. "Now, turn around, real slow."

Deacon turned and took a long look at the two men in the room. He had never seen either of them before.

"What do you want?"

"We got what we want. You."

Deacon looked from one man to the other. "Me, what do you want with me?"

Both men had their guns out, and they were pointed at Deacon. One of them waved his gun toward the cot. "Sit down."

Deacon did as he was ordered. "Back to my question, what do you want with me?"

One of the men smiled, showing stained teeth. "Seems that while you were in St. Louis, you stirred up some shit. We followed you so's we can put a stop to you. You are way over your head in this cowboy. Which, by the way, is where you will be once this tub gets under way." He smiled. "You are going to take a little swim, never to be seen or heard from again." Both men laughed.

Deacon leaned back on the cot with his back against the wall. "If you knew that I wasn't already dead, what has happened to Big Joe?"

Both men laughed. "Now that is the funny part. He has been charged with your murder. He's sitting in jail right now waiting for his trial and then hanging." They laughed even harder.

"I told you cowboy, you are way over your head in this. This outfit is bigger than you can even imagine. But you don't have to worry about it. Because, you ain't going to live much longer anyway."

One of the men took the bottle of rye and pulled the cork. He poured some into each cup. "Sure was mighty nice of you to bring us something to drink."

Deacon frowned. "Didn't bring that for you, and I'm going to be plenty upset if you drink it all."

"What's it matter? You're going to be dead in little while anyway."

"Okay, since I'm going to be dead, and you are drinking up my whiskey, tell me about this outfit. Who's running it; how does it work? Where are these kids taken, and how are they transported?"

At that moment they could hear the captain calling out orders to his crew as they prepared to pull away from the dock. The boat started moving.

The man closest to Deacon smiled. "Won't be long now. All we got to do is wait for most of the crew to bed down, and then you will take your swim."

One of the men took the only chair and placed it by the door and sat down. He looked at the other man as he took a sip of the whiskey. "Amos, don't tell him nothing."

Amos turned his cup up and drank the contents. "I ain't. Not that it would matter, cause, he's going to be dead in a little while anyway. And dead men don't talk." He laughed.

Deacon picked his right foot up and placed the heel of his boot on the edge of the bed. He pointed at the bottle. "I paid good money for that bottle. The least you could do is let a dying man have a drink from his own bottle."

Amos looked at the bottle, then at Deacon. He picked the bottle up and poured some in the cup he had set on the table. He handed the cup to Deacon as he pointed the gun at him. "I'll keep the bottle."

Deacon took the cup. "Thanks." He took a small drink.

Amos eased back to the table and placed one hip on the edge of the table. He took a long drink from the bottle.

The other man was watching. "Amos, Take it easy on that bottle."

Deacon smiled at the man. "Yeah, don't drink it all. I'm going to want some after I kill the two of you."

Amos cocked his pistol and pointed it at Deacon's face. "I could just shoot you right now."

"You could. But if you did, you would never get off this boat alive. There is only one way out of this hole we are in and when you pull that trigger that door way is going to be full of *"Betsey Ann"* crew members. They will take you apart. So, we both know you ain't going to pull that trigger."

"He's right Amos. Don't shoot him just yet."

Amos lowered the hammer on the pistol and took another long drink from the bottle.

Deacon smiled at him and took a sip from his cup. "You going to tell me about this outfit?"

Amos took another long pull from the bottle. "What'cha want to know?"

"Keep quite Amos. Don't say another word."

"What's it going hurt; he's going to be dead in a few minutes anyway?"

Deacon asked him again. "Who's in charge?"

"Amos, keep your mouth shut. Don't tell him!"

Deacon looked at the other man, then at Amos. "Well, who is it?"

Amos took another drink. He held the bottle up like he was saluting someone. "That would be none other than the mighty Stanley Crawford."

"Damnit Amos, I told you to be quiet."

Deacon took a sip from his cup. "I think I knew that already. Where do they unload the kids, how far down river?"

Amos' brow tightened; he was thinking. "It's just the other side of Memphis. Don't know the name of the place."

Deacon looked at the other man, who was shaking his head back and forth. "How do they move them across land and where do they take them?"

"How else, by wagon."

"How many men?"

"Depends, sometimes four, sometimes more, but never less than four."

Amos took another drink from the bottle.

Deacon sat on the bunk thinking about what he had just learned. The other man got up and took the bottle from Amos. "You are an idiot. If Crawford finds out you told him this he will kill you himself."

How's he going to find out. I ain't going to tell him, are you?"

"I should, but I won't. I like you, Amos, but you got a big mouth; and it's going to get you kilt one of these days."

Chapter 9

Deacon sat on the cot watching the two men, waiting for his opportunity. It came quicker than he expected. The door burst open and Captain Stumpy came barging in. "I thought…" he didn't get to finish what he was about to say.

Both of Crawford's men turned toward the door. Deacon pulled his knife from his boot and threw it into the heart of Amos as he sprang from the cot. He grabbed Amos before he fell and pulled his pistol from his belt. The other man turned and shot at Deacon hitting Amos in the back. Deacon fired and hit the other man in the heart. He was dead before he hit the floor. Deacon let Amos down on the floor. He too was dead.

Captain Stumpy took a drag off his cigar and let the smoke out. "I hate the smell of gun powder and blood." He looked into Deacon's eyes and pointed his cigar at him. He cocked his head to one side and squinted one eye. "I thought me and you was going to have a drink. And here I find you been having a party without me."

Deacon looked around on the floor for the bottle. He picked it up and looked at the contents. "Just about enough for each of us to have one drink."

Captain Stumpy nodded. "Now, best I can tell here, you three didn't get into a fight over a card game. So, what started this ruckus, politics or religion?"

Deacon laughed. "Neither. These two were sent to kill me."

The captain looked the two over and shook his head. "To bad for them. Like I said I hate the smell of gun powder and blood. Grab them two cups and that bottle, let's go to the wheelhouse. I'll send someone down to clean this mess up."

Deacon bent down and picked up the dead man's hat that was lying on the floor. It wasn't what he would prefer to wear; but since Big Joe had thrown his into the river, he needed something. He placed it on his head. It would have to do till he could do better.

As the two men entered the wheelhouse, the captain pointed to a chair. "Take a seat; now tell me why those two wanted you dead."

Deacon placed the cups on a small table and uncorked the bottle. He poured the remaining contents of the bottle into the cups. He set the bottle down and picked up the cups. He turned and handed one to the captain. "I have uncovered a slave trade. The head of this monster lives in St. Louis and is a powerful man. But he made a big mistake when his men took Senator Bennet's daughter."

"Let me guess who this man is, Stanley Crawford?"

"How did you know?"

"I always thought that he wasn't someone to trust. He seemed to be doing some pretty shady deals. I suspected he was running guns or something, but I never thought about slaves. Hell, the war is over. No one is buying nigger slaves anymore."

"Mexico is."

"Mexico?"

"Yeah, but not like you are thinking. They are buying white girls for sex and young men and children to work the silver mines."

The captain sipped his drink and shook his head. "That's terrible. Why ain't something being done about it?"

"I'm not sure. All I know is I was called in to find the senator's daughter and stumbled into this. Now there are people in danger because I figured out what was going on."

"How so?"

"I got some information from one of those men before he met with his final fate. For one thing, Big Joe has been arrested and is going to be tried for my murder."

"But you're not dead."

"I know that, and you know it, but the authorities in St. Louis don't. And I'm sure that when the trial starts there will be plenty of witnesses that will testify against him."

"Then you need to go back and set things right."

Deacon shook his head. "I wish I could, but I can't."

"And why the hell not?"

"I got to go find those kids. He will have to sit in jail till I can get back to St. Louis."

"What if you don't get back before he's hung?"

Deacon drew in a deep breath and let it out. "I have to. That is just one more reason for the urgency of this mission. I have to locate those kids and get back to St. Louis before it's too late to save Big Joe."

Chapter 10

The captain turned and looked down the river. "We got to find the "*Naomi*" soon. "

He turned back to Deacon. "Did those men give you any information to where these kids were being off loaded?"

Deacon nodded his headed. "Yeah, one of them said it was a place just the other side of Memphis."

Captain Stumpy took a long drag from his cigar and let the smoke out slow, while he looked at the floor. He looked up at Deacon. "I know the place. It's not some place I would normally dock. And it's not some place a stranger would live very long."

"I'll take my chances; you just get me there."

The captain walked over to the man who was at the big wheel. "Can you navigate the river at night faster than this?"

The man spat amber into a bucket at his feet. "You bet I can, Captain. I know this river like the back of me' hand."

"Okay, take her up."

"Yes sir."

The captain walked back to where Deacon was sitting and pointed toward the east side of the river. "You see that bluff up there?"

Deacon turned and looked out the window. The bluffs he was looking at were high and straight down to the river. "What about them?"

"This is where I lost this arm. Did you serve during the war?"

Deacon took a sip from his cup. "Not really."

"I don't understand, either you did, or you didn't."

"I stayed out of it till close to the end and then I

started a one-man campaign against the union. One group in particular; the ones who killed my wife and child."

By the dim light from the oil lantern hanging nearby the captain looked into Deacon's eyes. Deacon was staring back at him. The captain decided not to push the issue. "Anyway, as I was saying, here is where I lost my arm."

Deacon looked back toward the bluff. "Want to tell me about it?"

"I'd love to. I want to hear it myself. It was September of '61, General Leonidas Polk, who was also known as the Bishop of Louisiana, brought his forces from Tennessee to occupy the heights at Columbus, Kentucky. He also established a camp at Belmont on the Missouri side of the river. The rest of that fall and winter close to nineteen thousand men worked day and night, making Columbus, Fort DeRussey, impossible to overrun."

Deacon listened as Stumpy relived those days of the war.

Stumpy smiled as his thoughts took him back. "We took river steamers and made gun boats out of them. A huge chain, a mile long was floated across the river on log rafts tied off to two big sycamores on the Missouri side and a huge anchor held it on the Kentucky side. A capstan allowed the anchor to be raised and lowered to allow boats to cross. The links of that chain were almost a foot long and six inches across. That anchor weighed close to six ton and was nine feet from point to point."

He looked at Deacon. "We owned that damn river. Nothing was going up or down that river unless we let it. There were a hundred and forty cannons setting up there, and one on them was the "Lady Polk," named in honor of General Polk's wife. She weighed eight ton, had a rifled barrel, and could fire a cone-shaped projectile for three miles."

He shook his head and turned to look out the window. "We dug trenches, filled corn bags with sand, and built bunkers. General Polk, Pillow, Cheatham, and McGrown were there with us day and night digging those trenches. There were bombs called torpedoes made from cast iron placed in the river. They would be exploded by a wire that was floating below the service of the water if hit by a boat. Them things would hold up to two hundred pounds of gun powder."

Deacon cleared his throat to get Stumpy's attention. "Did the Union forces try to take Columbus?"

Stumpy laughed. "Oh, hell yeah, they tried, and we sent them running with their tails between their legs." His countenance saddened. "But not without a price. A lot of good men, from both sides, died."

He paused and walked over to a cabinet and took down a bottle and poured himself a drink then poured some in Deacon's cup.

"Grant had already seized Cairo, Illinois, and Paducah, Kentucky. He needed the Mississippi open so union supplies could be transported down river. He brought his forces in on the Missouri side and took Belmont. Polk sent troops and artillery up the east bank to reinforce his troops. Colonel Cheatham landed with reinforcement and attacked Grant. Grant's forces were trying to silence the guns from the bluff but couldn't stop them. Grant retreated with heavy losses. Rumors have it that as they loaded the river boats in retreat that he was almost left behind."

"I was commanding one of the gun boats. We were doing our part to help out. That's when I took a bullet in this arm. It ended up getting infected and ad to come off.”

“I heard that the heat from firing the Lady Polk during that battle caused the barrel to expand. It was left loaded and four days later when it was fired, it exploded. It broke into three pieces, killing eleven men and wounding twenty more.”

“Did the Union ever take Columbus?”

“Yeah. In 62 Fort Henry on the Tennessee River and Fort Donelson on the Cumberland was captured by the union opening the rivers for union supplies to be transported south. After that, Polk was ordered to evacuate Columbus, which resulted in the opening of the Mississippi River to the union as well.”

Deacon thought on this for a moment. “That had to be a major turning point for the union side.”

“Yeah, it was.”

Deacon stood and walked to the door. “I’m going down in to that hole and try to sleep.”

“Sleep well, I’ll wake you if anything comes up.”

Chapter 11

Anita Bennet sat in the bottom of a wagon, her wrists bound with iron shackles. Her knees were pulled up close to her chest. She was hungry, thirsty, and dirty. Her auburn hair that normally hung in perfect curls was now dirty and lay in tangled ropes. The beautiful powder blue dress that she was wearing when she was abducted was torn and filthy.

She looked at her hands, her wrists were bleeding from the scrapes caused by the shackles. Her hands were dirty and her perfectly manicured nails were now broken and dirty. She looked around at the other captives that were in the same predicament as she. There were ten all total; four others were in the wagon with her and five more were in another wagon.

Her boyfriend, Richard Kelly, lay in the bottom of the wagon unconscious. He had just been thrown into the wagon by two men.

She could tell by his shallow breathing that he was still alive. She eased over to him and with the hem of her dress she wiped the blood from his face and mouth. Tears ran down her face. His lip was split, and he had a cut over his eye. "Richard, Richard, wake up, please wake up. I need you; please wake up. I can't do this alone." She started crying harder.

Richard coughed and then moaned. He looked up at Anita. "I think they busted a rib this time. I can hardly breath." He grinned at her.

She wiped her tears. "Oh Richard, I thought they had killed you for sure this time. Please stop fighting with them; you can't win. There are too many of them; and they will kill you if you keep this up."

He struggled to sit up, and with her help he managed

to sit and lean against the side of the wagon. "Yep, they busted one of my ribs."

He looked at the others in the wagon, three girls and one boy. "Somehow we have to escape. If we don't our lives won't be worth living. As for me, I would rather be dead than to have to live where we're going."

Fifteen-year-old Cindy spoke up. "Do you know where they are taking us?"

He looked at her pretty blond hair. "Sadly to say I know where you are going. I heard my pa and a man talking the other day in the store. They didn't know I was listening. This man told pa that young girls were being taken to Mexico and made to be whores."

They all looked at each other. Cindy started crying.

Anita slapped him on the leg. "You shouldn't have told them that."

"Look, we got to get out of this mess. We need a plan."

Anita looked around at the others. "How do you think that we, as young as we are, could develop a plan to get away from these men? This obviously isn't the first time they have done this. They watch us like hawks."

"I know, but we have to get away somehow."

The wagon had started moving and did so till after dark. The passengers inside tried to ignore the fact that they were thirsty and hungry. The wagon stopped, and the tailgate dropped down.

In the dim light from the moon and stars, they looked at the man who was holding them captive. His name was Red Harding. He stood a little under six foot and weighed close to two hundred pounds. His red curly hair hung over the collar of his grimy gray shirt. His beard was darker than his hair, could have been because of the tobacco juice that stained it. He rarely went without a wad of chewing tobacco stuffed in his jaw.

He spat in the dust. "Get out. We'll be spending the night here."

As Richard got out of the wagon, Red took him by the shirt collar. "Boy, you try to run again, and it will be the last time you ever run. You're worth a lot of money to me but I'm tired of your shit. If you try to escape again, I will cut the back of your heel." He spat, and amber ran down into his beard. He didn't bother to wipe his mouth. "That's how we stopped our niggers from running off. Now get over there and sit down."

Richard looked around at their surroundings as the others climbed out of the wagon. It was an abandoned homestead, the barn, house, smokehouse and work shed were still standing but in bad need of repair. One of the men went into the house and he could now see a light through the window.

Red pushed him. "You kids go into the house."

As they walked in, the other man inside pointed to a back room. "In there."

Richard and the others filed into the room. It was dirty and smelled of rats and mice. The floor was covered with rat droppings. Anita turned to the man who was building a fire in an old cook stove. "Can we at least sweep this floor before we have to sleep on it?"

The man closed the door on the stove and stood to look at her. He turned without a word and walked to the corner of the room and picked up an old homemade broom. He tossed it to her. "Knock yourself out; and when you finish that room you can do this one."

One of the smaller girls, Glenda, tugged on Richard's shirt. "I gotta pee."

He glanced over at the man. "What about it. We been bouncing around in those wagons for hours. We all could use a trip to the outhouse."

The man went to the door and looked out. "Ain't got no body to watch you just now. Everybody is busy taking care of the horses and stuff. You'll have to wait a little while longer."

"But I can't. I got to go now."

He turned and gave the girl a hard look. "I said you'll wait."

She started crying.

"Oh hell, come on." He walked to the back door. "You go to the outhouse and I will stand right here so I can watch you and them. Now go and be quick about it."

She went to the door and looked toward the outhouse which was about thirty feet away. "It's dark; I don't want to go out there by myself."

Anita spoke up. "I'll go with her."

"No, she goes by herself; I can't trust you to go out there. You might decide not to come back. Now go if you're going; I got things to do."

Glenda pouted and looked toward the outhouse. She started running to it and went inside. The door slammed shut and few seconds later she started screaming.

Chapter 12

The man watching the children pulled his gun. He turned to them. "Stay Here!"

He ran to the outhouse and jerked the door open. Glenda was laying on the floor going into convulsions. There were also two Copperhead snakes, one was crawling over the top of Glenda and the other was coiled, ready to strike. He shot the one coiled; and as the other made its way clear of the child, he shot it.

The children in the house had gathered at the door and were watching as Red and the other men came running around the corner of the house. One of the men picked the girl up and started toward the house with her.

Red holstered his revolver. "Lou, what happened?"

The man looked at Red. "She said she had to go."

"And you let her go by herself?"

"Boss, I had no choice. The rest of you were busy. I stood at the door, so I could watch her and the others at the same time. I had no idea that there were snakes in there."

Red turned and went to the house. As he entered the room, he looked first to make sure the rest of the children were all there. They were. He walked to the table where they had laid the girl. She was breathing but barely. He noticed a bite on her neck, one on her hand, and another on her leg.

He turned and pointed a finger at Lou. "You got two choices. You find me another girl, or she comes out of your pay."

"Boss, that ain't fair. It wasn't my fault."

"Not your fault, who was watching them when she got snake bit?"

"I was, but I didn't know there were snakes in there.

And besides, she ain't dead."

Red turned and looked at the girl lying on the table. "No, but she soon will be. She may have lived through one of them bites, but there ain't no way she is going to live through three of them."

Some of the children started crying. Anita went to the girl. "Isn't there something we can do?"

One of the men shook his head. "I don't think the best doctor in the country could do anything for her. That bite in the neck took that poison straight to her heart and to her brain. I'm surprised that she has lived this long." He turned and walked out the door.

Red turned to Anita. "You know how to cook?"

"Yes."

"Good, help Lou here whip up some grub. And get this girl off our eating table. Let her die somewhere else." He walked out the door.

Richard watched him walk out. "I swear I'm going to kill that cold-hearted bastard."

Lou looked out the door and then turned to Richard. "Be careful boy; words like that will cause you a lot pain."

Richard's steel blue eyes burned into Lou's. "I mean it. Somehow, some way I'm going to kill him."

Lou smiled. "Better men than you have tried; best thing you can do is walk a wide path around him. That is if you want to live."

He picked the girl up and lay her on a make shift bed in the other room. He checked her breathing. She was gone. He took an old blanket that was lying nearby and covered her.

"I'm sorry darling. I didn't know there were snakes in there, honest I didn't. Besides you are probably better off, considering where you were going."

After everyone had eaten their fill of pork roast,

beans, potatoes and biscuits. Red pushed his plate back and looked at the other men in the room. "Lou, you, Jed, and Baxter take that dead girl out back and bury her before you turn in."

He looked over his shoulder where the kids were crowded into the small room. "You kids go to sleep; we will be pulling out early."

The next morning after everyone had eaten they were ushered outside to the wagons. The wagons had canvas stretched across wooden bows to protect the contents from the weather and also to conceal what was in the wagon from prying eyes.

Richard looked around at the men that were guarding them. He had learned their names, except for the two that had joined them when they got off the boat. They were the ones who were driving the wagons. He helped the girls into the wagon and climbed in behind them. "We got to get out of this mess."

After about an hour of jostling around in the wagon he looked out the back. The second wagon was following about twenty feet behind them. Lou was riding a horse to the left of that wagon. He eased over so he could see if he could see Jed and Red. They weren't at the back of the wagons. He got up and made his way to the front of the wagon. He could see Red in front of the wagon leading the way and Jed was riding on the right side of the wagon.

He stuck his head out the opening over the seat. "Hey, can I ride out here on the seat?"

The man driving the team elbowed him in the mouth. "Get back in there and sit down."

Richard fell back into the wagon. He rose up and rubbed his jaw. "I'll take that as a no."

Jason, the other boy in the wagon glared at him.

"What did you see out there?"

"They are watching close. There is no way to get out of this wagon without being seen. We'll have to wait and watch for another chance. If we can just get one person out, they can go for help."

"Maybe we can slip away at night while they sleep."

Richard looked at his hands. His wrist was bleeding and hurting. He shook his head. "I don't know. Whoever runs had better get away. Because, if they're caught, it won't be good for that person."

"You giving up?"

Richard glared at him. "Hell no, I ain't giving up. We got to get away. And it looks like if we do, it will be up to us. There is no one looking for us. If there had been, we would have been rescued by now."

Chapter 13

The *"Betsy Ann"* eased up toward the west bank of the Mississippi River. A gang plank was laid so Deacon could go ashore. Captain Stumpy stood watching with a cup of coffee in his hand. Deacon, we ain't seen nothing of the *"Naomi."* Are you sure this is where you want to get off?"

Deacon set his coffee cup down and looked up at the sky. The morning sun was making its way over the top of the trees. "Stumpy, I don't know. The man said it was a little ways past Memphis; that's all I got to go on. Only thing I know to do is get off here and ask around. Maybe somebody knows something."

Stumpy frowned. "Don't envy you none at all. From what I hear, this place can be dangerous, especially for strangers. You watch your back."

Deacon turned to walk away. "Thanks, Stumpy, I'll do that."

He made his way off the boat and walked a short distance to the edge of the small town. Not much was going on at this early hour of the day. He looked for a livery stable; he needed a horse. At the far end of town, he could see what might be a stable, so he strolled down the street. He could feel the hair on the back of his neck raising. Someone was watching him. He checked his gun on his left hip and slid the thong from the hammer, just in case.

He walked up to the corral fence and placed his saddle bags over the rail, propped his rifle against a post, and looked at the horses in the corral. Not much to pick from. Then he noticed a claybank standing in the shadows. He slid through the rails and eased over to him. The horse watched him as he walked around. He never raised his head, but his ears followed Deacon.

He was a palomino with a dark stripe down his back that ran into his white tail, which caused a dark streak in the tail. His legs up to his knees were the same color as the stripe down his back. His mane was white; other than that, he had no other markings. There was no brand to indicate that he belonged to any ranch hand.

Deacon placed one hand on the horse's neck and the other on his nose. The horse raised his head slightly. "Easy boy, I'm not going to hurt you."

He looked in the horse's mouth; he looked to be a six-year-old. He patted the horse on the neck and walked around him. He was in good shape, pretty head and ears; his legs were straight, wide in the shoulders and big in the hips. He looked like he could run if called on. As he turned to walk away, the horse followed him to the rail.

An older gentleman came from the stable as he was climbing the rail fence. "Looks like you made a friend, stranger."

Deacon smiled and glanced at the claybank. "Is he for sale?"

"Sure is, if you can stay on him." He stuck his hand out to shake hands with Deacon. "Name is Sam Breedlove. You might be better off with one of them others; he's thrown everybody that's tried to ride him."

Deacon took his hand. "Is that a fact? He looks calm and gentle."

"He is, till you get on him. He belonged to some cowpuncher who drifted in here about a month ago. Poor lad crossed paths with someone faster with a gun. I need to sell him to pay for his owner's funeral expenses and for his board. Problem is, ain't nobody been able to stay on him. I've had to refund money several times."

"Is that a fact? How much you want for him?"

"You saying you want him after what I done told you about him?"

Deacon grinned. "I'm not sure but shoot me a price for the horse and a saddle."

The old man scratched his chin whiskers. "Tell you what, I got the man's saddle in there, I'll throw that in and take forty dollars for horse and saddle."

Deacon shook his head. "Nope, you done told me; can't nobody ride him. And here you are trying to sell me a horse that's a bucker, and I haven't seen the saddle, for forty. I'll give twenty if the saddle suites me. And when I ride away, or if I have to lead him away, you'll be shed of this bronc."

"Twenty dollars. That's robbery; I'll take thirty-five."

"I'll do you a favor and give you twenty-five, and that's my top bid. You aren't going to get a better offer than that and you know it. All he's going to do is stand in there and eat your feed. He's costing you money every day you keep him, and you know it."

"Mister, you drive a hard bargain. But I'm going to trade with you on one condition."

"What's that?"

"You get out of town and fast."

"Why?"

"Cause, I like you, you seem like a nice feller; and most nice fellers don't last too long around here."

Deacon smiled and walked to the corral gate. "Bring me that saddle and a bridle."

Sam returned shortly with the saddle. "Here you go."

Deacon caught the claybank and led him to the gate. He placed the bridle and saddle on the horse. As he was cinching up the saddle, he noticed the horse backed his ears and turned his head slightly to look at him.

Deacon rubbed him on the neck and then backed up

to look at the horse. He saw that the horse was bowed up, and his tail was pulled in tight.

He walked back up to him and rubbed his neck. He looked into the horse's eyes; something's wrong. He undid the cinch and took the saddle off. He checked the underside of the saddle and found nothing that might be causing the horse pain. He could see Sam out of the corner of his eye watching him.

"Mister what are you doing?"

"Just checking this saddle." He picked up the blanket and turned it over, that's when he found the thorny burr. He pulled it off the blanket and handed it to Sam. "Is this yours?"

Sam took the burr and looked at it. "No sir. I ain't never seen that before."

"I bet you haven't."

"Honest mister, I ain't. I run an honest business here. I know what you are thinking; and I don't do business like that."

Deacon saddled the claybank. This time the horse never flinched. He stepped into the saddle and turned him to ride off. He trotted him down the street a short way and loped him back to where Sam was watching with his mouth open in amazement.

He rolled the burr between his fingers and looked up at Deacon. "Well, I'll be hornswoggled. I ain't never seen anything like that."

Deacon smiled. "It's an old cowboy trick. Cowboy rides into a strange town. He places a burr under his saddle when he gets off. Keeps anybody from stealing his horse."

Sam looked at the burr. "And to think this little burr kept me from making some good money from the sell of that hoss."

"If you had used a different blanket, he would have been okay."

"How did you know he wasn't a bucker?"

Deacon got down and rubbed the horse on the neck. "I didn't. I took a gamble, and I was right."

"You sure were; he's a nice horse."

"What do you call him?"

"Been calling him Dusty, you can call him whatever you like, he belongs to you now."

"Dusty suits him. Sam, I'm going to give you a chance to get more money."

"What are you talking about?"

"I got some questions I need some answers to. If you can supply me with the answers, it's worth ten bucks."

"What kind of questions?"

Deacon pulled the picture from his pocket. "Have you seen this girl?"

Sam looked at the picture. "Nope. Who is she?"

"Never mind who she is. Has anyone come through here in the past few days who may have gotten off a steam boat?"

"Mister, I don't know who you are or why you are looking for this girl. But you're fishing in the wrong pond. I don't know nothing. Keep your money. It ain't worth it."

Sam turned to walk back to the stable. Deacon followed him. "Sam, Sam, wait up. You know something, and I need to know what you know."

He turned and glared at Deacon. "Look mister, I don't know nothing, so leave me alone." He turned away.

Deacon took him by the arm. "Sam, I need to find that girl. Now, you can tell me, or I have ways to encourage a man to talk. I don't want to do that, so talk."

Sam looked at the hand on his arm and shook his

head. "If they find out I said anything, they will kill me. Who's going to take care of my family?"

"I can appreciate your problem. But somebody is taking kids and transporting them to Mexico. I aim to find them kids. Now tell me what you know."

"Look mister, I don't know much but I'll tell you what I've seen. A few days ago, two men came in here driving wagons with covers on them. They hung around and pretty much stayed to themselves. Then two days ago I saw them, and three more men headed out of town. They were coming from the river. That's all I know. Now get out of here before someone sees you here. I'm beginning to think you're not as nice as I thought you were."

Chapter 14

Deacon thanked Sam and left after retrieving his saddle bags and rifle. He rode to the general store and stocked up with supplies and bought a new hat and a rain slicker. He then went to the saloon. As he entered all heads turned to watch the stranger as he walked to the bar.

A young cowboy standing at the bar looked the new comer over. "I see old Sam slipped that yeller horse off on you." He laughed. "Good luck on riding him."

Deacon leaned against the bar. The cowboy doing the talking was young; his gun rig hung low and was tied down. "Already been riding him; he's a sweet ride." Deacon turned to the barkeep as he laid his money on the bar. "Give me a bottle of rye."

The young cowboy sauntered toward Deacon with his thumbs hooked in his gun belt. "You telling me that you rode that line back yeller horse?"

Deacon glanced at the man. "Yep."

"You must be some kind of a bronc buster to have ridden him. I tried to ride him; he shucked me off in about three jumps."

Deacon turned and smiled at him. "He never bucked with me."

"Why not?"

"To ride a horse, you got to be smarter than the horse."

The young man stood with his mouth open and stared at Deacon for a few seconds. "What are you saying, mister?"

Deacon picked up the bottle of rye by its long neck and turned to the young man. "I'm not saying anything. I'm leaving."

"You ain't going nowhere. We ain't done talking."

Deacon dropped his chin and gave the boy a hard look. "Don't do this. I got no quarrel with you."

The man backed up two steps. "I'm calling you out, mister."

Deacon spun the bottle of rye in the air and pulled his pistol. Before the young man could realize what was happening, Deacon had caught the bottle, and his gun was aimed at the would-be gun slinger's head.

"I told you that I have no quarrel with you. Now pull that pistol with two fingers and place it on the bar. He did as was instructed. "Now slide it to me." Again, he obliged.

Deacon placed the bottle on the bar and picked up the pistol placing it in his belt. He picked up his bottle from the bar where he had placed it and backed toward the door. "I'll leave this shooter at the edge of town. You can come and get it later. Don't follow me; if you do, I will kill you."

He mounted his horse and loped the short distance to the end of town. As he passed Sam's Livery Stable he tossed the gun into a water trough. He tipped his hat to Sam, who was leaning against the corral talking to another man. The claybank never broke stride.

He short loped for over a mile then reined his horse back to a walk. He turned in the saddle and looked back toward town. The country side was flat, so he could still make out the tops of the building in the distance; no one was on his trail.

He rubbed the horse on the neck and settled down into the saddle. It was good to be back on a horse. He clucked, and the horse eased into a trot.

After what Sam had told him, he was pretty sure he was on the right trail. And, in his estimation, he was no more than two days behind them. He had to cover some ground to catch them. But he also figured that he, on horseback, could travel faster than two wagons with a cargo load of kids.

The area he was riding in was pretty flat, with a few rolling hills, with very few trees. He noticed the dirt was dark, almost black. There were a few homesteads scattered along with row crops nearby. He could see farmers working their fields with mules pulling plows turning the black soil.

He rode hard all day stopping only long enough to let the horse drink and graze for a few minutes before moving on. He rode into a small clump of trees at dusk and dismounted. He stretched his legs and back; then unsaddled his horse and placed his saddle near a tree. He reached into the saddle bags and pulled out a stick of peppermint candy that he had bought while in town. He placed it between his teeth and walked back to his horse. He hobbled him and slid the bridle off. He broke off a piece of candy and gave it to the horse. He ate it and started looking for more.

"You got a sweet tooth, big boy?" He broke off another piece and gave it to him. "Here you go; now go eat some grass."

By the time the sun had set, and darkness had surrounded him, he had a fire going and coffee on. He unrolled the bed roll that belonged to the cowboy who had previously owned the horse and saddle. He unbuckled and checked the saddle bags. If there had been anything of value in them, Sam had taken it. He did find a letter from a Gail Hawthorn addressed to Bret Hawthorn. He read the letter, and in short, Gail must have been Bret's mother. She was asking him to come home to help with the farm. Since his father had taken sick, there was no one to help out.

"Sorry lady, He's not coming back." He folded the letter and placed it back into the saddle bags.

He glanced over at the horse; he was grazing and staying close to camp. He drank his coffee and chewed on beef jerky while watching his horse. Suddenly, the horse raised his head and whinnied. Deacon stood and eased over to where the horse was standing. He rubbed his neck and looked in the same direction as the horse. He couldn't see anything. But for sure there was something or someone out there.

To be on the safe side, he removed the hobbles and brought the horse in close to the fire. He fashioned a halter from his rope and tied the horse to a low hanging limb.

He shook out his bed roll and lay down to sleep with his head resting on his saddle. When he woke the next morning, the fire was out. He hobbled the horse and let him graze while he prepared the fire and coffee. While the coffee was heating, he saddled the horse and chewed on some jerky and cold biscuits that he had bought in town.

When the coffee was ready, he poured a cup, and walked to the edge of the clump of trees and looked back in the direction he had come. He wasn't sure, but he thought he saw a wisp of smoke in the distance. Could be nothing, and then he could have someone trailing him.

He finished his coffee, stirred the ashes of the fire and poured some water from his canteen on the coals. He mounted his horse and rode to a nearby creek. As the horse drank, he filled his canteen; then rode out onto the trail. He looked back but could see no one. He rode for an hour or so and occasionally he would see wagon tracks in the trail dust. He had no way of knowing if this was the wagons he was looking for. All he could do was keep following the tracks, and hopefully, they would lead him to the girl.

He rode to the top of a hill and reined up. He took his field glass out and searched the trail in front of him. There was nothing that would lead him to believe he was on the right trail. He turned and looked behind him. That's when he saw the man on horseback. He was still a good piece off but for sure was riding the same trail as he was. "Could be nothing, and then… we'll see." He clucked to the yellow horse and started off in a slow trot.

Chapter 15

The wagon Richard and Anita were in stopped. The flap on the back opened, and the tail gate dropped. Red was standing there. "Okay, everybody out."

As they got out of the wagons, they were escorted to a fallen tree and told to sit. It was almost dark; they had been in those wagons for three days now and Richard had no idea where he was. He twisted around so he could look behind him. Nothing, as far as he could see; there was nothing. "Where the hell are we?" The question wasn't addressed to anyone in particular.

Red overheard him; he turned and smiled. "On the trail to hell." He laughed and walked away.

Richard watched him as he walked off. "I'm going to kill that sonofa...." Somebody slapped him on the back of his head. He turned as Lou was bending over to whisper in his ear.

"I done told you to stop that kinda talk, boy. That man will eat you for breakfast. Now keep your damn mouth shut."

The man call Baxter climbed up on one of the wagons and drove off. He was gone for around three hours; when he returned, Lou and Jed walked to the wagon and unloaded some supplies.

Richard sat watching. He turned to Jason. "We got to be close to a town. He hasn't been gone more than three hours and he brought fresh supplies back with him."

Jason nodded. "Tonight, we slip away and find that town and tell the law."

"You have to go alone. I'm not leaving these girls by themselves. So, you will have to go it alone."

Jason shook his head. "I don't know, I ain't never been to good at being out in the dark by myself."

Richard glared at him. "You scared?"

"Hell yes, I'm scared!"

"You better be more afraid of what is going to happen to you once we get to where we are going."

Red walked up about that time and stood in the middle of the children who were sitting in a huddle. You girls go to that wagon over yonder." He pointed toward one of the wagons. "Boys to the other. In each wagon you will find buckets of water and soap. Strip off all your clothes and bathe. You will find fresh clothes in the wagons. They may not be as nice as what you was wearing when you started this trip, but they will be cleaner than what you got on now."

The four girls went to their wagon, and the boys went to the other. There was a guard at each wagon. Lou was standing by the girl's wagon. He removed their wrist shackles. "Get in there and take everything off and toss it out on the ground. Wash off and put on the fresh clothes."

Anita looked into the wagon and then at Lou. "You going to turn your back?"

Lou smiled. "Yes ma'am. I ain't going to watch and ain't no one else as long as old Lou is standing here."

She smiled at him. "Thanks."

"Yes, ma'am."

By the dim light of a lantern the girls washed and put on the fresh clothes. There were even some laughing and giggling going on inside the wagon as Lou stood guard outside.

He listened to the girls and made up his mind right then that this was his last trip. He couldn't do this no more. The money was good, real good, but the thought of what was happening to these kids was tearing him up on the inside.

Freedom Rides
R. D. Gregory

As the girls came out of the wagon, he replaced the shackles on their wrist. He then escorted them back to the fire. The boys were there already; Anita smiled at Richard. "I do feel better. I usually bathe more often than every two weeks."

Richard smiled back. "Yeah, me too."

Lou walked up and glanced at the children. "Time to bed down." He took the boys and shackled them together around a tree, while Jed was doing the same thing to the girls.

Richard protested. "What are you doing? Why? You've never done this before."

Lou frowned. "Boss' orders. He's worried that you might try to escape. This way he can rest the night and not have to worry about you getting away. Figures; we are too close to town. If you got away, you could get help." He double checked the locks, walked to the camp fire, and poured himself a cup of coffee. He sat down and stared into the flames.

Red walked up. "Are the kids secure?"

Without looking up Lou nodded. "Yeah, all secure."

Richard leaned back against the tree. "This does us in. No way one of us can get away now."

Thirteen-year-old Zack, lay down the best he could under the conditions and started crying. "I want to go home."

Jason kicked him on the leg. "Shut up. We all want to go home."

Richard jerked the shackle that was connected to Jason. "Leave him alone. Go to sleep; tomorrow is another day."

Chapter 16

Deacon made camp that night after a hard day of riding. The yellow horse had given him everything he had asked for. He cooked some smoked bacon and beans for his supper and drank coffee. After he had kicked out his bedroll, he poured some rye into his cup of coffee and settled down against his saddle.

He woke before daybreak and started a fire for coffee. After daylight and while the coffee was heating, he saddled his horse and checked his back trail. He could see smoke from a camp fire in the distance; he was still back there. "Who is this guy?"

He looked at the sky which was gray with clouds. "Best get going before this rain sets in."

He rode out of camp at a slow trot. Around midday he topped a hill and less than a mile away was a small town. He could also see the wagon tracks leaving the trail to the left. He sat there a moment looking at the tracks. He looked at the darkening clouds and decided to ride into town and check if anyone had seen the wagons.

There was a small stable at the edge of town. He pulled up at Casey's Livery Stable and stepped down at a watering trough.

There was a man under a horse nailing on a shoe; he set the foot down and straightened up. "You need something?"

"Not just now. Watering my horse is all. I would like to ask you a question."

"I don't charge nothing for answering question, so shoot." He smiled as he walked toward the stranger.

"You seen any strangers in town in the past couple days?"

"Nope, can't say that I have."

Freedom Rides
R. D. Gregory

"Okay, thanks." He looked at the clouds rolling in. "How about you put my horse in a stall and grain him for me. Don't take the saddle off; I'll be leaving before dark."

The man took the reins. "Sure thing."

Deacon walked up the street to the only saloon in town. As he went in, he looked around. The place was empty except for the barkeep. He eased up to the bar. "Kinda dead in here."

"In case you didn't notice when you rode in, this town is dead. We get a few strangers coming through on occasion but not many, not anymore."

"Anybody in the last couple days?"

"In fact, there was a man in here last night right about dark. He bought a couple of drinks and left. Are you going to drink or ask questions?"

Deacon smiled at him. "Tell you what I'll do better than that. I'll take a beer and something to eat if you got anything."

He sat a big jar of pickled boiled eggs on top of the bar. "Two cents per egg or I can fry some steak and eggs, if you prefer."

"I'll take that beer, two of these, while you fry me up two more and a steak."

The man gave a big smile. "Coming up." He handed Deacon his beer and went through a door at the end of the bar.

Deacon went to a corner table with his beer and the jar of eggs. He pulled his knife and fished an egg from the jar. As he ate the egg from the point of his knife blade he glanced out the window. It had started raining, so he settled in and relaxed, waiting for his food.

His thoughts were on Anita and the rest of the kids who were somewhere out there. If indeed the man that came in here the evening before was one of the people holding them, then he had to be close.

His food arrived, and he asked for a cup of coffee to go with it. After his meal, which wasn't anything to brag about, he went down the street to the general store. As he walked in, a man with thinning gray hair and wearing wire rim glasses raised up in his chair. "Howdy mister, what can I do for you today?"

Deacon looked around the store. Seeing nothing that he really needed he stepped up to the counter. "Give me a box of forty-fives and a box of forty-four-seventies."

The clerk placed the cartridges on the counter. "Will there be anything else?"

"There was a stranger came to town last evening. Did he come in here; and if so, what did he purchase?"

"There was a man in here okay, but he weren't no stranger. I've seen him before. He bought some supplies, grain for his horses, some flour, salt, canned stuff, and some smoke cured meat."

"Does he live around here?"

"Not sure, but I don't think so. He's been coming in here three, four times a year now for the last three years."

"You know his name?"

"Never ask. He always pays on the spot. Don't talk much. What's this all about?"

Deacon lied. "I'm looking for an old friend; heard he may be hanging his hat in these parts."

The clerk looked at the cartridges on the counter and then at Deacon. He smiled. "Good friend, is he?"

Deacon gave a sheepish grin. "Not really. He's got something that doesn't belong to him, and I aim to take it back to the rightful owner."

"Wish you wouldn't kill my customers."

"If it's the man I'm looking for, you wouldn't want him

as a customer. As far as killing him, that will be up to him." He reached into a large mouth jar and pulled out three sticks of peppermint candy.

"You got a sweet tooth?"

"My horse does."

He paid the clerk and walked to the livery stable. His horse was munching on hay; he looked up as Deacon entered the building. Deacon broke off a piece of candy and gave it to him.

The rain was still coming down in a slow drizzle. He put on his rain slicker and walked over to the man who ran the livery. "How much I owe you?"

"Shucks, mister, he didn't eat that much, I mean you ain't been here no time a-tall. Don't worry about it. I'll see you next time you're through here. Maybe you'll stay longer."

"Much obliged." He stepped into the saddle and rode out the big stable door and headed for the other end of town. When he passed the saloon, he noticed a bay horse tied in front. He reined to a stop and looked the horse over. "Could be that's the gent that has been on my tail for the past couple days."

He clucked to his horse and rode on out of town.

Chapter 17

Deacon picked up the wagon tracks about a mile out of town. He put his horse into a short lope and started following them. The rain had let up, but the sky was still a dark gray. There would be no camp fire tonight. Everything would be too wet to burn, and chances are the ones he was following wouldn't have a fire either.

He rubbed the horse on the neck. "Guess we just as well ride on, no fire means no coffee." He reached into his saddle bag and took out some jerky; with his jaw teeth he tore off a piece and let it lay in his mouth.

He rode on following the tracks that were fresher now. The rain had made the ground soft, and the wagons were leaving an easy enough trail. As darkness began to surround him, he stopped on a small hill and looked around. Not far away stood a grove of cedar trees.

He rode into the cedars and dismounted. He unsaddled his horse and placed his gear under a cedar. He placed hobbles on his horse then gave him a piece of candy.

He spread his bedroll under a cedar tree and leaned back against the tree. A dead limb was poking in his back. He pulled his knife and cut it off and leaned against the tree. He started whittling on the limb. After a few strokes with the knife on the limb, he noticed that the limb was dry. He kept cutting shavings off the limb until he had a nice size pile. He got up and broke off some small dead limbs from the nearby trees.

He placed the shavings in a pile and lit them with a match. Once they were burning, he started placing the smaller dead limbs on the fire. He kept this up till he had a nice size fire going. It was creating a lot of smoke, but it would heat coffee. He stood and smiled. He made the coffee and set it on a rock next to the fire and waited for it to heat.

He walked away from the fire out into the dark to check on his horse. He could see the yellow horse grazing nearby.

He turned to go back to the fire when he saw movement about fifty feet away. His horse had seen it, also. He was standing with his head up and looking in that direction.

Deacon pulled his gun and stood his ground waiting. Whatever it was moved again slowly toward the fire. Deacon squatted down in order to get a better view of the intruder. It was a man and he was slipping up on the campfire looking for the man who built it.

Deacon eased around so he could place himself behind the man. He could see him better now; the man was looking around trying to find him. Deacon slipped up closer as quiet as a cat and cocked his pistol. "I'm right here."

The man's body stiffened. "Mister Deacon Reeves, I mean you no harm. 'Cept maybe to impose on you for some of that coffee."

"Ease on in closer to the light so I can get a better look at you. And keep your hands above your shoulders."

"Anything you say."

The two men walked to the fire, and Deacon walked around the man in order to see his face. He was little less than six foot, in his forties, square jawed and medium build.

"Who are you and why have you been dogging my trail?"

"My name is Jordan and I work for the agency."

"You got any proof of that?"

"I do, if you will allow me to reach into my pocket."

"Go ahead." Deacon had already noticed the gun he was wearing had the same engraving on the handles.

The man pulled out his credentials and handed them to Deacon across the fire. "Like I said, I mean you no hurt. I came to assist you in bringing back the Bennet girl."

Deacon looked at the paper work and lowered the hammer on his pistol and placed it in his holster. He handed the man back his credentials, walked over to his saddle bags, and took out another tin cup. He tossed it to the man. "Coffee should be about ready, help yourself."

Deacon was still unsure of the man, so he kept his eye on him. "Why is it you are just now contacting me?"

"Mister Deacon, you didn't give me much of a chance. In fact, you should have come to see me when you arrived in St. Louis."

"Why would I have wanted to do that?"

Jordan picked up the coffee pot and poured some into a cup. He handed it to Deacon. Then he picked up the other cup and poured coffee into it. He sat the pot down and took a sip of coffee. He nodded his head in approval.

"Ever since that girl went missing, I have been working this case. I found out some things that would have helped us get her back."

Deacon smiled and went to his bed roll and sat down. He leaned back against the cedar tree and stretched his long legs out in front of him. He took a sip of his coffee and looked at the man. "Is that a fact?"

"Yes sir. I know that they are taking a group of young people to Mexico to sell them to the Mexicans for child labor."

"And what is your plan to stop them from doing that?"

"Well, I thought we would locate them and then notify the local lawman to arrest them."

"Now that is a plan. Jordan, you did say your name is Jordan, didn't you?"

"Yes."

"Well Jordan, if you will take your coffee and go to that ridge over there. Walk to the top of it and look to the south, and west, then turn to the north. Stay there for a few minutes and watch, looking in all directions. Then come back and tell me what you saw."

The man did as he was instructed. As he walked off, Deacon pulled the bottle of rye from his saddle bags. He poured some in his coffee cup and waited for Jordan to return.

Jordan walked back to the campfire. He squatted down and looked at Deacon.

Deacon offered the man the bottle of rye. He took it and poured some into his cup. "Well, what did you see?"

"Nothing, it's darker than hell out there."

"So, you didn't see anything, no camp fires, no lights from windows? No distant lights from towns or nothing?"

"Nope. Nothing"

"Then how do you propose to notify the law if you find these people when there is no law to be found? Out here you are on your own. There is no law, except the law to survive."

"I see."

"Where is your horse?"

"I tied him to a tree back yonder."

"Go get him. You can bed down here."

Jordan drank his cup empty, set it down, and walked off into the night.

Deacon sipped his drink as the man walked away and

thought to himself. "If you can find him."

Jordan returned with his horse, and the two men settled into their bedrolls to get some much-needed sleep.

Chapter 18

The next morning Deacon was up early. He got a fire started and put the coffee on. As he was saddling his horse Jordan came up to him. "You don't like me, do you?"

Deacon turned toward him. "I don't know you well enough to say one way or the other."

"It's okay if you don't. We don't have to be friends, but I would like to ride with you to help get those kids back."

Deacon pulled the cinch tight on his saddle and glanced over at him. "Well, if you are riding with me you best saddle up."

Jordan dropped his chin and smiled. "Yes sir." He walked off to get his horse.

The sun broke through the clouds as they crested the nearby hill when they rode out of camp.

They were still following the wagon tracks when they came to a place near a creek where the kids had spent the night before.

Deacon looked down the trail in the direction of the tracks. "We'll catch them today. I figure we're no more than two hours behind them. Before dark we will have them in sight."

Sure enough, late afternoon they could see the two wagons in the distance. Deacon reined up. "There they are, let's take our time and let them stop for camp."

"Why not take them now?"

"If we ride in now they will see us coming. They might suspect something and be ready. We would be out gunned. No, we'll wait till dark. That way we will have the element of surprise in our favor."

After dark the two men left their horses tied in a small

thicket two hundred yards from the campsite where the kids were being held. As they crept in slow and quiet Deacon stopped. He pulled his pistol and checked the rounds. "Check your shooter. We won't need any misfires."

As Jordan was checking his pistol, Deacon was watching him. "You know how to use that shooter?"

Jordan nodded. "Yeah, I can use it."

"Okay, when we get closer, we split up. I'll go to the far side and you wait on this side. When you see me come in to their camp, you come in. When it starts it will be fast; shoot to kill and do not shoot any of the children. Got it?"

"Got it."

As they got closer to the camp Deacon circled around to the other side of the camp. He slipped in close and squatted down. He surveyed the campsite. The two wagons were setting about twenty feet apart. The campfire was placed in the middle between them. The horses were picketed not far away with their harness and saddles still on them.

The girls were shackled together at one wagon, and the boys were shackled to the other wagon. Three men were drinking and playing cards by the fire. One was standing over by the horses with a rifle cradled in his arms. He would have to go down before any other moves were made.

Deacon rose to a crouch position and crept around to where the horses were. As he came near the horses, the one on the end got restless. Deacon placed his hand on the horse and rubbed his neck. He calmed down but not before he drew the attention of the guard. The man was coming toward the horses.

Deacon eased under the horse's neck and squatted

down. He pulled his knife and waited. As the man walked by, Deacon grabbed him from behind with his hand over his mouth and cut the man's throat. He caught the rifle as it slipped from the man's hands and placed it on the ground. Slow and easy he dragged the dead man away from the horses, for fear that the smell of blood would spook them.

He came back to the edge of the campsite and squatted down. The three men playing cards were still at it. There had to be at least one or two more around somewhere.

On the other side of the camp, Jordan was waiting on Deacon to make his move when someone stuck a gun barrel in his back. "You stand real still mister." The man took his pistol and placed it in his belt. "Now walk over toward that fire so I can get a look at you."

Deacon watched as Jordan came into the circle of light created by the campfire. The men playing cards stood as Red escorted the new comer to the fire. "Look here what I found snooping around out in the bushes while I was relieving myself." He spat amber.

"Who is he boss?"

Red placed his gun at the base of Jordan's neck. "Start talkin'. Who are you, and why was you snooping around?"

"My name is Jordan, and I was riding through and saw your camp fire. Was going to come in and ask for some coffee."

"Is that so; then where's your horse? I didn't see no horse out there."

Deacon frowned and spoke under his breath. "This is not the way I wanted this to happen." He stood and walked toward the men at the camp fire. Their attention was on Jordan, so they didn't notice him till he walked to the edge of the fire light about twenty feet away. "Everybody stand real still."

Red turned in surprise. "Mister, I don't know who you are; but if you don't put that gun down, your friend is going to die."

Deacon smiled at him. "Maybe, maybe not. If the four of you will put your guns down, I won't kill you."

Red was standing behind Jordan, not a good shot to have to make. The other three were starting to separate. The man in the middle went for his gun. Deacon shot him. As he was falling, Deacon aimed at the man to his left and squeezed the trigger. He went down with the front of his shirt soaking up his blood as it poured from the hole in his chest.

Red had Jordan by the back of the shirt and was pulling him backwards out of the light and into the trees. He was using him as a shield while shooting at Deacon. Jordan was stumbling backwards as Red dragged him but was able to keep Red's aim off.

Bullets were hissing by Deacon as he shot the other man; but not before he felt the hot lead and the shock of the impact as a bullet tore through his right side. He could feel the warm blood running down his side. He touched his side with his right hand and glanced at his hand as he sprinted in the direction that the other man had gone with Jordan.

He saw a flash and heard the gunfire. He made his way in that direction looking for the other man when he saw Jordan lying on the ground. He went to him and knelt down.

Jordan no doubt in a lot of pain and with a grimace on his face looked at Deacon. "It's bad, he shot me in the back. I... I can't feel my legs. Go get that sonofabitch."

Deacon squeezed his shoulder. "I'll be back." He could

hear a horse running away from the camp. He ran to where the horses were and could see the man riding off in the distance.

Deacon went back to Jordan and knelt beside him. "Jordan."

Jordan opened his eyes. "Did you get him?"

"No, he got away."

"Pity. I'm dying and the man who did this to me got away."

"Sorry, I couldn't go after him. I need to see to these kids."

"I know." His eyes closed, and his body went lax.

Deacon stood and touched his side. It hurt like hell, and it was still bleeding. He went back to the camp fire, then over to the wild-eyed boys shackled to the wagon wheel. "Where's the key?"

Richard pointed to one of the dead men. "He has them."

Chapter 19

After unlocking Richard's shackles, Deacon handed him the keys. "Unlock the rest of them." He looked at one of the other boys as his shackles were being unlocked. "Go back down the trail about two hundred yards. In a clump of trees, you will find two horses, bring them here."

The boy stood and rubbed his wrist. "Yes sir." He ran off to find the horses.

Deacon removed his vest and shoulder holster. He pulled his shirt tail up and looked at his side. The bullet had passed through not hitting anything vital. A girl with auburn hair of about sixteen walked over to where he was standing. "You've been shot."

Deacon looked at her and smiled, he recognized her from the photograph. "You're Anita Bennet."

"Yes I am. How did you know?"

"I've come to take you home."

She gave him a big smile and tears ran down her face. She took hold of his arm and placed her head against his shoulder and started crying. "I don't know who you are, and I don't care. You are an angel from God. Thank... thank you so much."

The rest of the children had gathered around him and were staring at his bloodied shirt. One of the younger girls started crying. "Oh no, he's going to die, and we'll be out here in this place alone. What will we do?" Which got the rest of the kids shook up and they all started chattering at the same time.

Deacon held up his hand for them to be quiet. "First off, I'm not going to die. But if I do, you will do whatever it takes to stay alive. You head northeast till you come to the river and follow it back home."

He started removing his shirt. "Now, one of you fetch me a bucket of water so I can clean this blood off me. The rest of you drag those dead men over into the bushes so we don't have to look at them the rest of the night."

The kids were watching him. He could tell from their expressions that most were still scared. He couldn't blame them. He pulled his knife from his boot and started cutting his shirt into strips. His horse arrived, and he went to the saddle bags and pulled out the bottle of rye and a small sewing kit. He washed the blood from his side and soaked a rag in rye.

As he was threading the needle Anita came to him. "Do you need some help?"

"I could use some. Do you know how to sew?"

"Yes, but... but I've never sewn on a person before."

"No time like the present to learn, if you're willing."

"I'm afraid I will hurt you."

"Oh yeah, it's going to hurt. But if I don't stop this blood from leaking out of me, I'm going to bleed to death."

She looked at Richard. "Bring that lantern over here closer so I can see better. Mister, you might want to lay down for this, just in case you pass out."

"Call me Deacon, and you see the other scars? Most of these I did myself. I won't need to lie down."

She looked at his scars. "I see that you're not much of a seamstress either."

He grinned at her. "You are a funny lady." He turned the bottle of rye up and took a long drink from it. "Now, funny girl, get to sewing."

She took the bottle an poured some on the needle. She handed him the bottle, and he drank some more. Richard was holding the light and Deacon was watching him as Anita pushed the needle into his skin and out again. "Boy, are you going to be okay?"

His face was pale, and he was sweating profusely. His eyes rolled back into his head; and Deacon grabbed the lantern as his knees buckled, and he passed out.

Anita looked at him then to Deacon. "Is he alright?"

"He'll be okay. He's just a little weak stomach. He'll come around. Keep doing what you're doing."

When she finished, she cleaned the needle and returned it to the sewing kit. She cleaned her hands, then took bandages and wrapped him. He put his clean shirt on and looked around at the kids.

"All of you come over here so I can talk to you." They all gathered up, even Richard had come around. He was still looking a little pale, but he would be okay.

Deacon looked into every face, and what he saw in most of them was fear. "My name is Deacon, and I am here to take you back to St. Louis. Thing is, I am going to need your help. You will have to do what I tell you, when I tell you, no questions asked. Can I count on you to do that?"

They all nodded their heads and said yes.

"Okay." He pointed to Richard. "You look to be the oldest of the boys. What is your name?"

"Richard Kelly."

Deacon smiled and looked at Anita. "Is this the young man you were secretly sneaking off to be with?"

Anita dropped her head and blushed. "Yes, how did you know?"

"Never mind that now." He turned to Richard. "I am placing you in charge of the horses. It will be your job to see to them and make sure they are ready to go every morning and secured at night. Can you handle that?"

"Yes sir, I think I can."

"Good, I'll help, and so will others. We will be needing fire wood each night and also, someone who can cook."

Anita spoke up. "I can cook." "Good, get some of these other older girls to help you. It's going to take me a few days to learn all of your names, but I will learn them."

One of the boys asked. "What if that man comes back?"

"What's your name son?"

"Jason."

"Jason, if he comes back, I will kill him. Now we need a shovel. There is someone we need to bury."

The smaller of the boys jumped up and ran around one of the wagons. When he came back, he had two shovels.

Deacon nodded. "Good, somebody get the lantern and you boys come with me." He led the boys into the woods to where Detective Jordan lay. He checked his pockets and took his valuables and personal stuff.

They gathered around him and picked him up and took him to the nearby clearing. They dug a shallow grave and put him in it. Deacon took his hat off. "Wish I could do better for you, Jordan."

Richard looked at Deacon. "Did you know him well."

"Didn't know him at all. Only met him yesterday. Let's go bed down boys; tomorrow is going to be a long day."

Chapter 20

The next morning Deacon was up before the sun. In fact, he hadn't slept much during the night. He got the fire going and the coffee on. As the kids started rolling out of their sleep, they gathered around the fire. When it was light enough, Deacon gathered the guns from the dead men and placed them in a pile in the back of one of the wagons. One by one he replaced the spent cartridges with fresh ones.

Richard wandered over with a piece of beef jerky and a cup of coffee. "Mister Deacon."

Deacon looked up from what he was doing. "No mister. I'm just Deacon. What 'cha need?"

"I brought you some coffee and a piece of jerky."

Deacon laid the gun down and took the coffee and the jerky. "Thanks Richard."

"Do you think the man that got away will come back?"

"Yes, I do, and he won't be alone."

"What are you going to do?"

"I am going to do my best to stay alive and keep you kids safe."

"Give me one of those guns, I'll help you."

"Richard, I appreciate the offer. But if you're not shooting at them, there is a good chance that they won't shoot at you."

"Sir, I would rather be dead than to be going where they are going to take us."

Deacon stared into the young man's eyes. He smiled as he remembered him fainting the night before. "You may have a weak stomach, but you got grit."

"Thanks."

"Do you know how to use a gun?"

"I'm better with a rifle or shotgun. But yeah, I can

use a pistol."

Deacon took a sip of his coffee. "We'll see when the time comes." He looked around at the others. "Okay, it's time to get rolling. Let's get the horses hooked up to the wagons."

"Yes, sir."

At that he ran over to where the others were gathered. The three boys went to the horses and led them to the wagons. Deacon chose not to help; instead he watched. He wanted to see if these kids could do it without him. While the boys were making up the hitches, the girls cleaned up the campsite and put everything away in the wagons.

When the boys were finished with the teams and had saddled the horses, Deacon walked around and checked the collars, traces, hames, and breeching.

Everything was in good condition. He turned and looked at his crew. "Well done. Now who can ride and who can drive a team?"

Most all of them said they could ride but no one had ever driven a team.

Deacon pointed to Richard. "I want you on a horse. You will ride our drag at least two hundred yards behind us. Watch our back; and if you see anything, you will let me know. Got it?"

"Yes sir."

"Anita, you ride a horse and stay close to me." He looked at the next oldest girl. "What's your name again?"

"Cindy."

"Okay, Cindy, you drive the wagon in the back and Jason, I want you to drive the lead wagon. Everybody else in the wagons. Tie the extra horses to the back of the wagons. Mount up; let's roll out."

Anita looked over where the dead men were lying on

the ground next to the trees. "What about them; aren't we going to bury them?"

Deacon looked at the men and then at the children who were all staring at him. "No, we're not. That would take too long, and we need to be heading north. Hopefully their friends will take care of that job."

He turned to Jason. "Get one of those shovels and place it over by them. I'm sorry kids, but that's the way it has to be. Now everybody load up."

They started down the trail the way they had come, with Deacon riding in front and Anita riding close behind. They had been on the trail for about two hours when Richard came galloping up beside Deacon. "Mister Deacon, can I ask you something?"

"Shoot, what's on your mind?"

"Is there a town close by?"

"Yeah. We should be there before dark."

"Sir, I been thinking. Night before last when we made camp, one of those men went off with a wagon; and when he came back, he had supplies."

"Yeah, so what's your point?"

"Well, he also brought us fresh clothes, and they weren't new. They had been cleaned and mended."

Deacon stopped and turned in his saddle, so he could look at Richard. "So, you are thinking that these men might have friends in the town, or at least close by?"

"Yeah, that's what I'm thinking."

Deacon looked due north at the country and the lay of the land. "Okay, let's get off this trail and head across country. Hopefully we will come across another trail after a few miles. You go back, and ride drag, and keep your eyes open."

Richard turned his horse to ride off, when Deacon called to him. "Richard."

He stopped and turned in the saddle. "Sir."

"Thanks for bringing that to my attention."

Anita sat her horse smiling as she watched Richard ride to the back of the wagons. When she turned her horse, she noticed Deacon with a smile on his face as he watched her. She blushed and turned away.

Deacon chuckled under his breath as he nudged his horse into a trot.

As they made their way across country, the going was slower. Deacon was leading the way and trying to pick a route that would cause the wagons less problems. Having to go around ditches, gullies and wooded areas was eating up the daylight. They had stopped for a short time around midday and now it was getting close to dark.

Deacon spotted a creek with running water near a grove of trees. He directed the wagons in close to the creek and instructed the boys to set up a picket line for the horses.

The girls were gathering fire wood from the edge of the woods while Deacon started a fire. Cindy dropped an arm load of sticks next to the fire. When she looked up, she gasped. "Mister Deacon!"

Deacon turned as he stood and looked in the direction she was pointing.

He could see four men on horseback following the wagon tracks headed straight for them. "Cindy, go tell Richard to come here; then tell everyone else to get behind the far wagon."

Deacon stood watching as the men rode closer. Richard came running up and stopped beside Deacon. "It's him, isn't it?"

"Yeah, I'm pretty sure that's Red, and as I figured, he brought help. You think you can handle a rifle if it comes down to it?"

"Yes sir."

"Okay, get one and a pistol and some cartridges from the wagon and go into the trees and hide behind a tree."

"Yes sir." He turned and ran off to the wagon.

To Deacon's surprise the four men kept coming. They rode into the camp, and Red rode up to within ten feet of where Deacon was standing.

Deacon looked the four men over and stared into Red's eyes. "You got a lot of nerve riding into my camp after what you've done."

Red glanced around the campsite. "Your camp? Looks like this is my campsite, seeing how them's my wagons, my horses and my kids. And I want them back."

Chapter 21

Deacon stood in front of the four men. He knew that coming out of this without catching lead was going to be slim.

"Red, can I call you Red? You're not getting these kids back. Not without stepping over my dead body."

Red shook his head and leaned back in his saddle. "Mister, there has been enough killing. I was hoping we could settle this another way."

"It's settled. Like I said, you're not getting these kids."

Red frowned and shifted in his saddle. Deacon read his move and pulled his gun with his left hand. As Red's pistol was clearing leather, the bullet from Deacon's gun hit him in the shoulder knocking him from his saddle.

Deacon pulled his other pistol and pointed each one at two of the three men left. None of them were making a move toward their guns. "You boys going for them guns or are you riding out?"

One of them spoke up. "Hey mister, we came along on the offer of fifty bucks apiece to help him drive them wagons. We don't know nothing about what is going on here between the two of you. So, if it is okay with you, we will turn around and ride back where we came from."

"That will be fine with me. But know this; if I see you on my trail, I will kill you."

"What about him?" The man was pointing toward Red.

Deacon looked over at Red who was now sitting up holding his right arm. "He stays with me. He has committed murder and kidnapping. I am going to turn him over to the law."

"Mister, I've known Red for several years and I also Know that he works for a mighty powerful man. I'm telling you this, because keeping him long enough to turn him over to the law may not turn out so well for you."

"Thanks for the warning, but I know all this. I'm taking him to jail."

The man doing the talking turned his horse; the others did the same. "Can't say I didn't warn you."

Deacon turned to Red. "Get up."

Red struggled to his feet. "You're a dead man."

"Seems to me that you are closer to death than I am, now get over there and sit on that fallen tree. I need to take a look at your shoulder."

Richard came out of the tree line and walked to where Deacon was. The other kids followed, and they all gathered around as Deacon looked at the bullet wound.

"Red, that bullet is still in there and needs to come out."

Red looked up at Deacon. "You go to hell. You ain't digging that slug out of me with no knife."

"If I don't, it could fester."

"I'll take my chances."

"Okay, it's your funeral. Richard get a set of them shackles from the wagon. Come on Red."

Deacon escorted him over to a wagon wheel and secured him. He then searched him and took a knife from in his boot.

Red smiled. "What's for supper?"

Deacon turned and walked away without answering. "You kids, all of you get over here."

They all met him at the fire. Deacon looked at the stern faces. "No one goes near him. And another thing. If anything happens to me, you head toward the river. I'm pretty sure that there will be a trail that will run parallel to it. Find that trail and go north till you reach a town. Work with the law there to get you on a steam boat to St. Louis."

Anita looked around at the others. "Mister Deacon, you can't leave us. We can't do this on our own."

"I don't plan on going anywhere, but in case something does happen, I want you to know what to do. You can do it alone if you have to. Work together and you can do anything. Now let's finish setting up camp and getting the meal behind us."

Late that night when everyone one was asleep, a man crept into camp. He looked at the kids asleep by the wagons, and Red was still cuffed to the wagon wheel. That meant that the person over by the fire was the one he was after. He raised his rifle and aimed at the person asleep. As he placed the sights of the rifle on the position of the head, the thought came to him. "Red is going to give me a lot of money for saving his ass."

He pulled the trigger. He ran over and jerked the blanket from the body, but it wasn't a body. He got a sick feeling in his stomach when he heard the hammer cock on the pistol behind him.

"Looking for me?"

The man straightened up and waited for the bullet.

"Drop the rifle."

The man looked down at the rifle in his hands. The hammer was down. Had he reloaded after shooting and let the hammer down. He couldn't remember.

Deacon spoke to him again. "Last chance, make your play or drop the rifle."

"Mister, I had it in my mind to come back and help Red. The other two, they wanted no part of it cause they were afraid of you. Said you meant what you said about killing us if you saw us again."

"You should have listened to them."

"So, you going to kill me?"

"Give me one good reason why I shouldn't."

The man laughed. "I ain't got one." He dropped the rifle and started turning to face Deacon. As he turned, he pulled his pistol. The man never had a chance, and he knew it. But for some unknown reason that no one will ever know why, he played the odds and lost.

Deacon went to him as he lay unmoving. He checked him for a pulse. He went to the wagon where the kids were standing watching. He pulled the shovel from the wagon. "Go back to sleep."

Richard followed him as he walked back toward the dead man. Without a word between them they took the man to the edge of the tree line and dug a grave for him.

When they were finished, Richard turned to Deacon. "How did you know?"

"Know what?"

"That he would come back and try to kill you."

"Something he said."

"What?"

"He said he had known Red for a long time. If that was true, then he knew what Red was doing. And he figured he could cash in on some easy money if he could kill me."

Richard nodded his head. "Makes sense after you put it that way."

Red was sitting up against the wagon wheel smiling as Deacon and Richard walked back into camp. "You got past that one, but will you survive the next one?"

Richard placed the sharp end of the shovel against Red's throat and placed his foot on it. "You shut the hell up or I'll cut your head off."

Red was sitting back against the wheel. He looked up at Richard and smiled. "You best hope I don't get free. After I kill him, I'm going to kill you real slow."

Deacon took Richard by the shoulder. "I told you to stay away from him. Now go to bed."

Chapter 22

The next morning after a restless sleep, Deacon rolled out of his bed roll under the trees to find a fire going and coffee on. He sat up and with unbelieving eyes watched as the children made breakfast and prepared the horses for travel. He smiled as he strolled over to the campfire. Cindy handed him a cup of coffee and a slice of fresh cooked smoked ham.

"Thank you, Cindy. Where did you get the ham?"

"It was in the wagon. There is ham, pork belly, beans and lots of other stuff in there. Red intended to eat good on this trip."

Deacon nodded his head and looked at Red shackled to the wagon wheel. "You fed him yet?"

"No sir, you told us to stay away from him."

He grinned at her. "Good girl. Now fix me a cup of coffee for him and some of that pork. I'll take it to him."

As he walked toward Red, Richard came by leading two horses, harnessed and ready to go. "Mister Deacon, we will have the teams hitched and ready to go soon. How long before we pull out?"

Deacon stopped and looked around at the children. Every one of them was doing something. "Richard, who organized this?"

Richard smiled and looked toward the campfire at Anita. "Me and Anita. We figured if you could keep us safe and get us home, we could take care of everything else."

"Good job. We pull out in about half an hour."

"Yes, sir."

Deacon handed Red the cup of coffee and the plate of food. Red spat out a plug of tobacco. "Thanks."

"How's the arm?"

"Hurts like hell."

"Let me look at it."

"Hell no. You stay away from me."

Deacon turned and walked away. "Okay. But you better let me doctor it."

When they pulled out Deacon took the lead again with Anita riding close behind and Richard riding drag. They rode on for most of an hour when Deacon pulled up and waited for Anita to ride up beside him. "I'm going on ahead to check things out. You follow my tracks. If you hear any gun shots from my direction, you stop. Pull off into some trees and wait for me. Otherwise follow my tracks."

"Yes, sir. You are coming back?"

"Yes, I'll be back."

He heeled Dusty into a lope and rode out of sight. As he topped the next rise, he reined up and looked around. As far as he could see, there was nothing except grass, weeds, and an occasional clump of trees. "There has to be a trail somewhere nearby." He took out his field glasses and searched the landscape again. Still nothing anywhere close. He looked back toward the wagons. The trail behind them was clear. At least no one was coming up from behind them.

He watched as Anita led the wagons closer to where he was sitting. This bunch of misfits will do okay, he thought. He turned his horse and trotted down the hill toward the north east, still hoping to find a trail that would lead them to the river.

Around mid-day, he rode back to the wagons. "Let's head for that clump of trees to let the horses rest for an hour or so."

As the wagons pulled into the shade of the trees, Deacon rode to the wagon that Red was in. He dismounted and pulled the flap back. "Get out, stretch your legs."

Red crawled out of the wagon. "You got a chew."

"Nope."

"I sure could use a chaw of tobacco right about now. I don't feel so good."

Deacon looked closer at him. "You don't look so good either." He glanced around. He took Red by the arm. "Come over and sit down. I need to look at that shoulder."

"I told you, you ain't digging that bullet out of me. Get me to a doctor."

"Sit down and shut up." Deacon pushed Red to a sitting position on a fallen tree. He pulled Red's shirt open and removed the bandage. The wound was red and angry looking. "Stay here."

Deacon went to his saddle bags and pulled a bottle of whiskey. He took it to Red. "Here, drink."

"Thanks. How about a plug of tobacco?"

"I told you I don't have any."

"Yeah well, there is some in that wagon, in that gunny sack."

Deacon was looking around at the kids. "Not now, Red. Drink up." He walked to were Anita and one of the other girls were talking.

"Have either of you seen Richard?"

Both girls turned and looked around. With a worried look, Anita tuned back to Deacon. "No, not since this morning."

Deacon went to Red. "Get up and bring that bottle." He took him over to the wagon and shackled him to the wheel. "You keep hitting that bottle, I'll be back dreckly."

He mounted his horse and rode back the way they had come looking for the boy. As he topped the next hill, he saw him riding toward him in a lope.

When Richard rode up beside him, he turned and looked back pointing. "Mister Deacon, I saw three men behind us. They didn't seem to be in no kind of hurry. They were following the wagon tracks for a while and then they rode off north east."

Deacon looked in that direction, he couldn't see anyone. "Come on, let's get back to the wagons." All was well at the wagons when they arrived. Red was still hitting the bottle and was getting pretty drunk. He had started harassing the girls.

Cindy came up to Deacon. "Can you shut him up. I'm tired of his filthy mouth."

Deacon looked around; those three men that Richard saw had him worried, and he didn't like the area. The under growth was too thick, and it would be too easy for someone to slip up on them. "Let's move out."

Cindy put her hands on her hips. "But we haven't rested, nor have we eaten anything."

Deacon was releasing Red from the wagon. He turned toward Cindy. "I told you not to question me, and to do what I said. Now let's move out. Eat some jerky." He helped Red into the wagon and handed him the bottle. "Keep drinking."

When everyone was loaded, he turned to Richard. "You stay close to the last wagon and keep your eyes open."

"Yes sir."

Deacon rode out in full alert. Instead of riding north east as he had been, he rode due east. He loped to the top of a hill and stopped. He took out his field glasses and surveyed the area. Still no trail in sight, no riders either.

As far as he could see there was no one on their trail either. I hate being followed by someone in front of me. This is a bad area. An ambush could come at anytime from anywhere. There were gullies and trees in every direction. No way to avoid them.

Chapter 23

The little caravan traveled all day without incident. As the sun was setting, Deacon stopped. He rode over to the lead wagon. "We'll make camp here for tonight."

He was unsaddling his horse when Cindy walked up to him. "Mister Deacon, I'm sorry I made you mad."

Deacon turned to her. "I'm not mad at you." He brushed a lock of hair from her dirty face and smiled at her. "I was concerned for you and how I can keep all of you safe. I was short with you, and I'm sorry. I'll try to do better. Forgive me?"

She nodded her head, then walked closer to him and put her arms around him. "Mister Deacon, will we ever get home. I've been so scared. Thank you for coming for us." She started crying.

He held her and stroked her hair. "Yes Cindy, I'm going to do everything in my power to get you home to your folks."

With his hand, he lifted her chin. "Now go get a fire started, it's going to be dark soon."

Deacon helped a very drunk Red out of the wagon and secured him to the wagon wheel. The fire was going, and the girls were busy preparing a meal. The boys had taken care of the horses. He walked to the water barrel that was attached to the side of the wagon and looked in. It was almost empty. He would have to find water tomorrow.

He went to the girls. "Anita." She turned to him. "We are running low on water, so don't waste it."

"Yes sir."

"I do need for you to put some on the fire to heat. I need to remove that slug form Red, and I will need yours and Richard's help."

After the water was heated Deacon placed a knife in the fire and went to Red. He helped him over beside the fire and laid him down on a blanket. He took out his knife and looked up at Richard. "Hold him still while I dig this slug out."

Red's eyes popped open and he screamed at Deacon. "Oh hell no. You get away from me."

Deacon placed a piece of leather in his mouth. "Bite down on this." He smiled at Red, who was watching him with wild eyes. "This is going to hurt you a lot more than it will me."

Deacon removed the bandage and started probing in the bullet hole. Red was screaming out with pain; then he went quiet.

Richard looked at Deacon. "Is he dead?"

"No, he has only passed out. This slug is lodged in the bone." He kept probing till it came loose. "Got it."

He held the slug in his hand, then tossed it on the ground. "Give me that knife that's in the fire." Anita handed him the hot knife, and he pressed it against the open wound. Red flinched and screamed out again. "Hold him Richard."

Deacon stood and turned to Anita. "If you would, clean that with warm water the best you can."

He walked off and when he came back he had some fresh bandages and a jar of salve. "Put this on it and bandage it up."

Red was awake and staring at him. "You sonofabitch, I told you I didn't want you digging that slug out."

"Red, I really don't care what you want. That slug had to come out, so I took out. Now it can start healing and maybe you will live long enough to hang. Now get up."

Deacon took him back to the wagon wheel and shackled him to it. "I'll bring you something eat."

"How about that chew?"

"Okay, I'll get you a chew."

After getting Red a chew of tobacco and a plate of food, he took a plate for himself along with a cup of coffee. He walked up the hill overlooking the camp and sat down cross-legged staring into the darkness toward the east. A few minutes later he heard foot steps behind him. He glanced over his shoulder and saw Jason coming up the hill.

Jason walked up and sat beside him. "Care if I sit with you?"

"Nope."

Jason plopped down beside him. "Care if I ask you something?"

"Nope."

"Do you know where we are?"

"Nope. All I know is we are somewhere west of the Mississippi."

"Are we going to make it back?"

Deacon placed his fork in his empty plate and turned to him. "Son, with everything that is within me, I will get you home. I am going to do all I can to keep you and the others safe."

He stood. "Come on let's go back to camp." As he started to turn, he saw something in the distance. He stopped and looked closer. It looked to be a campfire. "You see that?"

"Yes, what is it?"

"Could be nothing, and then it could be trouble." He started down the hill at a fast walk.

As he walked into camp, he called to Richard. "Saddle me a horse, something besides Dusty."

Anita ran up to him. "What's wrong?"

"Nothing yet. I have to ride out to check on

something." He turned and looked at Red. Who was smiling at him. He took Anita by the arm and led her away from the others. "If I'm not back by morning shoot him and leave him here. Take the wagons and head east. There has to be a trail no less than a day's ride from here."

"But Mister Deacon, I can't just kill him."

"You will, or he will kill you."

"You can't leave us."

"Those men that were following us earlier today are camped not far from here. I am going to go take care of them before they have a chance to ambush us on the trail."

"But Mister Deacon…"

"Just do as I say."

Richard walked up leading a horse and holding a rifle. "Thought you might need this, too."

He gave the key to Red's shackles to Richard. He stepped up on his horse and looked at the kids who had all gathered around. "I'll be back before morning. Set up a watch and keep your eyes and ears open." Heeling the horse into a trot he rode away.

It took him most of an hour to reach the camp site. It was nestled in the edge of a wooded area. There were three men milling about the camp fire making small talk. Tying his horse to a sapling he crept closer with his pistol in his hand. Squatting down he listened in on their conversation.

One of the men was talking. "Pa, I tell you I think them folks were lost."

"May be son, but it ain't none of our affair. They will be okay."

Deacon had heard enough. He stood and called out. "In the camp, I'm coming in."

All three men stood and looked in his direction. The older man pulled his pistol. "You're welcome if your friendly."

Deacon walked in slow with his hands away from his guns. "I'm friendly with them that will that will let me be."

"Could I interest you in a cup of coffee?"

Deacon smiled and relaxed a little. "I'd like that; I'm called Deacon, Deacon Reeves."

The man holstered his gun. "I'm Boyd Bohle, this here is my son and my brother's boy. What brings you out this way?"

One of the boys handed him a cup of coffee. He nodded his thanks. "Long story. I'm with the wagons that you were following today, and I must admit that I have no idea where I am."

"The man smiled. "Thought you was lost. Where you going?"

"I need to get to Memphis. I had to get off the trail a couple days back due to my cargo and I can't seem to find a trail."

"If you don't mind me asking, what are you hauling?"

"Actually, I would rather not say. But I do need to get it to Memphis in one piece. Problem is there are some people who want it badly."

"Is it gold?"

Deacon smiled. "No, it's more precious than gold. So, can you tell me how far to a trail, and which way I need to go to get to it?"

The man smiled. "You are on it, well almost. It's just the other side of these trees. Take a left and in a half a day you will be at the ferry crossing."

Deacon smiled. "I knew I had to be getting close." He emptied his cup and handed it back to one of the boys.

"Thanks, you folks have a good night."

He started back toward camp feeling good. Another day and he would be in Memphis and then a short trip up the river to St. Louis.

As he rode up to the camp Richard met him holding a rifle. "Mister Deacon is that you?"

"Yes, it is. And I have some good news."

"What?"

"We are only about a day from Memphis."

A big smile spread across Richard's face. "First thing I want when we get there is a hot bath."

Deacon nodded. "I hear you. I'm going to bed. See you in the morning."

When he got up the next morning there was an air of excitement amongst the kids. Richard had spread the word, and everybody was excited except Red.

As Deacon walked to the fire to get a cup of coffee Red called out to him. "Hey Deacon."

Deacon looked at him and poured two cups of coffee. He walked to Red and handed him the cup.

Red sipped the coffee. "What happens to me when we get to Memphis?"

Deacon squatted down and looked Red in the eyes, ignoring his question. "Red, I need some answers."

"Go to hell."

"I'm going to give you till mid-day to make up your mind to tell me what I want to know. So, you think on it. I want to know who is in charge of this operation, on this side of the border and on the other. I want to know where you are taking these kids and who your contact is. You have till mid-day and then the pain will begin." Smiling at Red he stood and walked away.

Chapter 24

After Deacon and the children finished their meal, they pulled out. On his adventure the night before Deacon had crossed a creek. The banks were too steep to cross with the wagons here at this spot, so he rode down the creek to find a suitable crossing. Once he had found one, he rode back and led them to it. As they crossed the creek, the horses were allowed to drink.

Deacon was sitting his horse on the far side when the last wagon, which had the water barrel on it, started across. He called out to Jason, who was driving the team. "Hold them there in the creek. Let's fill that water barrel before we move on, just in case."

Anita, Richard, and Cindy retrieved buckets from the wagon and started filling the barrel. Then they started pouring water on each other. Deacon hooked his leg over the saddle horn and watched as the rest of the children jumped in to join the fun. This went on for about fifteen minutes before they decided to get back into the wagons.

Everyone was soaking wet, but they didn't care. They were laughing and teasing one another. Deacon was pleased that they could relax and have a little fun under the circumstances.

As they pulled out Deacon rode to the back of the first wagon where Red was riding. He pulled the flap back at the tail of the wagon; Red was gone.

He cursed under his breath for being so careless. He rode to the front of the wagon. "Hold up."

Cindy stopped the wagon. "What's wrong, Mister Deacon?"

"Red's gone."

Cindy looked back into the wagon. "He was there

when we reached the creek."

"So, he can't be far. You kids take these wagons to that clump of trees and wait there for me."

He rode back to the creek and looked around. He could see where Red had slipped through the grass toward a stand of trees. He rode in that direction, thinking to himself. "How could I have been so careless?" When he got to the wooded area he dismounted and walked, looking for signs of Red.

He could see were something or someone had walked through the leaves. He followed it for about a hundred yards. Then he saw Red running through the trees about fifty feet away. He pulled his pistol and fired, hitting a tree right in front Red. Red stopped and looked at him.

"Red. The next one is for you. Now, come this way, or I will shoot you."

Red turned and started walking toward him with a smile on his face. As he got closer, he spat amber. "Damn my luck. You would have to check that wagon before you got too far down the road. Sure thought I had given you the slip."

Deacon holstered his gun. "Better luck next time. Let's go." He mounted his horse. "Start walking."

When they reached the wagons, Red sat down and leaned against a wheel. "I could use a drink."

Deacon dismounted and went to the water barrel. There was a dipper made from a gourd hanging on the side of the barrel. He took the dipper of water to Red as the children watched.

Red took the water and drank it down. He handed the dipper back to Deacon. "Thanks."

Deacon looked at the children. "You kids go off into the woods. Me and Red are going to have a little talk."

They all looked at him and then at Red as they walked

off.

Red sat staring at Deacon. "Wait, you said I had till mid-day."

Deacon unlocked the shackle from Red's left hand and pulled his right hand up and locked the shackle around the top of the wagon wheel. As he pulled his knife out he looked at Red. "I changed my mind, start talking."

Red looked at the knife. "What are you going to do?"

"If you don't tell me what I want to know I am going to cut your fingers off one at a time. Starting with this little one right here." Deacon took him by the hand and pressed the knife blade against the first joint of the little finger and the wagon wheel.

Red screamed out. "You can't do that. I can't tell you. If I do, they will kill me."

"You have three seconds to start talking. One... Two..."

"I tell you, they will kill me."

"Three." Deacon pressed on the knife and sliced it across the joint of the finger. The finger fell to the ground as Red screamed.

Deacon took hold of another finger and pressed it against the wagon wheel. "Same as before, now start talking. One... Two..."

Red screamed out in pain. "Stop... stop, I'll tell you what you want to know."

Deacon took a clean rag from the wagon and wrapped Red's finger. Red was staring at him with hate in his eyes. "You, sonofabitch, I'll kill you for this."

"Before you do that, tell me what I want to know."

Red started talking. As he did Deacon took a piece of paper out and wrote down names and places, and directions.

When Red was finished, Deacon folded the paper and put it in his pocket. "Now, that wasn't so hard. You could have saved yourself a lot pain."

Red looked at him. "They will kill me."

"I don't think you are going to have to worry about what they will do to you. With everything that you have done, you're going to hang."

Deacon released the shackle from the wheel and placed it back on his left wrist. "Let's go, get in the wagon."

Deacon walked around the wagon and called out to the kids. "Let's go."

They all came running. When they got to the wagon Richard gave Deacon a curious look. "What was all the screaming about?"

Deacon shook his head. "Nothing for you to get concerned about. Mount up everybody."

One of the smaller boys came around the wagon holding something. "Is this somebody's finger?"

Deacon took it from him. "Here, give me that." He threw it into the woods. "Let's go, mount up."

In less than an hour, they were on the trail, headed to the ferry.

Deacon rode up beside the wagon that Cindy was driving. Anita had chosen to ride with her in the wagon instead of riding the horse. "How is he doing back there?"

Anita looked back in the wagon at Red. "He's drinking on that bottle of whiskey."

"Let me know if he gives you any trouble."

"Okay. Mister Deacon, why did you cut his finger off?"

"I'm sorry. I wish there had been another way. I needed some answers to some questions I had. He didn't want to give them to me. I had to convince him that it would be in his best interest to tell me what I needed to know."

"That was cruel and beastly."

Deacon looked off and then back at Anita. "I suppose it was. But not near as cruel as what he was going to do with you kids." He heeled Dusty into a lope and rode on ahead.

A couple hours later Deacon heard a steam boat whistle. He looked back at the kids. They had heard it also. He rode up beside the front wagon. "What is Red up to back there?"

Anita looked back in the wagon. "Looks like he is asleep or passed out."

"Okay, I'm going on ahead to check out the ferry landing. Bring them on in, unless you hear shooting."

"Are you expecting trouble?"

"Always."

He nudged Dusty into a lope.

As he rode up to the ferry landing, he noticed five men waiting to cross. Three of them were the three he had seen the night before. They didn't concern him. It was the other two. He ignored them and road down to the river. The ferry was on the other side coming back. He turned and rode back to the little shack that was beside the road. An elderly gentleman came out of the shack. "Can I help you?"

Deacon stepped down off his horse. "Sure can, I got two wagons and some horses coming up the trail. I would like to get them to the other side."

"Ain't no problem. Depending on how many horses you got."

"Good. They should be here soon."

"Hope so, won't wait long on them. This is the last run of the day, and I'm ready to go home." He turned and walked back into the shack out of the sun.

Deacon mounted Dusty and started to ride off when Mister Bohle called to him. "Hey, where's them wagons?"

Deacon rode over to him. He glanced at the other two men as he smiled at Mister Bohle. "You know how it is, can't find good help these days. My teamsters are mite fresh. But they will do in a pinch." He tipped his hat and rode back to meet the wagons.

Fifteen minutes later he led the wagons down to the ferry landing. Mister Bohle walked up as he got down from his horse. He had looked this little caravan over and was shaking his head. "I thought you said they were fresh. Hell, they're just kids. And what are you hauling?"

Deacon nodded to him and looked at the kids as they gathered around. "The kids."

Mister Bohle pushed his hat back and looked at the children. "Okay, they are more precious than gold. But... but are they all yours?"

"Nope, none of them belong to me. Long story short I'm taking them back to their folks. Someone stole them and was going to sell them as slaves in Mexico."

"Rotten bastards. I hope you killed them."

"Not all of them. I have one in the back of that wagon. He's going back to hang."

"Mister, if you need any help, you let me know."

"Thanks."

He looked around at the kids again and shook his head.

The ferry landed and a man in a buckboard pulled by two horses unloaded along with a couple men on horseback. The wagons were loaded, and everyone else loaded on to the ferry.

Deacon noticed one of the men kept watching him

and looking at the kids and the wagons. Deacon kept his eye on him, but nothing happened.

They unloaded on the Memphis side without incident.

He paid for the crossing and the ragtag bunch headed to the heart of town.

Chapter 25

They stopped at the sheriff's office. Deacon got off his horse and went to the back of the wagon. He helped Red out of the wagon and escorted him into the office. When he opened the door, the sheriff looked up from his desk.

As they walked across the room, the sheriff looked Red over, noticing his injuries. He stood and looked Deacon in the eye. "What do we have here?"

Deacon explained the situation to the sheriff. "I would like to put him in your jail for safe keeping till I can book passage on a boat going north."

"No problem, follow me."

As they walked back into the office the sheriff put his hand out. "Name is, Asa Pruitt."

Deacon shook hands with the sheriff. "Deacon Reeves. He needs some doctoring. I'll pay for that and for the food he eats. If you could see to that, I would appreciate it. But right now, I have nine tired, dirty and hungry kids to see after."

"You go take care of them, I'll take care of him."

"Thanks."

They went down the street to Black's Livery stable. A big burly man was working on a freight wagon. He looked up from his work as Deacon and the kids pulled up in front. He wiped his hands on his pants as he walked their way. "Can I help you?"

"I hope so. I want to sell everything you see here except the claybank."

The man walked around looking at the horses and the wagons. "I don't know if I can afford all this, or if I can use it."

"Make an offer, I need to get rid of it all, and I'll sell cheap."

"Eight horses and two wagons, plus saddles." He ran his hand through his hair and took a deep breath. "Four hundred dollars."

"Four hundred?" Surely you can do better than that."

"You said, make an offer, I made an offer. Now, how much you thinking?"

"Them's good wagons, and those horses are first class. I'll take six fifty."

"Can't do it."

"Let's go kids."

The man looked at the kids and then at Deacon. "Five hundred and honest, that's the best I can do."

Deacon turned and shook hands with the man. "Deal, only if you will board my horse for free. Grain him good and give him plenty of hay."

"Mister, you drive a hard bargain." He gave a big smile. "But you have a deal. Come by tomorrow and I will have your money."

"Let's go kids." He removed his saddle bags and rifle from his horse and they walked up the street. He noticed the man at the ferry watching him from across the street, but then again, several people were watching them.

They entered a dress shop. A lady met them as they filed in. She looked at the kids and then smiled at Deacon. "Can I help you?"

"Yes ma'am. I want these girls to have new clothes. Nothing too fancy, something that would be good for traveling in."

She looked the girls over. "I think we can take care of that. How do you plan on paying for all this?"

Deacon reached in his inside vest pocket and pulled out some folding money. "Cash. If that is okay."

"Yes sir."

"You take care of these girls and I will go take care of

the boys. Oh, and by the way, they are not to leave this store till I come back."

"Yes, sir."

"Come on boys." They walked on down the street till they come across a store that sold men and children clothes. They walked in, and he looked around. "Okay boys, go get whatever you need."

A sales lady walked up to him. "Do you need any help?"

"Yes ma'am, see to it that they get everything they need."

Deacon picked himself out a new shirt and pants. Then he waited for the kids to get their shopping complete. When they were finished, he paid the clerk and the boys gathered up their packages. When they walked back into the dress shop; the girls were all giggling and having a good time. Even the saleslady was laughing with them.

Deacon smiled. "You ladies finished?"

They all ran to him and hugged him. "Thank you, Mister Deacon."

The lady walked behind the counter and started figuring the bill. As he paid the lady, she smiled at him. "Thank you, Mister Deacon."

Everyone gathered up their packages, and they headed to the Memphis Grand Hotel. The clerk looked them over as the trail dusty bunch of kids and the tall rugged man walked in.

Deacon walked up to the desk. "I need three rooms. I prefer that two of them be side by side and the other across the hall from them. I will also want ten baths."

"I can do that. Just sign the book."

Deacon signed the register book, and the man gave him the keys. "Up the steps and to the left. The baths will be ready in about thirty minutes." He leaned out over the counter and pointed to a pair of doors at the end of a hall. "Girls on the left, men and boys on the right."

Deacon led the group up the steps. He unlocked the first door and looked in. There was a bed and a chair. He found the same thing in the other two rooms. "Okay kids. I'll fix this, either with more rooms or more beds."

Anita spoke up. "Mister Deacon, we will be fine, if you can get us something to put on the floor. We have slept in a lot worse in the past few weeks."

Deacon frowned and shook his head. "Not if I can do anything about it. Now go into your rooms and stay. Take your baths and stay in this hotel. When everyone has cleaned up, we will go eat." He smiled. "Okay?"

Deacon went back down to the clerk's desk. "I need another bed in rooms twenty-four and twenty-six."

"That's going to cost extra."

"That's fine."

He walked out and went to the saloon across the street and ordered a beer. He took his beer and went to a table. He sat down and sipped the beer. It was cold. It was good. He ordered another and drank it. He went to the bar and asked for a bottle of rye. He paid and went back to his room where he sat down and uncorked the bottle. His head was spinning. So much had taken place. But he now had the kids out of danger. He leaned back in the chair and took another drank from the bottle. He drifted off to sleep.

Some time had passed when Deacon awakened. He took his new clothes and went downstairs to take a bath. After his bath, he stopped at the desk. "Can I get these clothes cleaned?"

The clerk looked at the clothes. He took a bag from under the counter. "Yeah, put them in here, I'll take care of it for you."

Deacon put the clothes in the bag. "Thanks."

When he got to the girls' room he knocked on the door. The door opened. Another bed had been set up in the room; the girls were all cleaned up and looked amazing. Deacon smiled. "I'm sorry, I have the wrong room." He acted as though he was closing the door.

Cindy called out to him. "Mister Deacon!"

He pushed the door open and smiled at them. "This can't be the same girls I dragged in here off the trail?"

All the girls smiled at him. "Yes, we are."

"Well, danged if you aren't. Are you ladies ready to go eat then?"

They all came running toward the door. "We are starving."

The door to the boys' room opened and they filed out into the hall. Deacon looked at the group. He smiled. "Let's eat."

Deacon led the group down the boardwalk to Granny's Cafe. Again, he noticed that same man across the street watching them. This guy was starting to get on his nerves. When he reached the cafe door he stopped and turned to look at the man. "Richard, you take them on in and get us a seat, I'll be right back."

He stepped off the boardwalk and started toward the man. The man turned away and walked off. Deacon watched him walk away; he turned around and went back to the cafe.

He sat down with the kids as a waitress walked up to take their order. "What will you be having this evening?"

"Take their orders and give them whatever they want."

Orders were taken, and the waitress walked away. Deacon sat back in his chair and looked around the table at the kids. "I must say, you young ladies look amazing, with your new dresses and ribbons in your hair."

They all smiled. Anita folded her hands on the table. "Mister Deacon, thank you so much for everything."

"Don't thank me yet; this isn't over till I get you all back home, safe and sound. And we still have a long way to go."

"Well, well, I'll be, if it ain't Deacon Reeves." Came a booming voice from across the room over the rest of the chatter in the cafe.

Deacon turned his attention to the man that was making his way toward them; it was Captain Stumpy. When he reached the table, he looked around at the children. "What have we here? I thought you were searching for one girl."

Deacon stood and shook his hand. "Captain, I am glad to see you." I was looking for one; but as you see I found more, and we are in need of your help."

Stumpy took a chair from a nearby table and slid it up beside Deacon's. "Make room kids." Chairs scraped on the wooden floor as the kids slid their chairs sideways to make room for the man. He sat down and looked around the table and stopped at Deacon. "What kind of help, you need money?"

Chapter 26

Deacon smiled at Captain Stumpy. "I need a ride up river for me, these kids, and my horse."

Stumpy pushed back in his chair and stared at Deacon for a few seconds; then he looked around at the kids, one at a time. He leaned up close to Deacon and whispered. "I don't haul people and livestock. I haul freight, not as much hassle."

"Captain take a long look at these kids. They have been away from home for a long time. They have been mistreated and shackled, forced to live in inhumane conditions. Captain, they just want to go home."

"But... But, damn it, Deacon, I don't transport people and livestock."

"But you can."

Stumpy stopped a waitress and ordered his meal. After she had walked away he looked at Deacon. "For you and these kids, I will do it."

Deacon smiled. "Thanks."

Stumpy shook his head. "Ever since I met you it has cost me. If we stay friends much longer, I'll go broke."

"Captain, I will pay you. I don't expect you to do this for nothing. I just want to get these kids back home as soon as possible."

"Deacon, I was only messing with you. Don't get me wrong, money is good, I like money. But I will do this for nothing."

Their food arrived, and the chatter around the table picked up from the kids. All else was forgotten for the time being. Deacon watched as the nine hungry children stuffed their faces. He smiled, and then he noticed that the cafe had grown deadly quiet. He glanced around the room at everyone staring and pointing at the children.

Stumpy had noticed it also.

Stumpy stood up. "What's wrong with you people, ain't you ever seen hungry kids before. No, I guess you haven't. How about I chain you to a wagon for a couple months. Then we will see how you act when a plate of good food is set before you."

Deacon took him by the arm. "Sit down. You are making it worse."

Stumpy looked at him and then at the kids. They had all stopped eating and were staring at him. He flopped down in his chair. "Oh Gawd, me and my mouth."

Deacon nodded to the kids. "Let's eat."

After the meal, Deacon and Stumpy made their plans. "I didn't get in till this afternoon. I got freight to unload tomorrow, and we can pull out first thing the next day."

"That sounds good. We will meet you at the docks day after tomorrow, say around eight."

"I'd like to pull out sooner if you can be there. That river is going to be busier than flies on a gut wagon by eight."

"Okay, as soon as I can roust these kids, we will be there."

"Good I'll see you then." He stood and shook hands with Deacon. "Sure am glad you found them kids." He turned and walked away.

"Okay kids, time to go back to the hotel."

He paid for their meal and the group went to the hotel. Deacon noticed that same man again standing in the shadows across the street. When the man realized that Deacon saw him, he walked away.

At the rooms Deacon informed them to stay in their rooms. "Do not for any reason leave them." When he heard the bolts lock on the inside he left the hotel and went to the saloon.

He went to a table and sat down. One of the working girls came over. "What a' you have mister?"

"A beer, and a shot of rye."

She left and came back a few minutes later. As she sat the drinks down on the table, he slid the money to her. "Thanks."

"Hey, ain't you the man with all the kids that the whole town is talking about?"

He picked up his beer and glanced up at her. "Yeah, I spect' I am." He took a sip from the beer.

"How did you go about having so many kids so close to the same age?"

"Long, story." He smiled at her. "They're not all from the same woman." He almost laughed, thinking, wait till that story gets around town. Bunch of busybodies.

"Oh, oh." She turned and walked away.

He finished his drinks and left the saloon. There the man was as he walked out the door, walking across the street.

"Hey, you there, stop." Deacon started toward the man. He turned and looked at Deacon, then ran into an alley. When Deacon reached the alley, the man was gone. And he wasn't about to walk into that dark alley, not tonight.

He went to the hotel and knocked on the girls' door. From inside he heard. "Yes, who's there?"

"It's just me, Deacon. Is everything alright?"

"Yes, Mister Deacon, we are fine."

"Good night."

He got the same response from the boys' room. He went to his room. Picked up the bottle of rye on the table, pulled the cork. As the rim of the bottle touched his lips, he took it down and replaced the cork. "I need to stay clear headed."

After removing his guns and his boots he lay on the bed. A thousand thoughts were running through his head. Finally, sleep came.

Chapter 27

The next morning, he awoke with the sun in his face. He got up, poured water from a pitcher into a bowl, and washed his face. He put on his boots and guns and went to the boys' room. He knocked on the door. When it opened Richard was standing there, dressed and ready to go.

Without a word Deacon went to the girls' room and knocked. Cindy opened the door.

He looked past her at the others. "Is everyone ready for some breakfast?"

They all yelled. "Yes!"

The group went to the cafe and sat down. Their orders were taken. Coffee was brought to those who wanted it and cold milk for the others.

In a few minutes, plates of eggs, bacon, hot biscuits and gravy along with pancakes were being placed around the table. Everyone started eating. Deacon sipped his coffee and watched as the kids laughed and picked at each other as they ate.

The sheriff walked in and strolled up to the table. "Mister Reeves, I need to speak with you about those wagons."

"I sold them wagons to the man at the livery stables. So, what's the problem?"

"The problem is not with the wagons, it's what's in them."

Deacon looked at the sheriff. "What are you talking about? There wasn't anything in them wagons except some old blankets and some food supplies."

"Last night Mister Black heard a noise out by his stable. When he went to check he saw someone messing around them wagons. He called out to the man and he ran off. It got his curiosity up so this morning he checked them wagons and found a false bottom."

"A false bottom?"

"Yep. He also found two dozen repeating rifles in them wagons and over a thousand rounds of ambition. You know anything about it?"

Deacon shook his head. "No, I had no idea. But that explains why they wanted them back so bad. Also, I been seeing a man watching me ever since I got here. In fact, I saw the same man on the ferry when we crossed the river."

"You see him again, let me know. I would like to have a talk with him."

"I will."

The sheriff looked around the table at the children. "Did you kids know that them guns were in those wagons?"

They all shook their heads no.

"Okay. Deacon come see me, we need to talk."

"Be there right after breakfast."

Without another word the sheriff turned and walked away.

After breakfast and out on the boardwalk Deacon handed Anita some money. "Why don't ya'll go look around town. Stay in a group and stay out of trouble."

"What's the money for?"

He smiled at her. "You may see something you want to buy. Like some candy or something."

"Thanks."

All the kid turned and started down the boardwalk.

Deacon went to the sheriff's office. When he entered the sheriff was pouring a cup a coffee. He turned to Deacon. "Coffee?"

"No thanks, I had plenty at the cafe."

Freedom Rides
R. D. Gregory

"Deacon, it's hard for me to believe that you were in those wagons for days and didn't know about them guns."

"Think what you will. I never got in those wagons. I was preoccupied with seeing after those kids."

"You need to tell me everything you know about this."

"Look Sheriff, I was on the trail of one girl, and it led me to this. Red and his men were taking them kids to Mexico to be sold. No way was I going to let that happen. I took the kids from him and there has been someone dogging me ever since. My main concern was keeping them kids safe, I knew nothing of the guns."

At that moment someone came in the office. "Hey Sheriff, we got these rifles out here in the wagon. What do you want us to do with them?"

"Bring em' in here and put them in one of the cells till I can find out what my options are." He paused and took a sip from his coffee cup. "Deacon, I don't like it. It ain't right for you to be trapesing around all over the country side with these young children and them not yours."

"Sheriff, I am taking them back to St. Louis."

"So you say. People are talking, and some have asked me to take them children from you."

"Sheriff, I advise you to not go down that road. The only way anyone is taking them children from me is over my dead body. I've done some pretty bad things in my life, but mistreating these kids isn't one of them. As long as they are in my care, they will get the best care I can give them. So, not you or any of the busybodies' in this town are taking them from me. And you can tell them that are concerned about their wellbeing, that those kids are going to be well taken care of until I turn them over to the authorities in St. Louis."

The sheriff took another sip of his coffee. "I don't like

you much, but I trust you to do the right thing."

"Sheriff, I don't give a tinker's damn if you like me or not."

"Another thing. What happened to Red's little finger? He said you cut it off."

"It was a misunderstanding on his part. I needed some answers to some questions."

"So, why did you cut off his finger?"

"Because he wouldn't answer my questions."

"So, just like that, you cut his finger off?"

"I did and was about to cut off another when he told me what I needed to know. This man is as low of a human as they get. He's selling kids for slaves to the Mexicans. I aim to stop him and the man he works for. If he has to lose a finger for me to get the answers to a few questions, then I have no problem in cutting it off."

"I see."

"Now, if you have nothing else for me, I have things to do. I will come around tomorrow morning to get my prisoner. And I hope there's not going to be a problem."

"No problem."

"Good."

Deacon left the sheriff's office and went to the livery stable. As he came close to the stable Mister Black came out leading a horse that he had just finished shoeing. He tied the horse to the hitching rail and turned to Deacon. "You come for your money?"

"Yes."

The man grinned as he reached in his pocket and pulled out the money for the wagons and horses. "I bought more than I bargained for."

"Yeah I'd say you did."

"Did you know them rifles were in those wagons?"

"Nope."

"You reckin' I'll get to keep them since I bought the wagons?"

"I have no idea. And I really don't care one way or the other."

"But, them rifles are worth a lot of money."

"I'm sure they are. But those rifles are none of my concern."

"Who did they belong to?"

"I'm not sure. I took them from a man called Red. Don't even know his real name. He's going to be hung before long and the man he works for is too. So, as far as I'm concerned you can have the rifles." He took the money from the man and turned to walk away.

"Mister Deacon, are you telling me that I can have those rifles for the purchase of them wagons?"

"All I'm telling you is, I don't want the rifles. They are really not mine, so I don't have any say in them. That will be between you and sheriff to decide. I'm using the money from the sale of them wagons to pay the expenses of getting those children back home. I figure the people that took those kids can pay for that. I'll be coming by tomorrow morning early to get my horse. Thank you and have a good day." Without another word he walked away.

While walking up the street he noticed the man that had been watching him was standing on the boardwalk up head, leaning against a post. Deacon walked into a nearby store.

The gentleman who owned the store looked up as he walked in. "Can I help you?"

"You got a back door to this place?"

"Well, yes. Why?"

"Show me."

The man led him through a back room to a door that

opened up into the alley.

Deacon opened the door and looked down the alley. "Can I get back to the street from this alley?"

"Yes. There is a small walk way between each of the buildings on this street."

"Thanks." Deacon made his way down the alley past two more buildings. He slowly and quietly eased down the walkway that led back to the street. He peeped around the corner of the building and could see the man still leaning against the post.

Silently, he eased up behind the man. "You looking for me?"

Startled, the man turned. When he saw it was Deacon he started backing up as he did his foot missed the boardwalk and he fell into the street. He rolled over and scrambled to get to his feet.

Deacon grabbed him by the arm and spun him around shoving him into the narrow walkway between the buildings. He took him by the throat and pushed him against the wall of the building. "Who are you and why are you following me?"

The man couldn't breathe, Deacon's grip around his throat was so tight it was about to crush his wind pipe. In a hushed raspy voice, scarcely above a whisper, he squeaked out. "I can't breathe."

Deacon eased up on his grip. "Talk."

The man took two deep breaths before speaking. "I don't know what you're talking about. I ain't following you."

Deacon tightened his grip. "You better start talking mister."

"Okay, okay. Turn me loose."

Deacon released his grip and took the man's gun from its holster and placed it in his belt.

"Look mister, all I was doing is trying to find out what happened to the kids and the rifles. When Red didn't show up at the next relay point I came looking for him and them wagons. I seed' where you had jumped em' and I figured you would head toward Memphis. Then I seed' you at the ferry so I been watching for a chance, to at least get them guns back. Now that the sheriff has em', I guess I might as well head back south."

"You aren't going any place except to jail. Now, who are you working for?"

"I ain't stupid, mister. If I told you that I would be a dead man."

"You're a dead man if you don't." He tightened his grip on the man's throat with one hand and hit him in the eye with his other fist. The man's head bounced off the wall behind him. His knees buckled, and he started sliding down the wall.

Deacon turned him loose and let him fall to the ground. He was out cold. Deacon stood looking at him in disgust. He took hold of his shirt collar and dragged him to a nearby watering trough. People on the street stopped and watched as Deacon threw the man on to the edge of the watering trough and pushed his head under the water.

A man ran over to him. "Sir, you are going to drown that man!"

Deacon glanced over at the new comer, then back at the man whose head was under the water. He was now trashing about trying to get his head above the water.

"Yeah, that's the idea." He ulled the man up out of the water. "You ready to start talking?"

The man coughed and shook his head. "I said too much already."

Deacon pushed him back under the water. He felt the

cold steel of a gun barrel press against the back of his neck.

"Turn him loose!"

Chapter 28

Deacon released his hold on the man and slowly turned around. He was staring down the barrel of a forty-five with the hammer cocked. Holding the pistol was a very upset sheriff.

The sheriff lowered his gun. He then reached over and took Deacon's guns. He stuck them in his belt, never taking his eyes off Deacon. "You are under arrest."

"Sheriff, this is the man that has been following me. I wasn't going to kill him, but I did need some answers."

The man was getting up. The sheriff helped him up. "Both of you are under arrest. Let's go." He pointed with his gun toward the jail.

After Sheriff Asa had the two behind bars he leaned against the wall. He could see Red was watching the man that Deacon had almost drown. The sheriff turned his attention to the man. "Do you know that fellow over there?"

The man looked at Red. "Yeah he's my boss."

"What kind of work do you do for him?"

"I'd rather not say."

Red spoke up. "You keep your mouth shut. Don't say another word."

Deacon was setting on his cot in the cell. "Sheriff, if you hadn't interrupted me I would have these answers already."

The sheriff looked at Deacon. "Yeah, if you didn't kill him first."

At that moment Anita and Richard ran in to the sheriff's office. They looked at Deacon in his cell. Anita walked up to the cell and then turned to the sheriff. "You have to let him out."

The sheriff took a step closer to Deacon's cell. "Now

why do I have to let him out?"

"Because, we need him to get back home."

"Well young lady he's not going anywhere till he goes before the judge. He almost killed a man."

Richard spoke up. "He wouldn't have killed that man. He was only trying to get him to talk. I saw the whole thing."

"Maybe, but from where I was standing it looked like he was going to kill him. So, he stays in jail."

Deacon stepped up to the bars. "Anita."

She turned to him as he motioned her to come closer. He whispered in her ear. She turned from him and took Richard by the arm. "Let's go."

After they left the sheriff kept questioning the man, but he wouldn't say anything. He wouldn't even give the sheriff his name.

Two hours later Anita and Richard came into the sheriff's office and handed the sheriff a telegram. He read it and without a word went to Deacon's cell and unlocked the door. "Okay Mister Reeves, you are free to go. I don't know who you know to have gotten the governor of Tennessee to send me a telegram demanding I turn you lose. But, you are free to go. I was also instructed to assist you in any way I can and not to hinder you in any of your dealings with these men."

Deacon went to the sheriff's desk and picked up his guns and knife that the sheriff had also taken from him. He turned and looked at the two men in the cell. Red was standing holding on to the bars in his cell watching him.

With his knife in his hand, Deacon walked to the cell where the other man was locked up. "Sheriff, unlock this door." He turned to Richard and Anita. "You kids get out of here."

Anita looked at the sheriff and then at Deacon.

"Please Mister Deacon, don't."

Deacon glanced at her. "I said for you to leave, now go."

The sheriff unlocked the cell door and stepped back. "I don't approve of this."

Deacon stepped past the sheriff. "You tried being nice and it didn't get you anywhere. Now it's my turn and if you don't approve, you best leave. Might want to go get the doctor."

The man was backing up. "What are you going to do?"

Deacon grabbed the man by the throat and pushed him against the cell wall. "That's up to you. If you tell me what I want to know, then nothing. If you don't then I'm going to start cutting parts of your body off." He placed the knife at the top of the man's left ear. "Like this ear, for starters."

"Sheriff, you can't just stand there and let him do this."

The sheriff shook his head. "Sorry mister, you're on your own. Best tell him what he wants to know."

A trickle of blood was running down the side of the man's jaw from the small cut at the top of his ear. He looked at Deacon with fear in his eyes. "What do you want to know?"

"For starters what's your name?"

"Corban Watson."

Deacon turned to the sheriff. "Get pencil and paper and write all this down."

And so it began. The questioning continued till Deacon confirmed most of what Red had told him, plus where the rifles were going.

Deacon being satisfied with the answers that Corban had given him he, left the cell. The sheriff locked the door and the two went to his office.

The sheriff shaking his head poured a cup of coffee and handed it to Deacon. He then poured himself one and went to his desk and sat down. He opened a drawer and took out a bottle of whiskey. Poured some in his coffee and offered it to Deacon.

"Thanks." Deacon took the bottle, poured some in his coffee and handed it back. "Now you see what kind of people we are dealing with."

"Yeah, you told me this already, but I didn't understand the full gravity of it all. It's all about the money, and they don't care who gets hurt. I deal with some riffraff here and some killings, but I had no idea this kind of stuff was going on."

"Sheriff Asa, this is only a drop in the bucket. I had to know who is behind all this if I'm going to stop it."

"Deacon, this has me to thinking. I've had reports of children missing here. I never did figure out where them kids got off to. My gawd, how could I have been so blind?" He took a drink from his coffee cup.

Deacon walked to the window and looked out. He could see Richard, Anita and the rest of the kids sitting on the boardwalk in front of the hotel. "Those kids out there are the lucky ones. I got them back before they arrived at their destination."

"Yeah, but what about the countless others that have been sold? What can be done about them?"

"I don't know. As you have found out I have ties with some pretty powerful people. I'll see what they can do after I get these children back home."

Deacon set his empty coffee cup on the desk. "I'll see you tomorrow morning."

When he walked out of the sheriff's office the kids saw him and came to meet him. He met them with a smile. "Who's hungry?"

At the cafe while waiting for their food Anita leaned up close to Deacon and whispered. "Did you hurt that man?"

Deacon whispered back. "No."

She leaned back in her chair and smiled at him. "Good."

The rest of the day and night went by without any problems.

The next morning Deacon rousted everyone early, they ate, and Deacon went to the livery to get his horse. He payed the bill at the hotel and went to the sheriff's office.

The sheriff was waiting for Deacon when he walked in. "I have Red ready to go, but what about Corban?"

"You have all the information you need to send him to prison. You keep him, but Red is going back with me. I need him to point a finger at Crawford."

The sheriff took Red by the arm and led him to the door. "I'll walk with you to the docks. He may have more friends around."

When they reached the docks Stumpy was ready for them. Dusty didn't want to walk the ramp that led to the boat but after a little coaxing he followed Deacon on board the boat.

Everyone settled in and the boat pulled out. The kids were all excited. They were now on the last leg toward home.

Chapter 29

When they reached St. Louis and debarked the boat, a throng of people started gathering. As they walked down the street, more people joined the group. One lady ran up to Deacon. She looked at the kids with tears in her eyes. "Mister, did you find by little girl?"

"Ma'am, if she's not here, then, no I didn't."

The lady sadly turned away and started crying.

Two police officers met them in the street. One of them took Red by the arm. "We'll take this man off your hands."

Deacon looked the two over. He recognized them to be the ones in the warehouse the night Tadpole had been taken. "I don't think so. He's my prisoner and I'm turning him over to the Chief."

"Then you are under arrest."

Anita stepped between Deacon and the two officers. When she did, Richard and the rest of the kids stepped in also. Richard was carrying a rifle; he levered a round into the chamber. "I don't think we are going to let you take him or Red."

The officer started to say something when he realized the throng of people that had gathered were closing in on him and surrounding them. He glanced around and turned to the other officer. "Let's go." Without another word they walked away.

Deacon placed a hand on Richard's shoulder. "You shouldn't have done that. I would have taken care of the situation. Now you are a marked man. Those two are involved in this somehow."

Richard watched the two officers walk away. He lowered the hammer on the rifle. "I figured they were, but I didn't care. You have put your life at risk getting us home. I wasn't about to stand here at let them take you."

"Like I said, I would have taken care of those two. Let's go."

Deacon gave Red a little push, and they started on down the street. As they walked close to Richard's father's place of business, his mother and father came running out of the store. His mother, crying, grabbed her son in a big hug.

His father took Deacon by the hand and shook it vigorously. "Mister, I don't know who you are, but I owe you a ton for saving my boy and the rest of these children. If I can ever do anything for you, please let me know."

"Mister Kelly, you don't owe me anything. But I do want to tell you, that you have raised a fine, brave young man. You should be very proud of him."

"We are. His mother has been absolutely devastated ever since he has been missing." He looked at Red, noticing the shackles on his wrist. "Is this the man who took him?"

"Yes, one of them."

"Leave him with me. I'll take care of him."

"I'd love to, but you know I can't do that."

"All I need is a few minutes alone with him."

Deacon smiled. "Can't do it. Let's go Red."

He started to walk off when Richard stopped him. "Mister Deacon."

Deacon turned to him. "Yes."

Richard put his hand out to shake hands with Deacon. As their hands grasped together, a tear fell from the corner of Richard's eye. "Thank you."

"Thank you for your help with this bunch. I couldn't have done this without yours and Anita's help. You'll do good son. You remember what I said about being a marked man, so watch your back."

"Yes sir, Mister Deacon, I will."

As the group traveled on down the street toward the police station, the mass of people grew larger. Red was starting to get nervous. He could hear some of the comments coming from the crowd; they were wanting to hang him.

When they reached the police station, Chief Atkins was standing there with several of his officers. "Mister Deacon, I see that you have found the missing girl, and it looks like you found others as well."

"Chief, this man is responsible for the kidnapping of these kids. If you will place him in your jail for safe keeping, I would appreciate it." He turned and looked at the crowd, then back at the chief. "This crowd is building into a lynch mob."

Chief Atkins was watching the crowd. "I see that it is." He looked at two of his officers. "Put this man into a cell. Deacon, you and the children follow me."

They followed the chief into his office. He sat down behind his desk, then looked at Anita and smiled. "Miss Bennet, it is good to see you back safe."

"No thanks to you."

"Now wait a minute. I..."

She cut him off in mid-sentence. "I don't want to hear any of your excuses. Me and some of the others were locked up here in a warehouse for days. If you had looked for us we would have been found."

Deacon placed his hand on her shoulder. "Anita now is not the time for this. Right now, we need to get you home."

The chief stood. "Yes, I agree." He walked to the door of his office and called out to one of his officers. "Go inform Senator Bennet that his daughter is here safe in my office."

He turned back and looked at Deacon and the group of kids. "Deacon, I will need a full report from you."

"Beg your pardon, but I don't report to you."

"I realize you don't report to me. But, I need to know what happened, when and where."

"Maybe you do, and I will tell you everything I know in due time. Right now, my concern is these kids. You help me find their parents, and I will tell you everything. The person you need to talk to is Red, the man I brought in. He can give you names and places."

"Okay, but I will need to know everything."

"Oh, and another thing. I understand that Big Joe is in jail for my murder. As you can see, I'm not dead; so, I want him released, immediately."

"I can't do that, not without direction from the judge."

"I suggest if you want to remain the Chief of Police, you will do it now."

The chief turned to an officer standing nearby. "Go get Big Joe and bring him here."

A commotion could be heard out in the hall, the door burst open, and a very excited Tadpole came running in all out of breath. A police officer was hot on his trail. "Sorry, sir."

Everyone turned to watch him as he rushed to Deacon. "I knew you would come back; I knew you would! Did you kill them bastards?"

Deacon squatted down and took Tadpole by the arms. "It's good to see you too. Now what did I tell you about using that kind of language?"

He smiled at Deacon. "Sorry. Did you, or did you just whoop up on em'?"

"You settle down. The chief and I have to talk, so I

want you to go sit in the hall until we are finished."

He dropped his head and pouted. "Okay." He met Big Joe coming in the door. He grinned at him. "He's back."

Big Joe ruffled his hair. "I see he is. Good thing too, huh?"

The Chief looked at Big Joe. "You are free to go."

Big Joe walked closer to the chief and looked down at him. "I tried to tell you, and you wouldn't listen. Now will you take note to what I tell you? You've got officers on your force that are taking bribes."

The chief stepped back. "Okay, I'll listen, but not now. I want to talk to you and Mister Deacon in private."

When Senator Bennet arrived with his wife there was a happy reunion. He hugged his daughter then went to Deacon. "Mister Deacon, thank you very much. When we got the wire from her, we were so excited. And here she is, safe and sound."

"She is a strong young lady. All of them are. They have been through some bad times, but hopefully they will put it behind them."

"Yes, yes of course." He turned to his wife and daughter. "Let's go home."

Mrs. Bennet and Anita stepped over to Deacon. Mrs. Bennet had tears in her eyes. "May I give you a hug."

Deacon smiled. "Yeah, I guess."

She put her arms around him and buried her head into his chest. "Thank you for bringing my baby home." She turned him loose and stepped back. Wiping her tears with a lace hanky. "I would like to invite you to the house tonight, for supper. Please come."

"I would be honored to join you."

Anita smiled at him. She gave him a big hug and looked up into his eyes. "Thank you, Mister Deacon. I will never forget you and what you have done for us."

"You are welcome, I'm glad I was able to locate you."

They turned to walk away, when Anita stopped and looked at the other children. To no one particular, she asked. "What happens to them?"

The chief spoke up. "I will notify the orphanage home to come and get them till we can locate their parents."

She put her hand to her mouth. "Oh no, you can't do that."

"I have no other choice."

She turned to her father and mother. "No, you can't let them go there after what they have been through."

Her father held her to him. "Dear, it will only be for a few days."

She pushed back and glared at her father. "No, not even for one hour. They are coming home with me."

"Be reasonable Anita, we can't take them home with us."

"They go home with me or I go with them. I will not leave them till I know they are safe with their parents."

Mrs. Bennet looked at her husband. She then looked at each of the children. "How would you like to come home with Anita?"

Senator Bennet turned to Chief Atkins. "I guess, we will be taking all the children to our house for the time being."

The chief nodded his head. "Very well. I will make arrangement for transportation." He walked out.

He came back in with an officer following him. "Each of you go with this officer and give him the necessary information we need to locate your parents."

The children followed the officer out of the room.

Chapter 30

After the children left, the chief closed the door. He motioned to chairs. "Please sit down, gentlemen. Would you care for some coffee?"

As Big Joe took his seat. "Is it the same mud that you gave me while I was locked up?"

"No."

"If that's the case, yes, I would love some."

The chief stepped out of the office and Tadpole came busting in. "Mister Deacon, I need to talk to you."

"Not now, I need to talk to the chief."

"But, but, it's important."

"Okay, what is so important?"

"I heard something."

"What?"

"I heard some men talking and they said they were going to kill you and Big Joe."

"When did you hear this?"

"Today, right after you got back. I didn't see who it was, and they didn't see me. But I heard them plain as day. One of them said that you had to die, and soon. And the other one agreed."

"Did you recognize their voices?"

"Not sure, but I think it was those two police officers."

The chief came back in with a pot of coffee and three cups. He paused when he saw Tadpole then went on to his desk and started pouring coffee.

Deacon patted Tadpole on the head. "Thanks, now go sit in the hall till we are finished here."

After Tadpole was gone, the chief took pencil and paper from his desk. "Alright Mister Deacon, tell me the whole story, and don't leave anything out."

"Do we have to do this now?"

"I think it's best if we get this over with."

Deacon leaned back in his chair, took a long breath. He started talking, telling the chief everything that he could think of, leaving nothing out.

The chief had been taking notes the entire time. He leaned back in his chair and shook his head. "That's quite a tale and several dead bodies."

"Not as many as it could have been." Deacon leaned forward in his chair. "Now I have a question for you."

"What's that?"

"What are you going to do about Crawford?"

"Not sure. I will have to build a case against him. You don't arrest a man as powerful as Crawford unless you have proof of a crime."

"You have proof. Red named him as the man in charge of kidnapping and selling these children, plus the selling of rifles to the Indians and the Mexicans."

"So you say. He has not told me that. All I have to go on is what you say he said. That is not enough for me to go charging a man."

Deacon stood. "I see what's happening. Crawford has you in his pocket as well."

The chief stood and leaned over his desk. "You have no call to accuse me of that."

"Don't I? I gave you all the information you need, and now you are telling me there is nothing you can do!"

"That's not true. I said I had to have proof. And soon as I get it, I will arrest him."

Deacon walked toward the door. Big Joe stood and followed.

The chief came around his desk. "Big Joe, I do want to say I am sorry for wrongfully charging you."

Big Joe glared at him. "Chief Atkins, I told you when you arrested me what was going on, and you wouldn't listen. Now Deacon is telling you the same thing. I do hope you do something about it. Because if you don't, well, I would hate to be in your shoes."

"Trust me gentlemen, I will look into this. And if he is behind all this, he will be charged."

Deacon opened the door to the office. "I hope so, and soon."

"By the way, Deacon, I must ask you to surrender your firearms."

"Chief Atkins, you can ask all you want to, but I'll not be parting with my pistols. There are people in this town that want me dead, and some of them are on your police force. Thank you, but I will be keeping them."

"I could call my officers and arrest you."

"Yes, I suppose you could, but I advise you not to do that. Several people would get hurt. I'll not give up my pistols to you or anyone."

The chief stood for several seconds staring into Deacon's eyes. "You are a hard man."

"Only when I have to be. Be reasonable, Chief, lives are at stake here. Mine, Big Joe's, the kids and maybe even Red's. Even though you have him locked up, he could be in danger."

"Okay, keep your guns."

Deacon nodded. "I'm glad you see it my way. If you need me, I'll be at the hotel." He and Big Joe left the office and as they walked past Tadpole sitting in the hall he jumped up and followed.

They left the building and walked into the street. Most of the people that had gathered had left. One of the men still there walked up to Deacon. "Sir, I hate to bother you, but do you know where my daughter is? She has been missing for over six months."

Deacon untied Dusty from where he had secured him

to a hitching rail. He looked the man in the eyes. "I'm sorry sir, no I don't. All I know is there is a place in Mexico where kids have been taken to. Where they went from there is anybody's guess. Again, I'm sorry."

The man turned and walked away, as did most everyone else. Deacon picked Tadpole up and placed him on Dusty. "Big Joe, I don't know about you, but I could use a drink."

Big Joe grinned. "Follow me." They walked to the closest saloon. Deacon helped Tadpole down from Dusty. "You stay here and keep him company, we'll be back in a few minutes."

Tadpole took Dusty's reins and with a pout on his face, he sat down on the boardwalk with his feet dangling off the edge.

Big Joe and Deacon ordered a beer each and went to a nearby table. Big Joe drank his mug of beer straight down, wiped his mouth, and held the mug up so the barkeep could see it was empty. "Bring me another and a shot of whiskey." He smiled at Deacon. "I sure am glad you got back. They had me scheduled to hang in a few days."

"I know. I heard about it, but there wasn't anything I could do. I had to go after those kids before I lost their trail."

Big Joe nodded his head. "I know. Them sonsofbitches railroaded me. Had everyone believing I had killed you. They wouldn't believe little Tadpole either."

"Big Joe, what about Chief Atkins, can I trust him to go after Crawford?"

The barkeep placed another round on the table. Big Joe picked up the whiskey glass and looked at Deacon. "Yeah, I think so. The chief is a good man, at least I think he is. I don't have hard feelings toward him. He tries to do the right thing, if the powers to be in this town will let him."

"How powerful is this Crawford?"

"Well, you might say he has this town by the throat, at least the shipping part of it. Which is a big part of this town. He pretty much controls the docks. Almost nothing goes up or down this river from here without his say so."

"How can that be?"

"He has a lot of people on his payroll. You don't work those docks without his say so. And the boats don't get loaded or unloaded unless he says it's okay."

"How about you, are you on his payroll?"

"Hell no!"

"How have you managed to work the docks then?"

"There are a few of us around. Most who do work for him don't like it, but they have to feed their families. Me, I don't have nobody but me to worry about, so I can be picky who I break my back for." He drank his whiskey and chased it with a big swallow of beer.

They finished their drinks and walked out where Tadpole was sitting holding Dusty. Deacon picked him up and placed on Dusty, he turned to Big Joe. "See you later. I need to see to my horse and get me a room. I'll be going to the senator's house for supper. I'll look you up later tonight."

"Right. You can find me at the bar down by the docks."

Chapter 31

That evening at Senator Bennet's house he was met at the door by Anita. "I've been watching for you. Oh, Mister Deacon, it is so good to be home." She put her arms around him and gave him a big hug. "Thank you, thank you. I can't imagine what my life would have been like if you hadn't saved us."

He smiled at her. "I'm glad I was able to help."

She took him by the hand and led him to the parlor where her father was waiting.

The senator stood as they entered the room. "Mister Deacon, can I fix you a drink?"

"Yes, rye whiskey, if you have it."

"Yes, of course." He poured the drink and handed it to Deacon. "Here you are. This is good Kentucky whiskey."

"Thanks."

Mrs. Bennet entered the room. "Good, you are here. Supper is being set, please come to the dining room."

The dining room was full of chatter as they walked in. All the kids were there, even Richard; and when Deacon entered the room, they fell silent. All were staring at him, their hero! He took his seat, and the chatter began again. He smiled as he looked at each of them. Mrs. Bennet had spared no expense. All of the children were wearing new clothes.

After the meal, Deacon and the senator went back to the parlor for drinks. "Deacon, there is no way I can ever repay you for what you have done. If you ever need anything, please let me know."

Deacon took a drink that was handed to him. "Actually Senator, there may be something you can do for me."

The senator smiled. "Name it, Mister Deacon."

Deacon sat down, took a sip from his drink. For fifteen minutes, he laid out a plan to the senator. When he was finished, the senator stood and walked to the table where the bottle was setting. He filled his glass and then refilled Deacon's, without saying a word. He placed the bottle back on the table and turned to face Deacon. "It's suicide."

"Can you help?"

"I'll do what I can. I'm not sure what I will be able to do."

"I understand, but if you will make the necessary contacts and have them to look in to it, I would be grateful."

"Yes, of course."

There was a knock on the door and Mrs. Bennet and the kids came in with pie and coffee. "The two of you slipped off before dessert was served. So, we brought it to you."

The senator took the coffee and pie from his wife. "Thank you, my dear."

Later that night after Deacon had left the senator's house and taken Dusty to the livery he went to the docks to find Big Joe. As he entered the bar, he could see Big Joe sitting at the table where he saw him the first time they met. Big Joe saw him when he walked through the door and waved to him.

Deacon went to his table and sat down. "I see no one has slipped a knife in your ribs yet."

Big Joe laughed. "Not yet, that's why I'm sitting here with my back to the wall."

"Not a bad idea."

The two sat drinking and talking till after midnight. Deacon pushed his chair back. "Big Joe, I'm going to bed.

I'll see you tomorrow sometime."

Big Joe stood. "Sounds like a good idea."

They left the bar together and walked down the street. At the next corner Big Joe turned and went his way as Deacon walked on to the hotel. He went to his room and went to bed.

The next morning as Deacon came out of the hotel, Tadpole met him. "Mister Deacon, the sun's been up awhile; where you been?"

Deacon smiled at him. "In bed, asleep. First good sleep I've had in several days. Now I'm hungry; have you had breakfast?"

"No. I drank a glass of milk, does that count?"

"Come on let's go grab some flapjacks."

After breakfast, Deacon headed to the police station with Tadpole tagging along beside him. He stopped suddenly. "Reckon what's going on?" He was looking down the street at a group of police officers coming his way, with the chief leading them.

When the group reached Deacon, the chief stopped. "I arrested the two officers that were indicated, and we are headed to the docks to check Crawford's warehouses. I was wondering if you want to join us?"

"I would love to."

When they reached the docks, the officers spread out, going to different building. Using crowbars, they pried off locks; and if they were met with resistance from of any of Crawford's men, they were arrested.

In their search they found areas where the children had been kept captive until they were moved down river. They also found rifles, ammunition and crates of silver.

They found some of the same things when searching Crawford's boats. Several men were arrested and taken to jail. Big Joe had joined them. He, Deacon and the chief were looking at several crates of rifles. Big Joe frowned at the chief. "Are you satisfied? Do you have enough proof now to arrest Crawford?"

"Yeah. Let's go. Meet me here in thirty minutes. I'm going after a horse and the police wagon."

When the chief returned riding a horse, he had ten officers with him along with a prison wagon. Deacon had saddled Dusty and was waiting. The group rode out and headed down the road to Crawford's house. Deacon looked at the group of police officers, noticing they were all well-heeled. "Looks like you are expecting trouble?"

"Yes I am. I think, by now he has heard about us searching his warehouses. I figure he has to know that I will be coming for him next."

"What happens if he has run already?"

The chief shook his head. "There's only so much I can do, and so far I can go. I'm stretching things a little by going to his house. He doesn't live inside the city limits."

When they reached the large two-story house, the chief sent men to the back of the house.

Everybody dismounted and pulled their weapons. The chief sent three men to the front door with instructions to break it down if it was locked. The door wasn't locked, and as the officers entered, gun shots were heard. Deacon ran to the door and peeped around the door facing. Two officers were on the floor, bleeding. The other was down behind a large piece of furniture.

He also saw two men, one was in a doorway across the room. The other was on the upstairs balcony, he was holding a shotgun. He could hear the officers coming in the back door. The man with the shotgun saw him and fired, just missing Deacon. He fired again. Deacon took this opportunity, while the man was reloading to rush into the room. He saw that the man in the door way was looking toward the back of the house. The man with the shotgun was reloading when Deacon's bullet struck him mid-chest knocking him off his feet.

The other man was turning back toward Deacon, when the slug hit him in the shoulder, knocking him down. Deacon ran to him, kicking the gun away. The officers helped him to his feet. The chief and the other officers came in, checked on their wounded, then came to where Deacon was.

Deacon turned to the chief. "He says there is no one else here, except for the house keeper and the cook."

"Where's Crawford?"

"He hasn't said, yet."

The man was standing between two officers. The chief looked at him. "I'm only going to ask you once. Where is Crawford?"

The man dropped his head. "I don't know."

The chief walked up closer and looked at the wound in his shoulder. He stuck his finger in the bullet hole and started pressing. The man started screaming. "He left. He left!"

Without removing his finger, he asked. "How and which way?"

The man was still screaming in pain. "He went south in a buckboard."

"When?"

"My gawd man, I don't know, fifteen, twenty minutes ago."

The chief removed his finger from the hole, looked at the blood on his hand, and wiped it on the, not so bloody side of the man's chest. "Get him out of here."

Deacon was headed toward the door when he heard the chief call his name.

He turned around. "What?"

"Where're you going?"

Deacon turned back toward the door. "After him, I'm not limited by boundaries or borders."

Chapter 32

Deacon walked out to where the horses were. He took the reins of his horse and then mounted the chief's horse. He turned to one of the officers that was standing near. "Tell the chief, I'm borrowing his horse."

He heeled the horse into a lope and rode south. He could see the buckboard tracks in the dusty trail. He loped the horse till it gave out and started slowing down. He stopped and dismounted. He took a set of hobbles from his saddle and placed them on the chief's horse. He mounted Dusty and rode off in a lope following the tracks.

He rode at a lope for several minutes and then slowed down to a long trot. When he saw the buckboard, it was traveling at a slow trot. So as not to draw attention, he rode up behind the buckboard slowly. As he drew nearer, he could see there were two people in the buckboard.

He heeled Dusty into a lope and went past Crawford and his man in the buckboard. When he was about twenty feet in front of them, he pulled up and spun Dusty around with his gun drawn.

With surprise and fear on his face, Crawford reined to a stop. The man with him was reaching for his gun.

"Don't do it mister, unless you have a death wish."

The man paused for a second with his hand on the butt of his revolver. He jumped from the buckboard and hit the ground in a roll. When he came up, his gun was out, but he never got a chance to use it. Deacon shot him in the left shoulder, knocking him off balance. Not willing to quit, the man regained his balance and was bringing his gun up when Deacon's next bullet hit him center chest. He fell to the ground, drawing his last breath.

When Deacon turned his attention back to Crawford, he was reaching for a rifle lying at his feet in the buckboard. "Mister Crawford, don't make the same mistake your friend made."

He straightened up and looked at Deacon. "Who are you, and what do you want?"

Deacon grinned. "They call me Deacon, and I am your worst nightmare. I've come to take you back to stand trial for kidnapping, murder, and anything else we can come up with. You are going to hang for what you have done or at least spend the rest of your life in prison."

"You can't arrest me; you're not the law."

Deacon waved the gun he was holding, in a sided to side motion. "This is all the law I need to take you back. Now turn that rig around, and let's get going. But before you do, pick that peace of trash up off the road and put it in the back of that buckboard."

Crawford stepped off the buckboard and picked the dead man up. He placed him in the back of the buckboard, noticing the trunk setting behind the seat. "Mister Deacon, can't we make a deal. I can make you a very rich man. All you have to do, is ride away. Why, you wouldn't even have to go back to St. Louis. You can go anywhere in the world."

"I don't make deals with people like you. Count yourself lucky that I haven't put a bullet in your worthless brain. Now get on that buckboard and let's go."

When they reached the police station, Deacon escorted Mister Crawford into the chief's office. "Here he is, back in your city limits."

The chief stood. "Well, well, Mister Stanley Crawford, you are under arrest."

"For what, you haven't got anything on me." He

pointed to Deacon. "This is the man you should be arresting. I witnessed him killing a man in cold blood."

The chief smiled at two officers who had followed them into the office. "Take Mister Crawford to a cell, while Deacon and I talk. I'll charge him later, after I have come up with all the charges I can bring against him."

The two officers escorted the complaining man out the door.

The chief opened a drawer and took out a bottle and two glasses. He poured whiskey in each glass and handed one to Deacon. He lifted his glass toward Deacon. "To you sir, for helping to rid this city of a major part of its scum problem."

Two days later Deacon was at the railroad station waiting on the train to take him back to Colorado. He and Big Joe had spent most of the night before drinking and talking. He had a bad hangover.

Tadpole was sitting next to him. "Mister Deacon, will I ever see you again?"

"Hard to say, little friend. Life has a way of bringing the unexpected. So, who knows? Listen to me Tadpole, you stay out of trouble and stop harassing the police. They can be your friend, if you will let them."

"Yes sir."

He heard footsteps coming; when he looked that way, he saw several people coming toward him. The Bennet family and some of the children, who as yet had not been picked up by their parents. Also, Chief Atkins and the Kelly family.

Deacon stood as Chief Atkins drew near. "Deacon, we wanted to come by and say our farewells. This city and its people owe you more than we can ever pay. You come back anytime you can. You can even wear your guns." He laughed. "I have your sworn statement, plus we have enough against Crawford and his men to put them away for a very long time. You take care."

They shook hands. "Thanks, I'm glad I could help."

The train conductor called. "All-a-board."

Senator Bennet stepped up and handed Deacon a sealed envelope. "Please take this to Mister Balancer." He then handed him another envelope. "This is for you, from my family and the Kelly family."

"Thank you, all of you."

The train break released, and the train started rolling.

"Got to go folks."

He ran to the steps and jumped on, walked up on the landing, and waved bye. He took his seat, gave the conductor his ticket and pulled his hat down over his eyes. As the train traveled down the track, the click-clack, click-clack of the wheels and the rocking motion of the car lullabied him into a deep sleep.

Chapter 33

When Deacon arrived in Denver, he took his horse to Wilson's Livery Stable. Shaw Wilson met him as he led Dusty through the door. "Mister Deacon, I see you made it back."

"Yeah, I'm back but not for long, feed him well and replace the shoes for me."

"Yes, sir. Where you off to this time?"

Deacon smiled at him. "Winter's coming, I think I'll go south."

"Can't blame you."

Deacon left the livery and went to his hotel room. He took a long hot bath and put on clean clothes. As he left his room, he ran into Luke in the lobby.

Luke's face lite up with a big smile. "If you ain't a sight for sore eyes. When did you get back?"

"Little bit ago. How are you?"

"Good. Let's go for a drink."

"I can't right now. I need to go see the boss."

"Okay, but look me up when you're finished with him. You and I have got some catching up to do."

Deacon slapped his friend on the shoulder as he walked past him. "I'll do that. Meet me at the Joker's Saloon in about an hour."

When he walked in the Balancer Detective Agency's office, he was greeted with a smile from Mrs. Edith Smith.

"Mister Reeves, it's good to see you back. I'm sure Mister Balancer is anxious to speak with you. I'll let him know you are here."

"Thank you."

She started toward Mister Balancer's door when it burst open. "Deacon, I thought I heard your voice out here. Come in."

Mister Balancer went to a liquor cabinet and took a bottle of rye and two glasses. "I understand that you found the girl and she is back home safe and sound." He handed Deacon the glass of whiskey. "Well done."

Deacon took the glass and gave Mister Balancer the envelope from Senator Bennet, and his report that he had written on the train. "You will find all the details in my report."

Mister Balancer went to his desk and sat down. He glanced over the report. "Very good. I see that my man in St. Louis was killed. I hate to hear that. I will have to get a replacement up there. Do you want the job?"

"No thanks."

"I didn't think so." He opened the envelope from Senator Bennet. Inside the envelope was a bank draft and a letter. He read the letter, nodding his head as he read.

"Well Deacon, Senator Bennet thinks pretty highly of you." He took a drink from his glass and stared at Deacon. "You have done it. You are now a free man. You can now do and go wherever you please. So, what are you going to do?"

"I would like to continue to work for you."

"Very well. I was hoping you would say that."

"I do have a request."

"What?"

"I want some time off. Winter is coming, and I don't like these Colorado winters. I would like to take some time and go south, till maybe spring. I'll stay in touch, and I'll be back in the spring."

Mister Balancer frowned. He leaned up and placed his hands together on top of his desk. "Don't bullshit me Deacon. I read over that report, you're going after those kids in Mexico."

Deacon took a sip from his glass as he looked out the window from where he was sitting in his chair. His gaze went from the window to his glass and then back to Mister Balancer. "Somebody has to."

"Don't be foolish. You can't do it alone, and the army nor the rangers will be able to go help you. It would be suicide."

"Maybe. But at least I will die a free man."

"I will not put my blessings on this. I can't say no; you can't have the time off. Because if I did, you would quit and do it anyway. But I do wish you would reconsider."

"I appreciate your concern, but I've made up my mind."

Mister Balancer took another drink from his glass, emptying it. He poured more rye in his glass and offered to refill Deacon's. Deacon declined. "No more for me, thanks."

Mister Balancer rubbed the back of his neck. "Okay, I see you're dead set on doing this, so, what can I do to help?"

"I don't know of anything you can do to help. This one is going to have to be all on me. I don't even know what I'm dealing with till I get down there."

"I can send Luke with you."

"I can't ask you to do that. He is needed here. Besides it may be a wasted trip."

Mister Balancer frowned and nodded his head. "When are you leaving?"

"As soon as I can. Going to take the train as far south as I can. That way I can cover more ground."

"Tell me what you know."

Deacon told his boss everything he had found out, giving him names and places.

"I'll have to say, I don't like this. It's too vague."

"Mister Balancer, I've been getting along fine for years with too little information. I'll figure it out."

Miser Balancer smiled at him. "I hope so."

Deacon stood. "If that is all, I'll be going. I got things to do."

"Yes, that's all. Deacon come back. And that's an order."

Deacon placed his hat on his head, ran his finger around the front of the brim, and smiled. "Yes sir."

Chapter 34

Deacon sat on Dusty looking across the Rio Grande at the barren rocky ground. It had been a long ride both by train and trail. Another day or day and a half he should be in Palau. From there it was only a short ride to the silver mines.

He heeled Dusty into a trot and rode into the river, headed for certain death in Mexico. His thoughts were not on his well-being but on that of the children that were being used as slaves.

At Palau he stocked up on supplies and rode out mid-afternoon. He set up camp in a gorge about a mile from the mine. He hoped that he was far enough off the main trail that he would not draw attention to himself. He wanted to do some scouting around before he made his move.

There was a small pool of water not far away and grass for the horse. He gathered some dried sticks and piled them for a fire later.

He rode out of the gorge and headed for the mine. He wanted to take a look around and get the lay of the land. He rode up on a hill that over looked the mine. As he dismounted, he took his field glasses and laid down to have a look.

There were several adobe style buildings inside a ten-foot adobe wall. There were several guards standing around and a Gatling gun posted on top of one of the buildings.

On a hill approximately five hundred yards to the west was the main house. There were more guards wandering around the main house. All total he guessed there were at least twenty guards that he could see. He wondered how many more there were that he couldn't see. In the mine there would be more.

He watched the entrance of the mine for a few minutes. There were men coming in and out, and then a cart came out being pushed by a boy. He pushed the cart over to a wagon and started taking the contents out of the cart and putting it into the wagon.

Once the cart was empty, the boy pushed it back inside the mine.

Deacon slid back from his position on the hill. Thinking to himself. "I have to get those kids out of there, but how?"

He crawled back to his position on the hill and took a closer look at the buildings. The larger buildings, he figured to be sleeping quarters for the prisoners and the guards. One would be where they ate their meals. The smaller one over by itself would be where the dynamite would be kept. There was a tool shed not far from it.

There was only one entrance into the compound and it was guarded by two well-armed men. The gates to the entrance were open at this time, but he figured they would be closed at night.

The main house also had an adobe wall around it, with only one entrance. The gates were closed and there were guards on the wall, one on each side of the gates.

Deacon lay in position till almost dark. And as he figured, the guards closed the gates. There was a lot of movement at the entrance of the mine as the kids were escorted out. He counted at least twenty. The anger rose in Deacon as he watched the kids, all ages, being pushed and struck by the guards. Some could hardly walk. They, no doubt, had been in that mine working all day.

"Hang on kids, I'm coming and soon."

The kids were lined up in a line, and each was given a small clay bowl. A heavy-set Mexican came out of one of the building packing a large container. He set it down on a table, and the children came by one by one as he placed some kind of mush into their bowl. Another man was standing at the end of the table breaking off pieces of bread and giving to each child.

He watched as the children used the piece of bread to sop the contents of the bowl. When finished, each placed their bowls into a container and were marched into one of the buildings. The door was locked, and a guard took a seat by the door.

Deacon was so upset when he slid back from his position and walked to his horse. It was all he could do to keep himself from charging in right now, guns blazing.

He rode back to his campsite and started a fire. He threw out his bedroll and put on a pot of coffee.

After a meal of beans and smoked pork, he sat watching Dusty munch on grass. He rolled a smoke, placing it between his lips he struck a lucifer on the butt of his gun. After lighting the smoke, he inhaled deeply and let it out slow. "I have to get into that compound." He thought to himself. "But how?"

He lay on his bedroll and slept for a few hours. When he awoke he saddled Dusty and rode into Palau. It was after midnight, and mostly quiet. A drunk Mexican was passed out near one of the cantinas. He grinned to himself as he dragged the man into an alley and removed his clothes, saying to himself. "Is he ever going to be surprised when he comes to!"

He took the clothes and rode back toward his campsite. As he was leaving town, he noticed a burro tied to a rail. "I might be able to use that little feller." He rode over, loosed the rein, and led the burro back to the campsite.

He put on the drunk man's clothes, consisting of, dirty

off-white cotton pants and shirt. The clothes were a little small, but they would have to do. With the clothes, there was a red, black and white poncho made of wool. He slipped it over his head, then crowned it off with a sombrero. "With this I should pass as one of the locals. And, with a little luck I can get into the compound."

The next morning as the sun was coming up, he went back to the hill that over looked the compound. As he lay there watching, he noticed someone several hundred yards away doing the same thing. He thought to himself. "Now reckon what he's up to?"

Deacon eased off the hill and came around behind the man. As he slipped up closer to the man, he could see that he was an American. With his gun at ready, he crept up closer. "Mister, don't make any sudden moves, and roll over so I can get a good look at you."

The man tensed up with surprise, then rolled over and sat up. He looked Deacon over in the Mexican clothes, and in a slow Texas draw he said. "You speak good English for a Mex."

"Yeah, and you speak good English for a Texican. What are you doing so far from home?"

"Them sombitches have got my son down there. I come to get him."

Deacon holstered his pistol. "I see. You got a plan on how you're going to that?"

"Nope, not yet. Got me some help over yonder in that gorge. Guess we'll just ride in there and start shooting."

"Good way to get killed. Did you see that Gatling gun on top of that building?"

"No."

"You'd be cut to pieces before you were ten feet inside that gate."

The man stood and looked back toward the compound. "I got to get him out of there." He turned and looked at Deacon. "Who are you, and what do you care?"

"They call me Deacon, and I come after those kids."

Chapter 35

Deacon walked closer to the man. "You got a name besides Tex?"

He smiled at Deacon. "Pruitt, James Pruitt."

"Okay James, let's me and you go talk to the rest of your friends and see if we can come up with a plan to get them kids out of there without us all being killed."

As Deacon and James rode up to the campsite, four men stood and came to where they were dismounting. James pointed a thumb at Deacon. "This here is Deacon. I met him while I was taking a look around. Says he's come after the kids."

James pointed to each man as he introduced them. "This here is Charlie, Deek, Randell and Hugo."

A big man with broad shoulders walked up to Deacon. "You got another name besides Deacon?"

"Yep, but it's not important for you to know. All you need to know is I'm here and I have a plan."

The man turned to James. "I don't trust this Mexican looking piece of trash. He could be one of them."

"Now Charlie, let's hear him out. If he wanted to kill me, he could have done it already."

Deacon glanced around at the five men. "I've come a long way to help these kids, and I will do it with or without your help. But if we can work together, there is a good chance we can get them kids out of there alive."

James turned toward the campfire. "Let's have some coffee and talk about this."

As Charlie poured the coffee, he glanced over at Deacon. "Okay mister, start talking, we're listenin'."

Deacon sipped his coffee. "For starters, there are about fifteen or twenty kids, so we are going to need wagons to get them back across the border."

James sat up straighter and looked around at the others. "Twenty kids, wagons? Where are we going to come up with wagons? I just want my son back."

Deacon gave him an, I can't believe you said that look. "So, all you're concerned about is your son? You just going to grab your son and run, and to hell with the rest of those kids?"

James dropped his head. "I... I don't know what I was thinking. I been so worried about my boy, I ain't thinking good. Of... of course, we got to get the others, too. But how under God are we going to do that?"

"The wagons are there, in the compound, we'll use them."

Deacon picked up a stick, and with it he laid out a sketch of the compound in the dirt. Then he pointed out the main buildings.

He looked at James. "One of you needs to go into town and pick up some whiskey and a pack for my burro."

Charlie gave him a questioning look. "What for?"

"I'm going in there tonight. I'll take several bottles of whiskey with me. If we can get them drunk, we will have a better chance."

One of the other men, Deek, spoke up. "That's a good idea. But how you going to get them to drink?"

Deacon smiled. "Men like these, like their whiskey. They'll drink if it's available, especially if it's free."

James turned to Deek. "Take Randell with you and go to Palau; get the stuff he needs."

"Yes sir." He turned to leave when Deacon stopped him. "Here, you'll need some money. Get six or eight bottles of cheap whiskey, and don't forget the pack."

"Got it. We'll be back before dark."

Deacon turned to James. "I'm going after my stuff at

my campsite. Everybody needs to stay here and out of sight till tonight." He mounted Dusty and rode off.

By the time he came back it was almost dark. Deek had made it back with the whiskey and a pack for the burro. As they placed the pack on the burro and secured the bottles of whiskey to it, Deacon laid out the plan.

"I'll get in there and spread the joy. Later tonight, after they are full of this rotgut, I will open the gates. When you come in, be slow and quiet. Bring my horse and leave the horses outside the gate. If this goes bad, we may need to make a quick getaway."

James looked across the burro at Deacon. "Why are you doing this? What's in it for you?"

Deacon placed both hands on the burro and stared into James' eyes. "The only thing I'm getting out of this, is the satisfaction that this bastard is shut down. And this is what I do best. I put assholes like this in prison, or I kill them."

"From what I have found out, his name is Alexander Crabtree. He came here after the war from Georgia, still flies the rebel flag and dresses in a Confederate uniform. Thinks the south will rise again. He has a group of supporters, and they're trying to rebuild an army."

"Hell Deacon, the war has been over for years."

"Not in his eyes. He says he hasn't surrendered. Says he is just regrouping."

"Sounds to me like he's crazy."

"Yeah, he's crazy alright. James, when we leave here, he's going with us. I'm taking him back to stand trial for what he has done."

James glanced back at the others who were standing around listening, then turned back to Deacon. "What the hell? How many men does he have?"

"I don't know, and I don't care. He's going back, or he

is going to die tonight."

James turned and walked away. "I don't like this. I just want my boy back."

Charlie took James by the arm. "Get a hold on yourself. Deacon is right. This man needs to be stopped. So, pull up your boots and let's do this." He grinned. "I ain't been in a good scrape in a long time."

He turned to Deacon. "I can't say for the rest, but I'm with you. Let's get this bastard."

Deacon picked up the lead rope to the burro. "Okay, I'm headed into the lion's den." He walked away.

As he got closer to the compound he took one of the bottles of whiskey and drank from it. He then poured some on his clothes, so he would smell like a drunk. It was dark by the time he reached the compound, and the gates were closed.

He beat on the door and called out in Spanish. Let me in, let me in!"

From the other side, a man called back to him. "What do you want?"

"Amigo, let me in, I am afraid. The wolves are close, and I am afraid."

The gate opened a few inches and a man looked out. He opened the gate further and stepped out. Once he was outside, he looked around some more. He stepped up close to Deacon and noticed the bottle in his hand and could smell the whiskey on him.

He looked at the whiskey bottles on the burro. He grinned. "Where do you go with so much whiskey?"

"I take it to my amigos in the hills. It is too far and the wolves are close. Please amigo, let me stay inside tonight. I will leave first light tomorrow."

The man opened the gate wider. "Come in, so you will be safe."

Deacon led the burro inside the compound and found a spot near the wall. He sat down and leaned against the wall. He took a long drink from the bottle. "Thank you, amigo. I owe you my life. Do you want a snort of my whiskey?"

The man grinned and took the bottle. He took a drink and handed it back to Deacon.

Deacon shook his hands at the man. "No, no, you keep the bottle. I go to sleep."

He pretended to sleep and watched as one by one the bottles on the burro were taken by the soldiers.

It was close to midnight when he got up and eased over to the building that had the Gatling gun on top of it. There was a ladder that led to the top of the building. He looked around to make sure no one was watching and then climbed the ladder. He peeped over the top of the building, there was no one there. He thought to himself. "Good, I feel better about this knowing no one is manning this gun at the present."

He slid down the ladder and made his way toward the gate. The man that was on guard was asleep, or passed out, either way he would soon be dead. Deacon approached the man with caution. He made his way to the wall and crept toward the guard. The man was sitting on the ground with the bottle of whiskey in his hand. His chin was resting on his chest and was in a deep sleep.

Deacon pulled his knife and crouched down beside the man. He drove the knife to the hilt into the man's heart. He removed the knife and wiped the blood from it on the man's shirt.

In a crouch, he ran to the gate and opened it far enough for the others to come in.

Chapter 36

After everyone was inside, Deacon closed the gate. James looked at him. "Why are you closing the gate?"

"Cause, we don't want anyone else coming in, till we are ready to leave."

James nodded his head with understanding. "Makes sense. Now what?"

"Now we get busy. First, we need to eliminate the rest of the guards. In that building over there should be some dynamite. Be quiet about it but break in there and get several sticks."

"Charlie, the rest of you, go to the stable and get the horses ready to hook to those wagons, and be careful. There may be some guards still awake."

Deacon ran to the dynamite shed where James was prying the lock off with a pick. James was able to bust the lock, and he and Deacon went inside. There were several cases of dynamite and kegs of gun powder stacked inside.

Deacon grinned. "We're going to make a hell of racket before we leave here. Tie four sticks of dynamite together on a short fuse."

While James was taking care of the dynamite Deacon took two kegs of gun powder, one under each arm and headed for the mine entrance. Ten feet into the mine, he saw another case of dynamite. He went a little further in and set the kegs down. With his knife, he burst open one of the kegs and poured some on the ground, he then placed the keg on its side in the middle of the gun power. He ran back and picked up the case of dynamite and took it to where the gun powder was. He set the dynamite on top of the keg of gun powder.

He burst open the other keg. Walking backwards out

of the mine, he left a trail of gunpowder to the outside of the mine opening. He checked to see how much was left in the keg. "Good, a little less than half. That should be enough." He placed the keg on the powder trail.

Charlie and the others were leading six mules from the stable and headed toward the wagons. Deacon went to where James was. "You got that dynamite ready?" He handed it to Deacon. "Fuse is too long." He took his knife and cut it shorter."

"Damn Deacon, you ain't given yourself enough time there. You better be ready to throw it when you light it. Four sticks of that shit is going to make a hell of a boom."

The door to the bunkhouse opened, and a drunk Mexican staggered out. He walked around the corner of the building away from Deacon and the rest, without ever looking their way. He was undoing the fly of his pants as he went out of sight. Deacon handed the dynamite back to James. "Hold this."

He ran over to the building and peeped around the corner. The man was relieving himself with his back to him. Deacon quietly walked up behind the man and with his right hand he reached around and covered the man's mouth while the knife in his left was cutting his throat.

Deacon eased him to the ground and went to the open door of the bunkhouse. They were all still asleep. He carefully closed the door.

He went back to where the others were gathered at the wagons. "Okay, so far so good. Now get the kids into them wagons."

James and Hugo went to the building where the kids were being kept. James busted the lock off the door, and the two went inside.

Deacon looked at Randell. "Go see if you can find some food and water for the trip. At some point, we are going to have to feed these kids."

"Charlie get on that roof top with that Gatling gun. Cut anybody that comes out of there down. Leave none of them alive."

Charlie took off in a trot toward the gun.

Deacon went into the storage building and came back with a case of dynamite, blasting caps and fuses. He set it down in one of the wagons and made up several single sticks.

The kids were coming out of the building and climbing into the wagons. Their ages looked to be from ten to about fourteen. James came up with a small boy under his arm, and tears in his eyes. "I found him, I found my boy." He picked the young boy up and put him in one of the wagons.

Deacon watched him for a few seconds with his son. "Okay James, Let's get these wagons over by the gate. But don't open that gate till I tell you."

He went to the bunkhouse, lit the dynamite, opened the door and threw it inside. He shut the door and ran. Four sticks of dynamite did make a hell of a boom. He looked up at Charlie who was standing on ready with the big gun. But no one came out.

Deacon walked toward the building with his gun in his hand. He looked up at Charlie. "Watch that trail leading up to the main house. We may have some company coming from that direction."

Deacon eased up to what was left of the building and looked around. There was fire inside the building and rubble everywhere. He could hear moaning. He went in and stumbled around the many bodies checking for life. When he came across someone still living, he put them out of their misery.

Randell found some jerky, smoked pork, venison,

canned goods, loaves of sourdough bread, and two goat skins of water. He also grabbed some metal cups and cooking utensils. He placed them in one of the wagons. "Deacon, I think I got enough to last us a couple of days."

"Good, our work here is about done."

About that time Charlie opened up with the big gun. The shooting lasted about five minutes and then all was quiet. Deacon called out to Charlie. "Is that it?"

"Yeah. So far anyway."

"Okay, come down." He opened the gate and ran to where Dusty was tied. He mounted and rode back inside. "I'm going to the main house. If I'm not back by daylight, take these kids, and get the hell out of here."

Deek was headed for his horse. "You can't go up there alone."

Deacon turned his horse toward the gate. "No other way. Stay here and help drive the mules."

He loped out the gate and toward the main house. When he neared the entrance, he called out in a frantic voice. "Open the gate, we are under attack!"

The gate opened, and two men were standing with rifles aimed at him.

Chapter 37

Deacon dismounted. "Amigos, I need to talk to Señor Crabtree. Many men are attacking. We need to get ready they will be coming here."

The two men looked at each other and lowered their rifles. One of them started barking out orders to get everyone on the wall ready for the attack. He turned back to Deacon. "Come with me. Mister Crabtree will want to talk to you."

Deacon followed the man, who sounded like he was from Georgia, into the house. Crabtree met them in the main room as they came through the door. "What the hell is going on?"

Deacon spoke up. "We are under attack. They are all dead."

"How many are there?"

Deacon pull his pistol and shot the other man in the face. He then turned to Crabtree. "Just me."

Crabtree's face went white. "What the hell? Who are you?"

"Your worst nightmare, and I've come to take you back across the border to hang for what you are doing."

Crabtree laughed. "You are one crazy sonofabitch. You will never get me back to good ole America. Hell, you want even get out of this house alive."

Deacon noticed a safe setting in the corner of the room. He pointed at it with his pistol. "Open the safe."

"Go to hell."

Deacon placed the gun barrel against Crabtree's forehead. "You first. Now I'm not asking again. Open the safe."

Reluctantly Crabtree turned toward the safe. He walked over and knelt on one knee. His hand was shaking as he operated the tumbler. He pulled the door open and started to reach inside for a pistol. Deacon hit him in the back of the head with his gun barrel, knocking him unconscious.

A young girl of about fifteen came into the room as Deacon was dragging him away from the safe. Deacon spun around pointing his gun at her. She looked at Deacon and then at Crabtree lying on the floor. She put her hands to her mouth.

Deacon lowered his weapon. "I mean you no harm. I'm here to take you back to America. Do you want to go home?"

She nodded her head yes.

"Are there others in the house?"

Again, she nodded her head.

"Can you go get everyone ready to leave?"

She turned to leave the room.

"Miss, can you find me some rope, so I can tie him up. Also, I will need a sack of some kind to put this money in.

"Will a flour sack do?"

"Yeah, a couple of them."

She hurried from the room.

Gunfire erupted from outside, and Deacon rushed to the door to look out. He could see the men on the wall shooting and he could hear a Gatling gun.

The young girl came back into the room with two flour sacks and some rope. "Mister, I got what you need."

Deacon took the stuff. "Thanks, now get everyone ready to leave, and hurry."

Deacon tied Crabtree's hands behind his back and then went to the safe. There was several thousand dollars in US currency and in Paseos in the safe along with some gold, and silver coins. He filled the sacks and tied the necks up with rope.

Four girls and two young boys came into the room along with a Mexican woman in her early thirties and a young American woman in her mid-twenties. The Mexican woman looked at Crabtree who was starting to come around and then she stared at Deacon. "You going to kill us?"

"No. I've come to take these kids home."

"I am glad. He is a monster. I kill him myself." She started toward Crabtree with a butcher knife.

Deacon grabbed her and wrenched the knife from her hand. "Oh no you don't. He's mine. I'm taking him back to America to hang."

She started to sob. "He is a terrible man. I want to kill him."

"I'm sure you do. His day is coming. Now do you want to go to America with us?"

"No. I will go home now and be with my family."

"Your choice lady." He tuned to the kids. "Grab them flour sacks and let's go. Stay behind me." He helped Crabtree to his feet. "Get up." He pushed him toward the door.

As they went into the yard Deacon could see several of Crabtree's men hunkered down behind the wall. Charlie was eating away at the wall with the Gatling gun. The men were afraid to put their heads up over the wall to return fire. And when one would, it was the last thing he ever did.

Deacon shoved the barrel of his gun into the back of Crabtree's neck. "Tell your men to put down their weapons."

Crabtree did as he was told and one by one the men threw their guns into the dirt.

The sun was starting to come up as Deacon marched Crabtree closer to the gate. Charlie had slowed down his firing of the big gun to a burst of rounds every now and then, letting them know he was still there.

Deacon looked at Crabtree's men, these men were Americans, probably Georgia boys. Deacon raised his voice, so he could be heard. "There is no reason for any of you to die. Come down off the wall and gather up over there." He pointed to one side of the gate.

The fifteen or so men did as they were told. Deacon pointed to one of the men. "Open that gate."

When the gate opened, Deek drove the wagon in, and Charlie was still behind the big gun. He had a smile on his face from ear to ear. "I ain't had this much fun since the hogs ate my little brother. He gave out a big rebel yell. You want me to kill these bastards?"

"No Charlie, I don't. I want you to escort them into the bunkhouse and lock the door." He looked at the group of what was Confederate soldiers. "You men should go home. The war is over. The south lost. Go home and get on with your lives."

One of the men spoke up. "We ain't got no homes or families. The Yanks saw to that."

Pulling his pistol, Charlie jumped down from the wagon. "Let's go boys. " He marched Crabtree's men into a building and locked the door. He turned back to Deacon. "This ain't going to hold them boys long."

"It'll do for now. Gather up all the weapons you can find and throw them in that well over there."

Deek and Charlie started picking up guns and throwing them into the well as Deacon was helping Crabtree into the wagon. Once in the wagon Deacon, climbed in and tied him to the wagon so he could not jump out.

Crabtree snarled at Deacon. "You won't get away with this. It's a long way to the border. And before this is done, I am going to take pleasure in killing you."

Deacon grinned at him. "I'm sure you will, if you get the opportunity." He jumped down from the wagon. "Let's go kids. Get in the wagon."

Deacon mounted his horse and looked around. "Hurry up Charlie, let's go back to the mine." He turned Dusty and rode to the corral where several horses were being kept. He opened the gate and rode to the back of the corral and started shooting his pistol. The horses in the corral spooked and ran from the corral and out the main entrance. "That should keep them busy for a few hours."

Chapter 38

When they arrived at the mine, Deacon dismounted. "James, Deek and Hugo, gather up your horses and tie them to the back of the wagons. Charlie, I want you and Randell on horseback." He went to where his clothes and hat lay next to the outside wall. He changed clothes, tossing the sombrero and the peasant clothes in a pile next to the wall.

He started to toss the poncho but decided to keep it. It would come in handy on cold nights. He walked back to where everyone was gathered. "Let's get the hell out of here. Charlie, lead them out; and if anything comes up, get back to that gun. Do you have plenty of ammo for that big gun?"

"Yes I do."

"Good. Randell, you ride drag. I got some things to do and I'll catch up. Now get!"

As the small caravan headed away, he ran to the building of gunpowder and dynamite. He took a keg of gunpowder and walked to where the piece of keg was setting. He set the keg down and burst a hole in the top. He then walked backwards leaving a trail of gunpowder to the dynamite building and poured a large amount in the floor.

He set the rest of the keg on the spilled gunpowder and walked to his horse. He rode through the gate and turned around. He pulled his rifle and aimed at the partial keg of gunpowder setting about half way between the mine entrance and the building full of dynamite. He fired, striking the keg, causing it to explode. Two trails of gunpowder were now burning, one leading to the mine, the other to the building.

When he saw the trails were burning, he turned

Dusty and kicked him into a run. He wanted to get away from there as fast and far as he could before the next explosions occurred.

The two explosions occurred almost at the same time. The ground shook, and the sound was almost deafening. He pulled Dusty to a stop and turned around. There was a fire ball going up several hundred feet. He sat watching his handy work for a short time, smiled, and rode to catch the rest of the group.

Randell smiled at him as he rode up. "That was quite an explosion."

"Yes it was. It'll take a lot of work to get that mine productive again."

"This has been easier than I thought it would be. I mean, I come along to help James find his son and it's been a long trip. We walked away from there with them kids without so much as a fight."

"Yes, we did. And I hope for everybody's sake it's over."

He heeled Dusty into a trot and rode up beside the rear wagon. Crabtree was sitting with his back against the side of the wagon and a frown on his face. "What's the matter, Crabtree, you look like you just lost your best dog."

"Go ahead, you bastard, have your laugh. We'll see who laughs last."

"Yes, we will." He heeled Dusty into a lope and rode to where Charlie was. "Charlie, Keep em' in a trot. We'll stop in a couple hours to let them rest."

Charlie twisted around in the saddle and looked back over the wagons. "How long will it take us to get across the border?"

"With these wagons, at least two or three days."

"You think we'll have any trouble from Crabtree's

bunch?"

"I think that would be a safe bet, so keep your eyes peeled."

"You should have let me kill that bunch when I had the chance."

"Maybe, I thought about it, but I couldn't bring myself to it. They are a bunch of misguided, fightin' men. They fought for what they thought was right, sadly they lost everything, but they weren't the only ones. A lot of people did, on both sides."

"Yeah, everybody lost in that war, if you ask me. Which side did you fight for?"

Deacon took a deep breath and let it out. "My side." They rode on in silence for some time, no one was saying anything. The only sounds were the crunching of wagon wheels on the hard-dry trail dirt, the creaking of leather, jingling of trace chains and an occasional snort of a horse or mule.

Deacon was ever mindful of his surroundings, watching in every direction, knowing that sooner or later trouble would be coming. But from which direction would it come? He reined his horse to a stop and waited for the first wagon to come along beside him. He looked at the wagon load of kids. "James, pull up. These kids need something to eat. I'm hungry, so I know they have to be starving."

Everybody stopped, and the kids got out of the wagons. Randell opened the sacks of food and gave everyone some jerky and a piece of bread. Water was poured up from the goat skins and passed around.

Crabtree was still tied in the wagon. He called out to Deacon. "Hey, what about me? Don't I get something to eat?"

Deacon walked over to him and stuck a piece of jerky

in his mouth. "Here, chew on this."

After letting the mules rest they started off again. Sometime later Deacon could see Palau in the distance. He rode up beside Charlie. "Let's skirt around Palau, no sense in borrowing trouble. And if we ride in there we may be asking for it."

They rode around the small village and headed for the border. An hour or so later Deacon noticed an adobe building to his right nestled up in a valley with high hills on three sides. He pointed to it. "Charlie let's check that out. We need water for the horses, and hopefully there will be water there."

He turned to James. "Follow us." He and Charlie pushed their horses into a lope and rode to the building. There were goats and a few sheep wandering around as they rode up. An old Mexican was sitting under a makeshift lean-to. He stood as the two rode up. A cur dog stood beside him growling.

The old man reached down and patted the dog on the head, and in Spanish told him to be quiet. Looking into the late afternoon sun, he was squinting at the two riders as he cocked his head to one side "Amigos, what brings you to my humble abode?"

Deacon pushed his hat back as he spoke in Spanish to the man. "Water. We need water for our horses and maybe spend the night. We can pay."

"I hear wagons, two maybe three. but they are not loaded very heavy. You are welcome, my God has brought you to me. I had a dream of you, a gringo on a journey would come. There, next to the corral, you will find water for your horses. I will kill a goat, and we will have a feast. You must tell me why God has brought you to my country. Go now and water your horses; you will find grain in the building next to the corral."

Freedom Rides
R. D. Gregory

Deacon and Charlie dismounted and led their horses to a watering trough, next to a broke down corral. As the horses were drinking, Deacon was watching the old man. He walked among his goats feeling of their heads and backs. When he found the one he wanted, he took his knife and knelt beside the goat. Deacon could tell he was talking to the goat as he cut its throat.

Deacon turned to Charlie. "He can't see."

Chapter 39

When the wagons arrived, Deacon met them. "Deek, place that Gatling gun out in front. Unhook the mules and water them. Make the needed repairs to that corral and put them in there for tonight."

James jumped down from his seat on the wagon. "We camping here tonight?"

"Yep. Get them kids unloaded and find a place to bed them down."

Deacon went to where the old man was dressing the slaughtered goat. "Can I help?"

"Si', if you like, you can start a fire while I prepare the goat."

"By the way, they call me Deacon."

The old man smiled at him. "I am called Juan. I am pleased that you came. I hear the children. If my wife were alive, she would enjoy the children. Now go, start the fire; we must feed the children. We will talk later."

After the meal of goat, beans, and potatoes Deacon sat watching some of the children playing with the goats. Three of the children were standing around Juan over by the fire. They were laughing as the old man told them stories of his childhood and raising his children here on this little plot of ground.

Deacon stood and walked out into the darkness away from everyone. The moon was shining big and bright, which lit up the night sky. He could hear coyotes in the distance, and the night birds calling, if indeed that was really what he was hearing.

He walked back to where the other men were sitting. "We best not get too relaxed. Let's set a watch in front and at the back of the house. Things don't feel right to me."

James stood and looked around. "You think we will have trouble?"

"Yeah, maybe not tonight, but tomorrow for sure."

Deek picked up a rifle and walked toward the wagons. "I'll take first watch."

James picked up his rifle. "I'll go around back. Don't expect nothing from that direction. Them bluffs are too high for even a goat."

Deacon turned to the others. "Get some rest."

Charlie stood. "I got a question."

"What's on your mind?"

"We been talking and well, who put you in charge? You been barking orders ever since you showed up, and we don't like it."

"I see. So, do you want to lead this bunch out of here?"

"Well, no… but we don't like you telling us what to do."

"I'm sorry, have I offended you? I didn't intend to. I am only trying to get all of us out of here alive. If I had left you to your own, you would all be dead right now. So again, I'm sorry if that offends you."

"Look mister, we could take James' boy and ride out of here. Then what would you do. If it hadn't been for us you would probably be dead too, you know."

"This may be true. I need your help to save these kids, but I can't make you stay. If you want to abandon these kids to a fate worse than death, then get the hell out of here. As for me, I came for these kids. By damn if it kills me, I'm taking them back across that border, with or without you. Now, make up your mind what you're going to do."

He turned and walked away, leaving Charlie and the others to decide if they were leaving or staying. He sat down beside Juan, who had been listening.

Juan was scratching in the dirt with a stick. "You have trouble my friend. These men, they do not have the same feelings for the children as you."

"I know, but I need them."

"Why did you come?"

"Juan, I came for these children and the man that was using them as slaves in his silver mine."

"This man, is he the one tied to the corral?"

"Yes."

"This man is going to cause you much trouble. You should kill him."

"Probably. I would rather take him back to be hung."

Juan grunted. "What is the difference? Either way he will be dead."

"True, and a few years ago I would have done that very thing. But now I try to do things according to the law."

"This man, he has hurt many young children for his pleasure and profit; he deserves to die. God will punish him in hell."

"I suspect he will, but unless I have to I will not kill him."

"You have a good heart Señor Deacon. Be careful my friend, it may get you killed." He sat up straight and cocked his head to one side. At the same time the dog started growling. "Someone is coming. One man on horse from the west."

Deacon stood and looked into the night. He couldn't see anyone. He walked toward Deek standing near one of the wagons. "You see or hear anything?"

"Nope."

Deek started to light a smoke, when Deacon stopped him. "Don't light that. A match can be seen in the dark for a long way. Stay here and don't move."

Deacon pulled his pistol and eased further away from the wagon and crouched down. He could now see a man on horseback coming toward him. He waited as the rider got closer. He could see it was an Indian, Apache.

When the rider got close, he stood and cocked the pistol. "That's far enough. What do you want?"

The Indian's horse shied from the sudden appearance of the man in the dark and reared up. The Indian stayed on the horse; and after it settled down, he stared at the gun that was pointed at him.

"I asked you, what do you want?"

The Indian looked toward the house and then back at Deacon. "You have Crabtree?"

"Yes."

"Give him to me, and you can go unharmed."

"How can I be sure of that?"

"I speak true. If you do not let Crabtree go free, we will kill all of you. You have till sun rises." He turned his horse and rode away.

Chapter 40

Deacon walked back to the wagons. The rest of the men had gathered and were looking at him. Charlie lowered his rifle, placing the butt on the ground. "Who was that, and what did they want?"

"It was an Apache, and he wanted Crabtree."

"That's all?"

"He said if we let him go then we could leave unharmed."

James turned to walk away, when Deacon stopped him. "Where are you going?"

"To cut Crabtree loose."

"No you don't. He's my prisoner, if anyone cuts him loose, it will be me."

James came stomping back toward Deacon. "Now look here, be reasonable. If we turn him loose then we can all ride out of here. If we don't then that bunch of Injuns is going to kill us all."

"You don't know that. What if there is only a half dozen or so of them? Besides, if we turn him loose, he is going to go back to doing the same thing he was doing. Do you want that on your conscious?"

"Well no, I guess not."

Deacon looked at the other men. "You all know where I stand; I say we keep Crabtree, so he can pay for what he has done. Now who's with me?"

Charlie looked at the others; no one was saying anything. "I'm probably going to be sorry, but I'm with Deacon on this. That sonofabitch has to be stopped. I say we fight."

At that they all agreed. Deacon smiled. "Does this mean you have all decided to stay and help with these children?"

The five men looked around at each other. Charlie cleared his throat. "Yeah, we ain't running out on these kids."

"Either of you want to call the shots or are you okay with me doing it?"

"Deacon, we ain't leaders."

"Okay, that means we may not get out of here tomorrow as we hoped. Let's get to it, we have a lot to do before morning."

Charlie spoke up. "What do you want us to do?"

"Line them wagons up across here. Take that gun out of that wagon and chop a hole in the wagon bed. Turn them wagons over to give us something to hide behind."

Everybody went to work making things ready. Deacon took the case of dynamite and tied several sticks of three together with pieces of white rag.

He then walked out into the night placing the explosives at different places about seventy-five yards from the wagons. The white rag would make them easier to see. He went back to the wagons which were now on their sides. "Good, now put the barrel of that big gun through that hole. When them red bastards come charging up here, they are going to have the surprise of their lives."

Deacon went to where Juan was sitting by the fire. "Señor Juan, may we put the children inside your house. I think they will be safer there."

"Si'. Please do. It may be crowded for so many children, but it will be safer for them."

Deacon walked to where the young lady was sitting with some of the children. "Ma'am, will you help me with the children?"

"Please call me Betty, and yes, anything I can do to help feel free to call on me."

"Thank you, Betty. We are expecting some trouble from some of the local Indians come morning. Would you gather up all the children and go inside the house? I know it will be crowded and stuffy in there, but it should be safer. Where are you from?"

"St. Louis. I was taken several years ago." She started crying. "They have mistreated me so many times."

"I'm sorry. It's over now, I won't let them hurt you again."

She walked away and started waking the children. Telling them to go inside the house.

Deacon went back to where Juan was sitting by the fire. "Señor Juan, I am sorry to have brought these troubles on you."

"Do not be sorry. God has brought you here, he has a reason for it. His ways are above our ways, he knows what is best. Now Señor Deacon, you must rest. I can hear the weariness in your voice, and tomorrow you will need your strength. Sleep, the dog and I will keep watch. I will wake you before morning."

"Señor Juan, I want to ask you something."

"Si'."

"Can you see?"

The old man smiled. "Not so much with my eyes anymore. But Señor, I see in other ways. I see with my ears and my touch. God has chosen to blur my eyes, so my hearing could be better."

Deacon stood. "I'm going to check on the other men." He went to the wagons, as he walked up he noticed that three of the men were asleep. James was sitting on the wagon tongue, with a rifle across his lap. Deacon looked around for the other man. "Where's Hugo?"

"He's around back of the house."

"Good, wake me in an hour or so and I will take over

watch." He laid down next to the wagon and was asleep almost by the time his head was on the ground.

Chapter 41

Deacon awoke in the calm of the predawn. He stood and stretched, working the kinks from his back and shoulders. Charlie was sitting on a wagon tongue with a rifle propped between his knees. He glanced over at Deacon. "Our red friends have been doing some whooping and hollering for the past hour or so. Other than that, it's been quiet."

Deacon looked to the west. "They're building up their courage. We better get ready."

He walked around waking up the other men. Everybody gathered at the wagons and stared off to the west, the direction from which the attack would come. Deacon checked the rounds in his pistols and his rifle. "When they come let them get to those sticks of dynamite. Shoot those white rags as they get close. Charlie, get on that Gatling gun and chew them up." We are going to have an advantage; the sun will be in their eyes. Plus, we have that big gun."

Juan came to them with a bucket in each hand. "Señor, I bring you water and something to eat. It is only boiled eggs. It is all I have."

Everyone took an egg and started peeling it. Deacon took the gourd dipper and scooped up a dipper of water from the bucket. After drinking, he handed the dipper to James. "Thank you, Juan. Now you get somewhere safe. I don't want you to get hurt."

"Do not worry for Juan. I will be fine."

Deacon looked past him to the cliffs behind the adobe house. "Juan is there a passage way up or down those cliffs?"

"Si'. It is not so easy, but a man on foot can make his way down the cliffs. I have done it many times when I was not so old."

Charlie swallowed a mouthful of egg. "We got company coming."

Deacon turned to see two riders loping up the valley. He and Charlie walked out past the wagons to greet the two riders. The two riders stopped their horses twenty feet from Deacon and Charlie. One of them was one of Crabtree's men, the other was an Apache.

Charlie whispered to Deacon. "I knew I should have killed that bunch."

"No use crying over spilt milk now."

Crabtree's man stared at Deacon. "Mister, we want Mister Crabtree. You going to give him up or do we have to take him?"

"Crabtree is going back to America to stand trial for his crimes against the American people."

The man laughed. "You ain't taking him across the border."

"I'll take him across or I'll kill him on this side, either way, he is done. Now the best thing you and your boys can do is get out of my way."

The man looked at the wagons and the handful of men. "Why are you doing this? There is no way you can win. I have close to fifty men, you can't possibly come out of this alive."

"That may be true, the outcome is yet to be seen. One thing is for sure, if you come after Crabtree there is going to be a lot less of you than there is now."

"So be it." He and his Indian friend turned their horses and rode away.

Charlie took a deep breath. "Half a dozen or so, you said. Looks like we got a few more than that."

"Yeah. You still want to stay with me?"

Charlie grinned. "Wouldn't miss it. When they come

up that valley, me and Nettie will cut them down."

"Nettie?"

"Yeah, that's what I named the Gatling gun. She reminds me of a gal back in Amarillo in my younger days. That gal was meaner than a cornered mountain lion. If you riled her, she knew more cuss words than a Missouri mule skinner. She could cuss you for fifteen minutes and never use the same word twice. That gal could spit out more fire and brimstone than the devil himself."

"Nettie, huh? What happen to her?"

"She's back on the ranch tending to our five kids. I married her, took her for better and worse." He laughed. "Damn, what a woman."

Deacon shook his head. "Come on, let's get back to the others."

When they walked back to the others he could see the worried faces. "They'll be coming soon, and there will be several of them. So, if any of you want out, now is the time to go. No hard feelings on my part, because none of you owe me anything."

Charlie pulled his pistol and checked the loads. "I'm staying, and it ain't for you that I'm doing so. It's for them kids and the ones that would be in the same fate if this man ain't stopped." He looked over at Crabtree still tied to the corral post. "Course, I could walk over there and put a bullet in his brain and put an end to this right now."

"You can do that, but it won't stop what's about to happen. They'll be coming, they want us dead, and they want those kids and don't forget the money from Crabtree's safe."

"James turned and looked at the others. "Money, what money?"

Deacon pointed to the flour sacks. "That money. I'm guessing somewhere from fifty to a hundred thousand dollars in US and Mexican bills and gold."

They all stared at the sacks. James swallowed a lump in his throat. "You aim to keep all that to yourself?"

Deacon shook his head no. "I didn't intend to keep any of it. I took it because it seemed like the thing to do at the time. Never gave much thought to what to do with it. Guess I'll give it to the kids. But I'm not against cutting all of you in with, let's say half of it, if you will help me get these kids and Crabtree across the border."

Randell spoke up. "Hell, I was going to help, and still will, with or without the money."

Deek and the rest also agreed with Randell. "No way would we run out and leave these kids."

Deacon looked each one in the eye. "Good, let's get ready. Deek, are you any good with that rifle?"

"I can manage."

"Okay, someone needs to watch that cliff back there."

Deek put his rifle on his shoulder and headed to the back of the house. "I got it covered."

"Alright everybody, take a position behind these wagons."

Everybody took a spot and laid out extra ammunition.

They waited, but nothing happened. An hour, then two hours went by with nothing.

Charlie left his spot behind the Gatling gun and walked to where Deacon was leaned against a wagon, chewing on a chunk of jerky. "Reckon what they're waiting for?"

"Don't know for sure. Could be they're waiting for the sun to be in our eyes. They know we can't get out of here, so they're taking their time."

"Did you notice that rifle that Injun was packing?"

"I did. It was a new Winchester."

"Do you think they will all be toten one of them?"

"I wouldn't be surprised if they aren't. Why do you think these Apache are getting into this fight? It's because that bastard over there has been supplying them with rifles, good rifles."

Charlie looked over at Crabtree tied to the post in the sun. "Another good reason to put a bullet in his brain."

"Yeah, I agree. A white man selling rifles to an Indian, so he can kill white men. Crabtree is about as low as they come."

A rifle shot rang out from behind the house. Deacon grabbed his rifle and ran toward the back of the house. "Stay here."

He heard two more shots before he reached the house. When he rounded the corner, he could see Deek taking aim at an Apache making his way down the cliff. He could also see two more, higher on the cliff with rifles, shooting at Deek. Deacon stopped; using the corner of the building as a rest he took aim and squeezed the trigger. One Indian down, he levered another round into the chamber. He took aim, but he was too late, Deek had already taken out the other two.

He heard Charlie yell. "Here they come!"

Chapter 42

Deacon called out to Deek. "You okay?"

"Yep."

"Keep your eyes peeled." He turned and ran back to the wagons. He could see the riders coming at full gallop. "Hold your fire!" He was standing behind the center wagon. He glanced both directions, everybody was aiming their rifles toward the riders, and they were coming fast.

He heard someone running and looked over his shoulder. It was Betty. "What are you doing."

Panting, she dropped to her knees beside him. "I can help."

"I don't want you here."

"I'm here and I ain't leaving, so give me some shells, I can reload for you."

Deacon dropped her a box of rifle shells.

Slugs were starting to hit the wagons and whizz by his head. As he took aim at the white rag tied around the dynamite he yelled. "Hold your fire, hold, hold, now!" He squeezed the trigger as the riders came close to the dynamite.

His first bullet hit the target and three horses and riders went down as the dynamite exploded. The others were having almost the same results.

Charlie opened up with the Gatling gun. Regretfully he was throwing so much lead that several horses along with their riders went down.

One of the Indians made it to the wagons, he was pointing his rifle at James when Deacon shot him. The acid smoke and dust was thick, as he emptied his rifle taking down a rider with almost every shot. Handing it to Betty, he pulled his pistol, and continued firing.

Crabtree's men along with the Indians were coming fast and putting out a lot of lead from those repeating rifles. Deacon saw Hugo go down and Randell had taken a slug to his arm but was still shooting with his pistol. Deek was up by the house and was coming toward the wagons, shooting as he came.

Deacon emptied his pistol and dropped to one knee behind the wagon for cover as he reloaded. Betty handed him his rifle. "Thanks, now go over and see about Hugo, stop the bleeding if you can."

She made her way to Hugo, who was laying on the ground, bleeding from a bullet wound to his chest. She took his bandana from around his neck, folding it, she placed it on the wound. "Can you hold this?"

"Yeah, I think so."

She turned back to look at Deacon as an Indian came off his horse with a knife in his hand. He knocked Deacon down and was sitting on top of him. Deacon had the man by the throat with one hand and his other was holding the Indian's wrist. The point of the knife was almost in Deacon's face. She picked up Hugo's pistol and aimed it at the Indian and pulled the trigger.

Deacon rolled the dead Indian off and jumped to his feet. He picked up his rifle and started shooting again. He felt the tug and the burning of a bullet as it tore through the flesh of his right arm. At that moment, he saw the man who was in charge, sitting his horse not twenty feet away. He was taking aim at him again, but he was too slow.

Deacon spun to his right as the bullet burned the air beside his face. When he came full circle, his gun was aimed at the man. He squeezed the trigger; and as if it was in slow motion, he saw the bullet hit its mark. The man slumped over in the saddle and rode away.

One by one the riders started riding away, what was left of them. Deacon leaned against the wagon and looked at his arm. There was a lot of blood.

As he started to remove his bandana, Betty ran to him. "You're hurt!" She bent down and tore off a piece of cloth from the hem of her dress and wrapped it around his arm, tying it tight to stop the bleeding. As she placed the bandage on his arm, he looked out at the dead men and horses. He then turned his attention back to his group. "How bad is Hugo?"

Betty finished tying the knot. "He's bad. He's going to need a doctor, or he ain't going to make it. May not anyway. There, all done."

Deacon looked at his arm. "Thanks, and thanks for helping me with that Indian."

She smiled at him, blushed, and turned away.

Deek and James were looking after Randell and Hugo. Charlie walked to where Deacon was reloading his weapons. "We gave em' hell, didn't we?"

"Yeah, I guess we did."

"You think they'll be back for more?"

Deacon stepped around him and walked out from behind the wagons. Heading toward the twenty some odd dead and dying men lying on the parched red Mexican soil. "I don't know, but I don't think so."

Charlie watched him as he walked away. As Deacon came to each body, whether it be horse or man, he would check for life. If there was life, he ended the suffering by putting a bullet in the head.

When he returned to the wagons with an arm load of rifles, James looked at him in disbelieve. "You are one cold bastard."

He dropped the rifles in a pile. "Don't call me that again. Call me cold if you will, but you nor I or anyone else will ever have to fight those men again. Now come help me pick up the rest of the weapons. Also, gather up all the ammunition you can find."

They gathered the guns and placed them in a pile. Deacon went to where Hugo had been moved to the shady side of the house. Juan was giving him a drink of water. Deacon squatted down beside him. "How are you doing?"

"Not so good. I could use something a little stronger than water. It might help with the pain."

Deacon went to his saddle bags and returned with a bottle of whiskey, but it was too late, the man was dead. He uncorked the bottle and took a long drink. "That one was for you, this one is for me." He took another and placed the cork back in the neck of the bottle. "Juan, I am sorry to have brought so much death to your home."

"Señor Deacon, it could not be helped. It is for the little ones. I will kill another goat, they must eat."

Deacon went to the pile of weapons, picked out three Winchesters, loaded them and laid them on the side of a wagon. "Charlie, how you doing on ammo for that Galling gun?"

"I about used it all. Got maybe two hundred rounds left."

"Okay stand watch, Deek go back to the house and watch that cliff. We don't want any surprises."

Chapter 43

The afternoon sun was hot as Deacon stood leaned against one of the wagons. He walked to the corral and caught Dusty. After he had saddled him he led him to where Charlie was at the turned over wagons. He picked up a rifle and slid it in the saddle boot. "I'm going to see what's going on. I would have thought if they were coming back they would have done so by now."

"Reckon they gave it up. I mean, we did give'em a walloping this morning."

He mounted his horse. "Could be. While I'm gone, right these wagons and get ready to pull out. If that bunch has left, we are heading for the border before they have a chance to regroup. Pick out six of those Winchesters from that pile and destroy the rest."

He rode out down the valley, passing all the dead bodies. As he neared the place where the bunch had spent the night he reined up and looked around. He noticed a couple of crippled horses wandering around near the campsite. He pulled his rifle and rode in closer, cautiously.

They were gone, except for two of Crabtree's men. They were lying face down in the dirt, dead. They had been scalped. As he started to leave, he heard moaning. He turned and rode to a large bolder. Sitting on the ground, leaned against the bolder on the far side was the man he had shot.

Deacon dismounted and with his pistol in hand he approached the man. His shirt was ripped open and he was covered in blood. His stomach had been sliced open and his intestines were on the outside of his body. He also had been scalped.

Deacon walked closer to him, as he squatted down he

holstered his pistol. The man looked at him and pleaded. "Help me."

"Not much I can do for you mister."

"Kill me then."

"Mister, after what you and your friends have done, I have no mercy for you. You deserve to die a slow painful death."

"Please, kill me."

"This is what happens when you associate with the Apache. They have no use for a white man unless it is for their benefit. Once your usefulness was over then they were done with you."

He stood and started to leave when he noticed the man's pistol lying nearby. He picked it up and checked the chamber. He walked back to the man and squatted down. The man stared at him as he handed him the pistol.

The man took the gun and aimed it at Deacon as he pulled the hammer back. "You killed them all, good men they were, and you killed them. Now I'm going to kill you." He pulled the trigger; the hammer snapped as it fell on an empty cartridge. He cocked the hammer again and squeezed the trigger. Again, it fell on an empty cartridge. Gun still in hand he dropped his hand to the ground and stared at Deacon with hate in his eyes.

Deacon stood, took a deep breath, exhaled and turned his back on the man as he walked toward his horse. He mounted his horse and rode up to where the man was sitting. He took a cartridge from his gun belt and tossed it on the ground near him. "I advise you to do the smart thing." The buzzards and critters will be making a meal of you soon. You don't want to be alive for that."

He turned Dusty and rode off in a trot.

A few moments later he heard the report from the pistol. He looked back over his shoulder at the dead man, then nudged Dusty into a lope.

When he rode up to the adobe house, he could see that the wagons were ready to go. Everyone was gathered up by the house eating. Juan was saying his goodbyes to the children.

He walked up to Charlie. "Has Crabtree had anything to eat or drink?"

Charlie swallowed a mouth full of goat stew. "Not yet. I was about to bring him something. What did you find out there? Are they gone?"

"Yeah, they're gone. For how long, that is the question? I'll fix Crabtree a plate, you finish your meal, then get everybody in the wagons, we're leaving."

He took Crabtree a plate of goat stew and a cup of water. He set the food down and untied his hands, so he could eat. "If you try anything, I shoot you in the knee."

 Crabtree looked at him with hate in his eyes. "You won that battle. But my men ain't done."

"Your men are all dead and in hell."

Crabtree looked at him in surprise. "All of them?"

"All of them. What didn't die here, the Apache killed. Now eat so we can get moving."

"Them damn Indians. I thought they were fighting men."

After he had eaten, Deacon escorted him to the wagon with the Gatling gun mounted in it. He secured him in the wagon and told Deek to keep a close eye on him.

He went to the house and fixed himself a plate of stew and sat down beside Juan. "Thanks for the food. Don't think I have ever eaten goat that tasted this good."

"Thank you, Señor. I am glad you came. I have had

pleasure with the little ones. But now you must go before the Apache come for their dead."

"Yes, we are going to leave soon. Come with us."

"Oh no Señor Deacon, I will stay here."

"You should come with us."

"I cannot. I must see to my goats."

"The goats will take care of themselves."

"But Señor, they are my family, they depend on me."

"Juan, your eyesight is failing you. In a few more months you will be totally blind. What will you do then?"

Juan smiled. "I will do as I have always done."

"Be reasonable, come with me. I have family in north Texas, I can take you to them. They will take good care of you."

"Thank you for your kindness, but I will stay here. This is my home. All of my family is dead and buried over there. I will stay here and die as well."

Deacon finished his meal and stood. "I wish you would change your mind."

"No, this is my home; this is where I belong."

Deacon walked to the wagons. James and Deek were putting Hugo's dead body in the wagon with Crabtree. Crabtree was complaining. "Get that stinking dead body out of this wagon."

James glared at him. "Shut the hell up or you will join him." He turned to Deacon. "I ain't leaving him here. We're taking him back home to Texas to bury."

Deacon nodded. "That's fine. I don't blame you. Randell, can you drive a team with that busted arm?"

"I'll manage."

"James take the lead wagon, Randell, follow him, Deek, bring up the rear with that Gatling gun. Charlie, follow us and keep your eyes peel to the rear. I'll lead out and ride ahead. Everybody keep your eyes open."

He went to the flour sacks and took out a hand full of gold coins. He went to where Juan was sitting. "Juan, I have something for you." He placed the coins in Juan's hands.

Juan handed them back to him. "I do not need this, nor do I want it. I have all I need. Now go, it will be dark in a few hours. You must travel as fast as you can before the darkness surrounds you."

"Good bye Juan, thank you for everything."

"May God be with you."

Chapter 44

Deacon heeled Dusty in to a lope and led the wagons down the valley and back to the trail leading to the border. The hot afternoon sun was beating down. They had been on the trail for over two hours when he reined up and looked back toward the wagons. The mules had been at a steady trot since they left Juan's. They were starting to show signs of weariness.

There was no shade anywhere to be found, but the animals needed a rest. He rode back to the first wagon. "Let's give them a little rest."

Everyone got out of the wagons and stretched their legs, except for Crabtree. The goatskins of water were passed around.

Crabtree was objecting to the fact that he wasn't allowed to get out of the wagon. "Hey, you going to let me out. I need to walk around. I been bound up for so long I can't feel my legs anymore."

Deacon took one of the goatskins and climbed into the wagon. "Here, have some water and shut the hell up. I could care less that you can't feel your legs."

"I'm going to kill you, real soon."

"You been dreaming again. Now shut up and drink, before I change my mind." He held the goatskin, so Crabtree could get a drink.

Deacon hopped out of the wagon and looked back at Hugo's corpse, wrapped in a blanket in the wagon with Crabtree. He went to where James was squatted down in the shade of one of the wagons. "James, that corpse is going to get pretty rank in this sun and heat."

James stood and looked at the wagon that held Hugo's body. "I know, but I ain't leaving him. I don't care how bad he stinks."

"Okay, it's your call."

"Deacon, he was my friend. Me and him been through a lot together down through the years. I can't leave him here. I've got to take him back and give him a proper burial. You understand, don't you?"

"I suppose so. Let's get moving."

As they pulled out Deacon heeled Dusty into a lope and rode ahead. He was a good way from the wagons when he reined to a stop to let them catch up. He wanted to keep them in sight, but he also wanted to make sure they weren't riding into an ambush.

He was walking his horse and looking around when he saw a rider on a hill to the west. He took out his field glasses and took a closer look. It was an Apache, and he seemed to be watching the wagons. With the glasses he scanned the area all around, he saw another one on the east side.

He heard a horse approaching from the rear; when he turned to see who it was, he was surprised to see Betty on one of the spare horses. She rode up beside him. "Mister Deacon, somebody is watching us."

He smiled at her. "Yeah, I see them."

"Who is it?"

"Crabtree's Apache friends, I imagine."

"Are they going to attack us?"

"I don't know. But it is a good possibility. If you would, ride back and tell everybody to stay alert. Also tell Charlie, I said to be ready to man that big gun."

Without a word, she turned and rode back toward the wagons.

Deacon heeled Dusty into a short lope and rode toward the border. He was hoping that it was over the next rise. When he crested the next hill, disappointment was all he had. The river was not in sight. He looked back at the wagons still coming at a trot. He checked on the Apache and only saw the one on the east side.

He kept watching to the west, looking for the other one when he saw not only one but two. He kept watching them when one of them rode off toward the north. He thought to himself. "This can't mean anything but trouble."

He waited for the wagons to come up the hill and stop. "Give the mules a breather. Looks like we may have trouble up ahead."

Charlie rode up beside Deacon. "How many you figure?"

"Don't know, I've only seen three."

"If you see three, there could be thirty you don't see."

"Yeah, and out here in the open we are sitting ducks."

"Don't forget, we still got Nettie girl and two hundred rounds of ammo."

"I haven't forgot. But know this, when they do come, they are going to want to stop that gun first and foremost."

"Yeah, I figured as much."

Deacon pointed out across the prairie to the hills to the north. "If I remember correctly the river is on the other side of that row of hills about a mile."

"It I'll take us the rest of the afternoon to get to those hills."

"You got any problems with crossing the river in the dark?"

"I don't. But what about them kids?"

"I don't foresee any problems crossing the river if we can get there."

"Why do you suppose them Indians still want Crabtree?"

"Not sure they do. They want us dead, we killed

several of their braves and they want revenge."

"I'm sure they do, but it's going to cost them several more braves if they come at us."

"They won't be so careless next time. They will be on us before we know they are around."

Charlie looked at the flat open ground toward the hills to the north. "There ain't nothing out there big enough for them to hide behind."

"I know. Even still, be sharp. They will hit us before we get to the river. Or they may wait till we are in the river."

"But if we don't cross till dark, they won't attack. They don't fight after dark."

Deacon smiled at him. "Where did you hear that?"

"I don't know. But that's what I heard."

"Trust me. They will fight after dark."

"Well hell, got so's you can't believe anything you hear now days."

"Okay let's get going. You go ahead and get in that wagon with that Nettie, as you call it. Put that wagon in front and by the way when it does start, try not to shoot any of us, or our horses or mules."

Charlie smiled. "I'll do my best. No promises though." He tied his horse to the back of one of the other wagons and climbed up into the wagon with the Gatling gun. "Deek, take us to the front. We're going to lead this parade for a while."

Deacon put Dusty into a fast trot and rode out a hundred yards or so in front of the wagons. He rode down the hill and out into the flat ground. He was watching all around, something wasn't right, where were they, which direction would they come from?

He rode on expecting a charge from any direction at any moment, but it didn't come. His nerves were on end and the hair was standing up on the back of his neck.

Dusty was uneasy, he kept shaking his head and biting at the bit, and he never acted this way.

About halfway across the valley it happened. The ground opened, and Indians were coming from every direction.

Chapter 45

Deacon was reaching for his pistol as Dusty was rearing, shying from the two Indians running straight at him. One of the Indians lunged, grabbing Deacon as the other one went for Dusty's head throwing him to the ground. All four fell into a heap of tangled arms and legs, of grunts and cursing.

One of the Indians was now on top of Deacon. He arched his back and using his arms and legs he managed to throw the Indian to one side. He rolled over and as he was scrambling to get to his feet, the other Indian hit him in the temple with the butt of his rifle. Lights and pain exploded in his head, then darkness took over. He was unconscious.

When Deacon came to, it was dark. He was lying face down in the dirt. His hands were tied behind his back and his feet were bound as well. His head hurt with a throbbing pain and his eyes were blur. He managed to roll over and sit up.

"You finally decide to join the living. Not that we will be living for long."

Deacon turned his head, to see Charlie sitting close by, also tied, leaning against a rock. He had dried blood on the side of his face, which was coming from a large gash on the side of his head.

"How long have I been out?"

"Not sure, I was out myself for a while."

"Where are we?"

"Don't know that either, my guess, still in Mexico somewhere."

"Where is everybody else."

"Randell is over here on the other side of this rock. He's alive but barely. I saw Deek take a bullet before my lights went out; I figure he's dead. As for James, the young braves have been using him for target practice. If you'll look over on the other side of that fire you can see him tied to a post with about twenty arrows in him."

"What about the kids?"

"Don't know, haven't seen them."

Deacon wormed his way to the rock beside Charlie. He leaned against the rock and looked across the fire at James. He looked to be dead, at least he should be with as many arrows he had in him.

He could see Crabtree sitting cross legged beside an older Indian. Together they had been watching as James was being used for target practice.

Deacon dropped his head. "Charlie, I'm sorry I got us in this mess."

"You got nothing to be sorry for. We done what we did because it was the right thing to do. And I would do it again." That sonofabitch over there is at fault. Look at him, eating and laughing with them red bastards while they kill a white man. I knowed I should have killed him."

One of the Indians standing nearby noticed that Deacon was awake. He went to where Crabtree was sitting with the chief. Crabtree stood and came to Deacon.

As he walked up, Deacon noticed Crabtree had his Colt stuck in his waist band.

"Good, you are awake. Now you get to watch while the rest of your friends die, and die slowly, I might say."

He squatted down so he could look Deacon in the eye. "These Apache have ways of killing a man that can last for days. I am going to take a great amount of pleasure in knowing you died a slow and painful death. I just wish I could stay around and watch, but I must be going. You took me away from some very important affairs that I need to return to."

Deacon looked at him with his cold dark eyes. "I'm not dead yet."

Crabtree turned and started walking away when Deacon called to him. "Crabtree, I'm coming for you. When I see you, I'm going to kill you."

Crabtree stopped, turned a quarter turn and looked at Deacon. He smiled. "You don't know when you are beaten, do you? And oh, by the way, thanks for the Colt and the horse. Don't figure you'll be needing either one anymore." He didn't wait for a response from Deacon. He turned and walked away.

Charlie glanced over at Deacon. "You been chewing on loco weed or something, we are going to die."

"Charlie, I'm not ready to die. I got some more living to do."

"Good luck with that."

Deacon looked around Charlie, trying to see Randell. All he could see was his feet. "Randell... Randell, you still alive?"

"Yeah, I'm hurting too bad to be dead."

"How bad you hurt?"

"I think I got some busted ribs and a lump on my head the size of a goose egg. Can't hardly breath my ribs hurt so bad."

"Don't give up and when they come for us don't show fear, no matter what happens. They respect that."

"What difference will it make?"

"If nothing else, maybe a quicker death."

"That's comforting to know."

Deacon squirmed around so he could get his hands closer to the rock he was leaning against. He started rubbing his bounds against the rock in hope of rubbing them thin enough to break loss. There was an Indian standing nearby, so he had to be careful not to be seen doing it. Charlie started doing the same thing.

Deacon stopped rubbing his wrist on the rock when he noticed the Indian standing guard turn toward them. "Hey Randell, did you see what happen to the kids?"

"Yeah, they are to our left out of sight."

"Did they harm them?"

"No, least I don't think so. That older girl got away. I saw her ridding like the devil himself was after her toward the border. Reckon she'll bring help?"

"That would be nice, but I'm afraid it will be too late in coming. No, if we get out of this we are going to have to do it on our own."

"You got a plan?"

"No, not yet."

Chapter 46

Deacon and Charlie continued to work on their bonds, to no avail. Charlie leaned his head back against the rock. "God my hands hurt. I think all I am managing to do is scrape the hide off my hands."

Deacon let out a long breath in a sigh. "Yeah me too. Lean up and let me have a look at your hands."

Charlie rolled to one side so Deacon could see his hands. In the light of the moon Deacon could make out the blood on Charlie's wrist and hands. "Yeah, they are bleeding pretty bad. And I can't see that you have done much damage to those rawhide straps at all."

Deacon sat in silence, watching as one by one the Indians went to sleep. There were two keeping guard, and they were staying alert. "If only them two would fall asleep we could put our backs together and maybe one could untie the other."

"Yeah, but it don't look like that's going to happen any time soon."

The night dragged on. Deacon and Charlie dozed off a time or two, but the Indians on guard stayed alert all night.

Just before dawn another Indian joined the other two guards. They talked for a few minutes and then the two that had been there all night left. The new comer came to where the captives were. He said something in his native tongue then spat on Deacon.

Charlie watched as the man walked away. "I don't think he likes you much."

"I don't either. What did I ever do to him?"

Charlie stared laughing, which got Deacon to laughing. The Indian stared at them and they laughed harder. He came toward them yelling something. He pulled his knife and squatted down beside Deacon, placing the knife at Deacon's throat.

Deacon was staring into the Indian's eyes and smiling at him. He spoke through clenched teeth. "I think he wants us to stop laughing."

Charlie was holding back his laughter. "Yeah, I think so."

The Indian stood; but before he walked away, he kicked Deacon in the ribs.

Deacon doubled over from the pain and looked over at Charlie. "Nope, he don't like me."

Around mid-morning four Indians came toward them. They cut the rawhide from their ankles and roughly jerked them to their feet. They then escorted them to where several braves had gathered. Once there, their hands, were cut free and their shirts were removed. They were forced to lay down on their backs and rawhide was tied to their wrist and ankles.

Deacon fought back as they tied the rawhide to his wrist. "I want to speak with the chief."

One of the Indians standing near-by stepped closer to him and stood so as to block the sun from Deacon's eyes. "Why do you wish to speak to Chief Mangas?"

"I'm a warrior of the Comanche tribe. To kill me like this would be a dishonor, not only to me but also, to the mighty Chief Mangas."

"You speak lies. You are white eyes."

"I am also Comanche."

"Let him stand, I will hear what he says."

Deacon was pulled to his feet, being held by his arms by two braves. The one Deacon was talking to stepped close to him. "I am Taza, Chief Mangas is my father. Tell me how you are white and Comanche, then I will take you to my father."

"My grandmother was the daughter of a Comanche Chief. The blood that flows in my body is Indian blood."

"Come, speak with my father, he will say how you will die."

Chief Mangas was sitting on a blanket not far away. He had heard the conversation between Deacon and Taza. He stood as they approached. "What do they call you?"

"I am called Deacon."

"Why have you come to my land to make war on my people?"

"I did not come to your land to make war on the mighty Apache. I came for the children to take them back to their people. I only kill the Apache because they were trying to kill me. I do not wish to fight with the Apache."

"You came to my land and you have killed many of my people, now you must die."

"To kill me like this would be a dishonor. I am a mighty warrior. I have fought many battles and counted many coup, yet I live. The Great Spirit rides with me. You can see the many scars in my flesh and I still live. If I must die, let me die in battle so my spirit may go to the happy hunting ground as a warrior."

"You are neither white or Indian, why do I care if you go to the happy hunting ground that awaits after death?"

"The Great Spirit would be very displeased with you for killing me like a dog tied in the sun."

A medicine man standing near the chief whispered in his ear. The chief looked at the medicine man, and then he looked toward the sky.

Taza stepped close to his father. "Father, let me kill him in battle. Then I will receive his strength when he dies by my knife."

Mangas nodded to his son and sat down on his blanket to watch the fight between Taza and this man called Deacon.

The two men stood before Mangas as a six-foot length of rawhide was tied to each of their left wrist. Once the rawhide was in place the two men were tied together with about four feet space between them. They turned to face each other. The Indians had formed a semi-circle around the two fighters leaving one side open, so the chief could watch.

Chapter 47

Two knives were thrown on the ground, one on each side of the semi-circle as Mangas yelled. "Begin."

Taza started to lunge for the knife that was near him but didn't make it. Deacon wrapped the rawhide around his hand and jerked Taza toward him, hitting him in the jaw. Taza fell to the ground and Deacon went for the knife. As he was about pick it up an Indian standing near it kicked the knife toward Taza.

Deacon spun around to see Taza scrambling to his feet with the knife in his hand, smiling. He started pulling on the rawhide, trying to draw Deacon closer to him. Deacon was resisting and trying to circle around to the other knife. But Taza stayed between it and him.

Taza came at him slashing the knife from left to right. Deacon jumped back, the knife barely missing his stomach.

Taza came at him again slashing the knife, Deacon jumped back but as the knife went past his body he hit Taza a hard blow with his fist in the ribs. The blow knocked the wind out of Taza.

Deacon didn't hesitate, he hit the Indian again, this time in the jaw, knocking him to his knees. He glanced around and saw the other knife was close. He snatched it up and turned to see Taza getting to his feet. The two men started circling, glaring at each other, watching for the right moment to make a move on his opponent.

Taza rubbed the corner of his mouth with the back of his hand and spat blood. "You hit like a squaw."

Deacon grinned at him, and fake lunged at him. Taza jumped back. "If I hit like a squaw, why does the mighty warrior fear me?" He fake lunged at him again, and again Taza jumped back. Deacon laughed. This infuriated Taza.

Taza came at him; as he did, an Indian standing near Deacon hit him in the lower back with the butt of his rifle. The blow knocked the wind from Deacon, and he went down on one knee. Taza stopped and looked at the Indian who had hit Deacon. In his native tongue he chided him. "Do not interfere again."

Taza turned to see Deacon starting to stand. "When I kill you, it must be by my power. This will not happen again."

Deacon was standing bent over looking at Taza, he nodded.

Taza started circling to the left as Deacon stood his ground. He came at him with his knife low and Deacon grabbed his wrist; and at the same time, he thrust his knife toward Taza's midsection. Taza, pushed the knife away before it made contact. He grabbed Deacon's wrist and forced the hand holding the knife up over his head.

The two stood only for a few seconds staring into their opponent's eyes. Deacon's hand holding the knife was coming ever so slowly toward Taza. He realized he could not over power Deacon's upper body strength. He fell back, dropping to his back and tucking his knees up close to his chest, pulling Deacon with him as he fell. Using the strength of his legs, he flipped Deacon over his head to the ground on his back.

Taza had lost his knife in this maneuver so he did not hesitate. He rolled to his feet and hands and charged Deacon as he was trying to get up. Taza hit Deacon in the back with his body, driving him back to the ground. He straddled Deacon's back and using the rawhide strap, he wrapped it around Deacon's throat.

Deacon's head was pulled back; he couldn't get his breath. He tried to pull the rawhide loose but couldn't. His knife was laying on the ground out in front of him. He reached for it but could only touch it with his fingertips. He pushed with his knee, inching himself forward; he was getting weaker.

He was able to grasp the knife as Taza pulled harder on the strap around his neck. With all the strength he had left he swung his arm around stabbing Taza in the leg. Taza screamed out in pain and released his hold on the strap. He rolled to one side to pull the knife from his leg.

Deacon got to his feet as Taza was starting to get up. Deacon kicked him in the face, knocking him to his back. Staggering, Deacon got to the other knife and picked it up as Taza was starting to get up. He ran to him; placing a foot in the middle of his back, he pushed him back to the ground. He put his knee in the center of Taza's back and took him by the hair pulling his head back. He placed the knife at Taza's throat and applied pressure.

Deacon looked up at Chief Mangas, who was still sitting on his blanket cross legged. The man looked disappointed and sad. He released Taza as he stood, and threw the knife, sticking it in the ground in front of the chief. He looked around at the Indians; when he came back to the chief, he was standing up with the knife in his hand.

Deacon turned and helped Taza to his feet as the chief approached. He looked at the chief. "I did not come to this land to make war with the mighty Apache. Today I give you life; and in return I ask for life, for me and my friends."

"Why did you not kill Taza?"

"I have no quarrel with Taza or you, I do not wish to be an enemy of the Apache. The Great Spirit came to me in a dream; he told me that I would be the victor, but that I must not kill the son of the Mighty Chief Mangas."

The chief took hold of the rawhide strap and cut it. He then took Deacon by the back of his right hand and placed the knife in the palm of his hand. He sliced Deacon's hand and then sliced the palm of his own hand. The two clasped their hands together.

The chief nodded. "From this day forward, you will be known by the Apache as, Kuruk, meaning Bear, blood brother to the Apache."

"It is an honor to be blood brother to Chief Mangas. The Great Spirit will be pleased. Now, can my friends and I leave so we may take the little ones to their home?"

"First you must come, we will eat, and we will talk."

Two hours later Deacon, Randell and Charlie were hitching the mules to the wagons. Charlie finished hooking the last tug to the singletree. He raised up and looked around. "Deacon, I haven't seen my horse."

Deacon smiled. "What do you think you were eating a little bit ago?"

"No… no, don't tell me that. You mean I was eating my horse."

"Yep, well maybe not yours, but it was horse meat."

"Damn, I liked that horse. I raised him from a baby."

Deacon looked around at the children who had gathered at the wagons. Speaking to one of the older boys, he asked. "Is this everybody?"

"Yes sir."

"What's your name son?

"Adam."

"Okay Adam, can you handle that team of mules?"

"Yes sir. Been working a team since I was five. I can handle them just fine."

"Good, then you climb up there and help Mister Randell. He's got some busted ribs."

As the kids were loading in the wagons, Deacon

looked for the bags of money, they were gone. Crabtree had taken them, he guessed. The dead body of Hugo was still laying in the wagon with the Gatling gun.

"Charlie, let's get James' body and take it back to Texas. It seemed important to him that Hugo be returned home, the least we can do is the same for him."

Charlie frowned at Deacon. "If you say so, but them dead bodies are going to get pretty ripe by the time we get them home. Hugo is already starting to stink pretty bad."

"I know, let's get them across the river anyway. Once on the other side we'll bury them."

Chapter 48

As they were preparing to leave, Chief Mangas and Taza walked up. Chief Mangas looked at the children. "Kuruk, go from our land; take the small ones to their families; do not return to this side of the river."

Taza stepped closer to Deacon. "If you return to Apache land I will kill you. You have made me small in the eyes of my people. I must kill you to prove that I am a mighty warrior and a leader, worthy to be chief someday. I would do so now, but my father has promised you safety."

Deacon looked Taza in the eyes. "Know this, if you come for me, I will kill you. The Great Spirit has spoken to me of this." He turned his head to look at Chief Mangas. "Speak to your son Taza. Do not allow him to anger the Great Spirit. I do not wish to kill him."

He turned his back on Taza and climbed on to the wagon seat.

Taza walked to the off mule and took hold of his rein. "Deacon, I call you Deacon and not Kuruk, because you are not my brother. You are neither Comanche or white. You are a dog in Taza's eyes. A dog that I will kill. And when you are dead, I will eat your heart, so I will receive your strength. I will take your hair and hang it on my war lance that all may see that Taza is a great warrior. The wolves and the birds will feast on your flesh, and your bones will be whitened by the sun. Your skull I will place on a pole outside my teepee forever, so all will know that Taza has taken the life of Kuruk. They will sing songs of my victory."

Deacon slapped the reins on the back of the mules and called on them. "Yhaa, let's go mules."

Taza released his hold on the mule as it walked off.

"When the sun comes up tomorrow, I will come for you."

With Deacon leading in the first wagon they headed for the border once again. They had been on the trail for almost three hours when Deacon pulled the mules to a stop. "Okay everybody out. Let's give the mules a rest and stretch our legs."

Charlie came up to him. "I got to ask you something. It's been bothering me for some time now."

"What's that?"

"Well... well aah, did this Great Spirit really come to you in a dream?"

"Deacon laughed. "No, but I know that the Indians are a spiritual people and they look to the Great Spirit to guide them. So, I used that to make them think I was something that I'm not. Lucky for us it worked."

"So, you're not part Comanche?"

"Do I look like an Indian to you?" Deacon was smiling as he walked away.

Charlie scratched his head. "Well, yeah, sort of. Hell, I don't know."

After a few minutes, Deacon called out. "Okay, everybody back in the wagons." Adam was about to climb onto the wagon seat when Deacon walked past. "Adam, how you doing with that team?"

"Just fine, sir."

"Good. Make sure you keep up."

"Yes sir."

They drove on for another hour when they came to the place where they were jumped by the Indians. Deacon saw what was left of the remains of Deek's body. Between the wolves, coyotes and buzzards the body was scattered over a large area. "You kids close your eyes till I tell you that you can open them."

After they had passed he told them they could open their eyes. A little boy sitting next to the wagon seat spoke up. "Mister Deacon, what was that?"

Deacon moved around in the seat, so he could get a better look at the boy. "Did you peek?"

The boy dropped his head. "Uh-huh."

"I told you not to look."

"Yes sir, I know. But I couldn't keep from it. What was it?"

"Well, son, it was Mister Deek, or what was left of him."

"Mister Deek was killed by them Indians."

"Yes, he was, and they left him there on the ground and the critters got to his dead body and tore at it."

"Mister Deacon."

"Yes."

"Can Mister Deek still go to heaven seeing how's he ain't all there?"

"Yes, he can. You see, when you get to heaven, you get an all new body."

"So, when I die, and I go to heaven and I see Mister Deek I will know him? Even though he has a different body?"

"Yes, you will."

"Good, cause, I never got to tell him thanks for getting me out of that bad place."

"That would be a good thing to do."

"Mister Deacon?"

"Yes."

"Are you going to die, too?"

"Someday, but no time soon I hope."

"Please don't die. If you and Mister Charlie and Mister Randell die who will get us home?"

Deacon turned in the seat. "Stand up."

The boy did as he was told. Deacon reached around him with one arm. Picking the boy up he swung him over the back of the seat and sat him down next to him. "What's your name?"

"Aaron."

"How old are you, Aaron?"

"Eight."

He handed the reins to the boy. "Here, you drive; I'm tired."

The boy took the reins. "I ain't never drove no mules afore."

"Well Aaron, you're not going to learn any younger. Now after you get the hang of this, if something was to happen to me you can drive. Okay?"

The boy smiled. "Okay."

They drove on up the hill and started down the other side with the river in sight. "Won't be long now and we will be in Texas."

Deacon noticed a large cloud of dust to his left coming toward them. "Better give them reins to me." He took the reins and stopped the mules.

Charlie bound off the wagon he was driving and ran up to where Deacon was. "What is it?"

"I don't know, but it can't be good. Better bring that big gun up here."

Charlie drove the wagon with the gun in it to the front. Deacon took a lead rope and tied the team he was driving to the back of Charlie's wagon. "You kids get down as low in them wagons as you can."

He climbed up in the seat beside Charlie. "You get back there on that gun, just in case."

They started on down the hill toward the river which was a good mile away. The cloud of dust was getting closer.

Chapter 49

Deacon could hear the sound of the horses running as they grew closer. He had the mules in a fast trot, but there was no way they would make the river before whoever it was coming got there. He pushed the mules harder, but they were too tired to go much faster.

A line of Mexican soldiers cut across the trail in front of them. Deacon reined the mules to a stop about three hundred yards from the soldiers. Charlie racked a shell into the chamber of the Gatling gun. "Want me to kill em'?"

"Not yet, let's see what they want."

"At this range I could take several of them out before they got close enough to do us any harm."

"I know, but I don't want to start a war between the United States and Mexico if I can help it."

"To hell with them wet backs. I'm close enough to home to smell my Nettie's cooking."

"Charlie, don't do it."

"Damnit Deacon, this bunch ain't here to give us a going away present. They aim to kill us."

Deacon jumped down off the wagon. "I'm going to parlay with them. If they kill me, you kill them."

"Deacon, I'm again' it, come back here."

Deacon ignored him and walked toward the soldiers. One of the soldiers rode out to meet him. Deacon could tell by the way he was dressed that this must be the captain. The man rode up to Deacon. "You and your amigos are under arrest."

"For what?"

"Murder, and kidnapping."

Deacon smiled. "Captain, I came for these kids to take them home. You know as well as I do that they were brought here as slaves to work that mine."

"Oh yes, that reminds me, also you are charged with destruction of property. Señor, I think you will spend many years in prison. Or maybe you will be shot for your crimes against Mexico."

"Captain, I'm not going to jail. If you and your men want me, you will have to take me dead. I'll not surrender. And if you try to stop me... well, several of you will die. My advice to you is to get out of my way, because I am taking these kids home. The crimes that were committed wasn't done by me, but by the man who kidnapped these kids and used them as slaves."

"I have many men, there is only three of you."

"Captain, my first bullet is for you. I may die here today, but so will you. Think on that, is my death worth your life as well."

Deacon turned his back on the captain and walked back toward the wagons. He climbed on to the wagon and picked up the reins. "Charlie, shoot off a few rounds in front of them. Don't kill any of them but let them know that we have this gun."

Charlie rattled off several rounds from the Gatling gun into the ground in front of the soldier's horses. Some of the horses reared causing quite a commotion.

Deacon waited to see what the captain's next move would be. He could hear the captain shouting commands to his men. Once they had their horses under control they split into two groups. One group stayed between them and the river, the other went to the left about two hundred yards.

"Deacon."

"Yeah, Charlie."

"Do you see what I see?"

"Yeah, they've split, making it harder to focus on a

single charge."

"No, not that. Look across the river."

Deacon looked across the river and to the right there was a large cloud of dust coming their way. "Reckon who that is."

"I hope it's the Calvary."

"Not much they can do from that side of the river."

As the riders rode up, they stopped at the edge of the river. The lieutenant pulled his field glass and assessed the situation. "Sergeant, form a single line; do not cross the river, and do not engage."

"Beg your pardon, sir. If them Mexs attack that group of kids, they will all be killed."

"I know Sergeant, but we cannot cross the river. If they can make it to the river, once in the river we can assist."

"Sir, they'll never make the river."

"We cannot engage till they are in the river. Now do as ordered."

"Sir. Let me take half of the men over."

"Absolutely not. And any man who crosses that river will be court-marshaled. The United States Calvary cannot cross into Mexico. Do you understand me, Sergeant?"

On the other side of the river Deacon watched as the soldiers between him and the river dismounted with their rifles and took a one knee kneeling position.

Charlie cleared his throat. "Deacon, what are you waiting on. Let's do this and get it over with."

Deacon looked back. "You kids get down in them wagons and stay down." He clucked to the mules and started toward the soldiers in a walk. "Charlie, hold your fire till I give the word."

"Deacon that bunch to our left is coming our way."

"I see them."

Across the river the Calvary was in a line, standing at the river's edge. The sergeant removed his hat and threw it on the ground and then he started unbuttoning his blue coat. The lieutenant looked at him. "Sergeant, what are you doing?"

"Sir, I may not be allowed to cross that river as a member of the United States Calvary, but I sure as hell can as a man." He tossed the coat on the ground as he heeled his mount into a trot into the river.

The lieutenant called out to him. "Sergeant come back here. That's an order." He looked down the line at his men; they all were removing their coats and riding into the river.

"What the hell." He pulled his saber and charged into the river. He loped across the water and ran up the bank on the other side. "Sergeant, gather your men."

The sergeant smiled. "Yes sir." And yelled out. "Form a column of twos."

"Sergeant, you and half the men stay here. I will take the rest to the wagons. We will put them in a cross fire."

The lieutenant charged past the Mexican soldiers and to the wagons. He reined up and looked at the kids. He then turned to Deacon. With his saber in hand, he saluted him. "Lieutenant Wilburn Gross at your service. You are Deacon, I presume."

"Yes, I am, and am I ever glad to see you and your men. But how..."

He was interrupted. "Not now sir, let's get back on our side of the river. He turned to his men. "Four of you men in front of this wagon, the rest split up, ride on each side. He rode to the front of the column. "At a walk. Ho."

He led the group down the hill straight toward the group of Mexican soldiers. The Captain of the Mexican

Army walked his horse out in front of his men. When the lieutenant reached him, he stopped.

Deacon drove the wagon to one side so Charlie could get a better aim with the Gatling gun. "Charlie don't do anything yet."

Chapter 50

The Mexican soldiers all had their rifles aimed at the Cavalrymen. The lieutenant looked at them and then at the Captain. "I have you out-manned and out-gunned. I advise you to put down your weapons and ride away."

The Mexican stared at the lieutenant for a few seconds. "Señor, you have no authority in Mexico. When your commanding officer hears that you come to my land, he will not be pleased."

"Me or my men were never in Mexico, Señor. Do you understand? Now get out of my way or we will ride over you. Your choice." He raised his arm. When he did every soldier pulled their pistol.

The captain looked at the Gatling gun and the soldiers. He twisted in his saddle and looked at the soldiers behind him and his men. He decided that this was not a battle he wanted to fight. He ordered his men to mount their horses and they rode off.

The lieutenant drew a deep breath of relief. He turned to Deacon. "Let's go to Texas."

Deacon jumped down from the wagon. "Okay Charlie, you get this team, I'll follow."

Once they were on the Texas side of the river, Lieutenant Gross called out to his sergeant. The sergeant rode up beside him. "Yes, sir."

"Sergeant, you and the rest of the men are out of uniform. You have ten minutes to be in uniform and ready to ride, or you will be placed on notice."

A big smile spread across his face. He saluted the Lieutenant. "Yes, sir!"

"And wipe that smile off your face."

"Yes, sir."

They traveled for two hours before they stopped to

make camp. The children were excited to be out of Mexico. They were talking with the soldiers as they set up camp.

Deacon went to where the lieutenant was unsaddling his horse. "Lieutenant Gross, thank you for what you did."

"I must confess that if it hadn't been for my men, I would not have crossed that river. If my commanding officer finds out I will be court-martialed."

"I realize that. And trust me, as far as I'm concerned, you didn't. Now, tell me, how did you know where to find me?"

"First, we were ordered to come and help you with the children once you crossed the river."

"By whose orders?"

"Sir, I don't know who you are, but you have got some friends in high places. That's all I know. My commanding officer ordered me to find you. We have been looking for you for over a week. Then this girl rides into our camp last night and said you had been captured by the Apache. Is that true?"

"Yes, Chief Mangas and his son Taza."

"How did you manage to get away, and bring the children with you?"

Deacon grinned. "Long story short. I fought Taza for our freedom and won. Now Taza has sworn to kill me."

"You should have killed him. He has been raiding the ranchers on this side of the river for years, and we haven't been able to catch him."

"At the time, I felt it in my best interest to let him live."

"I understand. What about the man that had the children."

"Unfortunately, he got away. His name is Crabtree,

most of his men are dead. But it won't take him long to recruit more. Did you know he was supplying rifles to the Indians and to the Mexicans?"

"We knew someone was, but we didn't know who."

"Yeah, well, he is a real piece of work, and I'm going back for him. But first I need some sleep. I'm going to bed down under that wagon. Wake me in four hours."

"Don't you want to eat something first?"

"No, right now I need sleep. I'll eat later." By the way where is the girl?"

"One of my men escorted her to the fort."

"Good, I'm glad she's safe." He went to one of the wagons and crawled under it. Within minutes he was sound asleep."

Four hours later Charlie awakened him. "Hey Deacon, your four hours are up, time to get up."

Deacon rolled out from under the wagon. He stood and stretched, getting the kinks out of his back. "What time is it?"

"Close to ten."

"Where is the lieutenant?"

"Over yonder, asleep."

Deacon started to walk off when Charlie stopped him. "Hey Deacon, we need to talk."

Deacon stopped and looked at him. "Okay, what about?"

"The money."

"The money is gone."

"No it's not, at least not all of it."

"I looked in the wagons before we left the Indians. It wasn't there."

Charlie grinned. "I hid a big part of that money inside that blanket with Hugo's body. Didn't figure anybody would be messing with that dead body. While you were sleeping, we buried Hugo and James, the money was still there. I have it hid in a safe place."

"I would like to see that the children get a share and that the rest of it be split up between the five of you that help rescue them. James, Deek, and Hugo's family should get their part."

"You should take your share."

"I didn't do this for the money; I don't want it. Charlie, I'm trusting you to do right by them kids and the families of the three that were killed."

"I will Deacon, you can trust me."

Will you stay with the kids till they reach the fort?"

"Course I will. I came this far, a few more days away from my ranch won't matter. But what about you, ain't you going to the fort?"

"No, I'm going after Crabtree."

"You're crazy. You can't go back there not now, not ever."

"I have to stop Crabtree. If I don't, he will continue doing what he's been doing."

"Deacon, you cross that river and you ain't coming back. There are too many people over there that want you dead."

"I've dealt with that for several years now. Someday it'll come; but till it does, I will continue to do what I do."

Deacon walked toward the fire and Charlie followed shaking his head, mumbling. "I sure don't ever want that man dogging my trail."

The children and the troops were all asleep except for the four guards that were posted around the camp. Deacon found a cup and poured himself coffee from a large pot that was hanging from a tripod. Someone had been thoughtful enough to leave him a plate of stew setting on the tailboard of a nearby wagon.

He propped one hip on the tailboard and picked up the plate of food. It was cold, but it would fill the emptiness in his gut. After he had eaten he woke the lieutenant. "I hate to wake you, Lieutenant, but I need a horse and a pistol."

"Why?"

"I'm leaving. I'm going back for Crabtree."

Chapter 51

Deacon rode out of camp in a lope. When he reached the river, he pulled up. He sat his horse and looked across the river before committing himself to the water. As he eased the horse in the water, he continued to watch the far bank, expecting an ambush at any minute. He made it across the river without incident.

Once on the trail on the Mexican side of the river he nudged his horse into a lope till he reached the crest of the next hill. He slowed to a trot and started down the other side. He was on edge his senses were heightened to full alert; they had to be; his life depended on it.

He rode on in the night covering as much ground as he could under the cloak of darkness. When he reached the valley that led to where Juan lived, he turned and rode in that direction.

As he got close to the house the scent of death was strong. He pulled his pistol and rode slow. The dead Indians were gone. The white men were still laying where they had fallen, at least what was left of them. He could see buzzards sitting on some of the carcasses and corpses of the men.

As he rode on toward the adobe casa, he saw a dead goat, then another. He stopped and looked around; then he saw Juan sitting against the house. Even from this distance in the dark, he could tell he was dead.

Deacon dismounted and made his way through the dead goats to Juan. He looked around; seeing no danger he knelt beside him. His dog was laying across his legs; he too was dead. Both had been shot, but at least Juan had not been tortured or mutilated. Deacon placed his hand on Juan's shoulder. "I am so sorry. You knew this would happen, and yet you helped us. Why?"

He stood and walked around the house. He found a shovel and went to where he had seen a gravesite. He buried Juan, and his dog beside his wife. With the shovel he pounded a crude cross made of pieces of firewood, tied together with rawhide, into the hard dry ground. He removed his hat and recited the Lord's Prayer.

He placed his hat on. "Thank you, Juan, for helping the children." He placed rocks around the cross to help support it and walked to where he had left his horse.

As he rode back to the trail that led to Palau, he noticed an Indian on a distant hill following him. When he reached the trail, he heeled his horse into a lope. He rode at this speed for about twenty minutes before pulling back to a trot. He had not seen the Indian since he started down the trail to Palau. This worried him.

When he rode into Palau, it was midafternoon. He watered his horse then went to the cantina for a drink and something to eat. A quick meal and a couple shots of tequila, and he was back on the trail towards Crabtree's small fortress.

When he was within five hundred yards of the adobe wall that surrounded the house, he stopped. He watched for several minutes and only saw two guards. The gate was open leading into the grounds. He rode up slowly toward the gate.

One of the guards met him at the gate. "What do you want, señor?"

"I've come to see Señor Crabtree about a job."

"You wish to work for Señor Crabtree?"

"Si'."

"Come, I will take you to him." The man walked toward the big house. As Deacon followed on horseback, he was looking around. He noticed Dusty tied to a hitching rail in front of the house. There were two other

Mexicans sitting in the shade, and one on the wall watching the trail.

When they reached the main house, Deacon dismounted. As he was tying his horse to the hitching rail, he looked at the Mexican. "How many men does Señor Crabtree have working for him?"

"There are only four of us now. Many men were killed; he is looking for more men to help with the mine."

"I see. How were his men killed?"

"I was not here, but I was told that many men came in and destroyed the mine and killed all the men who worked it. Also, they killed all of Señor Crabtree's personal guards."

"That's terrible; how many men were there?"

"Like I say, I was not here, but they say there was at least thirty."

"No kiddin', thirty men." It was all Deacon could do to keep from laughing.

"Si'. Come, we will go in the house to talk with Señor Crabtree."

When they walked into the spacious main room of the house, Crabtree was standing with his back to them pouring a drink. Deacon came through the door behind the Mexican; he pushed the door shut with his foot and pulled his pistol. He stuck the pistol in the man's back. "Drop the rifle, and don't move."

Crabtree turned to see who had come in. When he saw Deacon, he dropped his drink and pulled his pistol firing two shots. Both shots hit the Mexican. As he was falling, Deacon got off a shot at Crabtree as he ducked through a door going into the adjoining room. Deacon quickly locked the door so no one else could come in. He took the Mexican's pistol and stuck it in his belt.

He made his way across the room to the door that

Crabtree had gone through. He peeped around the door facing but did not see Crabtree. "Crabtree give it up. I come to take you back to Texas."

Crabtree laughed. "You tried that once already. I ain't going back. I got to know, how in hell did you escape Mangas?"

"Haven't you heard, me and the chief are good friends now. He let me go."

"Got where you can't trust anybody anymore. And, where is the rest of my money?"

Deacon ignored the question.

There was shouting from outside. The other guards were trying to get the door open.

Deacon fired a shot into the door. He could hear the guards running away.

Crabtree called out to them in Spanish to go to the back door.

Deacon wasn't sure what he had said to them, but it didn't take long for him to figure it out. He could hear the men running around the building.

Crabtree fired a shot striking the door facing that Deacon was hiding behind.

Deacon reloaded his spent shells, holstered the pistol and pulled the Mexican's pistol from his belt. He fired a quick shot through the door and went to the other side. From this angle, he could get a better view of the other room. He peeped around the corner and could see Crabtree down behind a desk. He fired two more shots into the desk.

Crabtree stuck his pistol over the desk and fired.

Deacon could hear the guards coming in the back door. One of the men was wearing spurs with large rowels. He could hear them dragging on the floor as he crossed the room, headed for a door to his right. Deacon waited; he saw the pistol before he saw the man.

When the guard stepped into the room Deacon shot him and sprinted to the door. The other two men were about half way across the room. They never got a shot off before Deacon shot them both in the chest. He dropped the Mexican's gun to the floor and pulled his.

He went back and glanced through the door at Crabtree, still behind the desk. "It's just me and you now. Give it up."

"Go to hell." Was the response he got back plus two more slugs in the wall he was hiding behind.

Deacon looked through the door. He could see Crabtree's foot sticking out from behind the desk. He took aim and shot his foot.

Crabtree let out a string of curses words. He lay on the floor and crawled to where he could look around the desk. He fired two more shots in Deacon's direction.

Deacon fired and ran into the room shooting again as he sprinted across the room. He rounded the desk at Crabtree's feet. Crabtree fired, but missed. Deacon didn't, his bullet hit Crabtree dead center of the heart.

Chapter 52

Deacon squatted down beside Crabtree; his life had ended. He took his pistol from Crabtree's dead fingers and reloaded it. Placing it in his holster he walked through the house looking around. He noticed that the safe was open. He took what money was there and went to the kitchen. There was a fire in the cook stove and a basket of eggs on the table. He found a pan and grease and fried four eggs.

After he had eaten, he walked out into the cool night air. He removed the saddle and bridle from the horse he had borrowed from the lieutenant and turned him free.

He rubbed Dusty between the eyes. His old saddle had been replaced with a black one with silver Conchos on it. He liked the new saddle, but he needed his gear off the old one. He led his horse over to the stable. As he walked into the dark stable, he looked around for a lantern; finding one, he lit it. He found his saddle and gear, taking everything but the saddle; he placed it on his horse with the new saddle.

There were four horses in stalls, so he turned them out. He didn't know how long it would be before someone came around and he didn't want the horses to starve to death.

He rode out the gate and headed toward Palau in a trot. By the time he reached the small village it was close to midnight. He saw no one out on the streets as he rode through. Once on the outskirts, he heeled Dusty into a lope. He had hopes on making the border in less than two days.

He had been riding hard for the last three hours so he reined up. Dismounting, he started walking, leading Dusty to give him a little breather. He walked for at least thirty minutes before he got back into the saddle. He rode on in the clear cool night. He could hear coyotes in the distance, and the night birds calling.

He rode on in the night with only his thoughts to keep him awake. What would he do now that his mission was complete? He had stopped the slavers, or at least this bunch. Were there others he wondered? Anyway, this bunch was finished and the man behind it all was dead.

He had his freedom to ride anywhere. Where would he go? What would he do with the rest of his life? His thoughts turned to Rat Dobbs.

"I can't be free not until Rat Dobbs is dead or in prison. I have to find him and put a stop to his killings and destroying people's lives." He rode on with his thoughts. Remembering what had transpired in Greenbrier, Texas. How that Rat had almost killed his brother and was the cause of Clara's death.

He had to put an end to Rat. There had been many lawmen who tried and failed. He wondered to himself if he was fast enough to take Dobbs. "One thing is for sure, if I get the opportunity, we will find out."

In the early dawn light, he could see a little village not far away. He rode in and went to the cantina. He ordered something to eat and coffee. After eating, he walked Dusty to a make shift stable down the street, where he bought grain and hay for him. "Señor, could I rest here for today?"

The man pointed toward the corner of the stable. "Si', you can rest there."

"Thank you."

He went to the corner and lay down and slept most of the day. When he awoke, it was late afternoon. He fed and watered Dusty then went to the cantina for something to eat.

When he rode out, the sun was hanging low in the sky. He rode all night only stopping long enough to give Dusty a short rest.

When the sun came up, he was tired and so was Dusty, both needed a rest. But he couldn't stop; there were too many people on this side of the border that wanted him dead. The entire Mexican Army for one and Taza for another. He was more worried about Taza than the Mexicans. Because he knew that the border wouldn't stop him.

He was in the valley, headed for the last hill before crossing the border. He turned in the saddle and glanced around. So far all was good; he couldn't see anyone on his trail. But he also knew that Taza wouldn't let himself be seen till he was ready to.

When he reached the crest of the hill he stopped to let Dusty rest. He dismounted and took out his field glasses to have a look around. As far as he could see in all direction, there was no human life. He put the glasses up and sat down on a rock.

Nearby a lizard scampered across the dry ground chasing an insect. Both the lizard and the insect doing what they must do to survive. This time the insect lost.

After a bit longer, he got up and mounted his horse. The border was in sight and he was anxious to cross over. When he reached the river, he let Dusty drink before riding across.

As he was crossing, he saw a rider coming toward him in a lope from a group of scrub oaks. He rode on to the bank on the Texas side and watched as the rider came closer. It was Taza, and behind him came four more braves.

Deacon pulled his rifle and waited. With an Apache yell, Taza kicked his horse into a run straight at Deacon, waving a lance.

Seeing the horse and rider coming at him and with the Indian yelling, Dusty wanted to run. Deacon held him, waiting on the charging horse and rider to get closer. As Taza came at him with the lance, Deacon heeled Dusty and swung at the lance with his rifle. Catching the lance, he pushed it downward. The point stuck in the ground and the lance broke from the forward motion.

Deacon spun Dusty around to face Taza. He put his rifle away and called to Taza. "You don't have to do this, Taza. I don't want to fight you."

Taza threw what was left of the lance down. "I must kill you, so my people will know that I am a mighty warrior."

"You are a mighty warrior already. Killing me is not going to prove anything."

"They will know I have taken the life of Kuruk, the Bear. All men will fear me; I will be Chief of all Apache." He pulled a tomahawk and threw it at Deacon.

Deacon made a dive for the ground as the tomahawk sailed by his head. He hit the ground hands first, rolled to one side and was getting to his feet when Taza ran over him with his horse, knocking him to the ground.

He sprang to his feet as Taza charged him again. Deacon jumped to one side and grabbed Taza as he went by, pulling him from his horse. They fell to the ground and rolled. Taza broke free from Deacon and leaped to his feet, pulling his knife.

As Deacon was getting to his feet he could see Taza coming at him with the knife. The broken lance was sticking in the ground nearby. He grabbed the lace and swung around as Taza came at him. The point of the lance entered Taza just below the rib cage, center mass, stopping him in his tracks.

Taza dropped his knife and looked down at the shaft of the lance. He took hold of it with both hands and slowly pulled it from his body, staring into Deacon's eyes as he did so. He raised it over his head and looked to the sky. He dropped to his knees, with his arms falling to his sides. He sat back on his heels and drew his last breath with his chin resting on his chest.

Deacon turned to the four braves that were sitting on their horses, less than a hundred feet away. "Taza has gone to the spirit in the sky. Take him to his father, Mangas, so he may grieve. Tell Mangas that I, Kuruk, with help from the Great Spirit, won the victory over this mighty warrior. Tell him I did not wish to take Taza's life, but he left me no other choice."

One of the Indians rode closer to Deacon. "We will do as you say, Kuruk."

Chapter 53

Deacon left the Indians to deal with Taza and rode north west. He had decided to go back to Colorado by way of New Mexico Territory. With a little luck he would run across Rat Dobbs' trail.

It was late-afternoon when he stopped and made camp. He hobbled Dusty and let him graze on what little grass was there. As the sun set he was drinking coffee and chewing on jerky. He tied Dusty to a sapling and spread out his bed roll.

The next morning, he was up before daylight; and by the time the sun was up he was on the trail. He rode into a small border town around noon. It seemed quite enough so he decided to stay a couple days, maybe catch up on some much-needed rest. He saw a sign that read, "Rooms for Rent."

He dismounted and went inside the adobe style building. A young Mexican girl was sweeping the floor.

Deacon removed his hat. "Ma'am, do you speak English?"

She pushed a lock of raven hair back from her black eyes and smiled at him. "Si'."

"I saw your sign; do you have a room that I could rent for a couple of days?"

"Si'. Follow me, I will show you the room."

He followed the girl to a small eight by ten room with a cot, a small table and a straight back chair. The room was clean, and the bed linen looked to be clean. There was an oil lamp hanging on the wall and a pitcher and basin for water on the table. There was one small window with dirty stained glass covering it. "How much?"

"Five dollars each night. I will prepare for you two

meals, one in the morning and another at night. I will keep the pitcher full of water fresh from the well." She smiled and blushed. "And if you want a woman to lay with you, I can arrange that also for another two dollars."

"I'll take the room."

"You must pay in advance."

He took five dollars from his pocket and paid her.

"Thank you, señor."

He walked out to his horse and gathered his belongings and took them to the room. As he went back out to where Dusty was, he noticed two men watching him from across the street. He ignored them and led his horse to the livery stable. The little man that ran the place was leaned back in a chair, taking a nap on the shady side of the building.

Deacon walked up to where he was and cleared his throat. There was no movement from the older man. Deacon looked closer wondering if he was alive. He could see him breathing so he tapped him on the arm. "Sorry to bother you."

The man jumped. "What... uh, who said that." He looked up at Deacon and squinted his eyes. "What do you want?"

"I'd like to put my horse up, if you got a stall for him."

He looked Deacon over from head to foot, and then he took a long look at the horse and saddle. He stood and walked over to the silver studded saddle. "That must have cost you a bunch."

"Yeah, a lot. Now, do you have room for my horse or not?"

"Look around you mister. Does this place look like it has a lot people coming and going? You're the first stranger I've seen in, hell I don't remember. Sure, I got a stall, I spose' you'll be expecting me to grain him too?"

"Yes sir, and hay. He's had several days of hard riding."

The old man turned and looked at Deacon. He closed one eye. "You the law?"

"Nope."

"You, running from the law?"

"Nope."

"What'cha doing way out here then?"

"You ask too many questions old timer."

The man turned and walked into the barn. "Name's Billy, not old timer."

"Why didn't you say so?"

"Say so what? Put him in there."

"Say what your name was."

"Don't recall you given your'n up." He pulled a bottle from the feed box and took a drink. He handed the bottle to Deacon.

"They call me Deacon."

Billy took a scoop of oats to Dusty's stall and poured it in his trough. "Are you a preacher man?"

Deacon smiled. "Nope."

As he walked past Deacon he, took the bottle and took a drink, then handed the bottle back to Deacon. "Well, why they call you Deacon fer?"

Deacon handed him the bottle and went to his horse. "It's a long story."

"I got all day."

"I don't. Some other time Billy, some other time." He pulled the saddle off Dusty and hung it on a rack. He started out the door when Billy called to him.

"Hey, where you going?"

"For a drink at the saloon."

Billy looked at his bottle. "Someten' wrong with my whiskey?"

"Nope, too much conversation."

Billy took another drink from the bottle and put the cork in the neck. "Hey mister."

Deacon turned and looked at him and smiled. "Name's Deacon."

Billy nodded his head. "You watch your back over there. Sometimes strangers don't last too long around here if you get my drift."

"Thanks Billy, I'll do that." Walking across the street, he could see the two men watching him. When he entered the saloon, he stopped inside the door and looked around. The barkeep was asleep in the corner; he was the only person in the room.

Deacon glanced out the door at the two men who were now on the move, heading toward the livery stable. He walked to the bar and slapped the top of it, waking the barkeep. The man got up and slowly walked to where Deacon was standing. "What cha' want?"

"A bottle of your best whiskey."

The man reached behind him and took a bottle from the shelf. "It's not only the best; it's also the worst. It's all I got, like it or leave it."

"Got a glass?"

He pulled a glass from under the bar but kept his hand on top of the glass to keep Deacon from taking it. "That'll be six bucks."

"Six dollars."

"Yep, It's my best." He smiled.

Deacon smiled back at him. "Six dollars it is." He paid the man and took his bottle and glass to a corner table. He sat down with his back to the wall, so he could watch the door.

He poured whiskey into the glass and looked at it. Picking it up and holding it so the light would shine through. He noticed the barkeep watching him as he took a sip. Just as he thought, the whiskey was watered down and not with very good water. He sat the glass down and stared at the barkeep. He took another sip and put the cork back in the bottle and poured what was left in the glass in the floor.

Deacon got up from his chair, picking up the bottle he walked back to the bar. The barkeep backed away as Deacon placed the bottle on top of the bar.

"Mister, I've been on the trail for several days. I'm tired, I'm irritable, and I'm thirsty for something more than watered down whiskey. You've got to the count of five to come up with a bottle of good whiskey or I'm going to get real upset."

"Two."

"Wait, what happen to one?"

"Four."

The man took another bottle down and placed it on the bar. "Here mister, try this bottle."

Deacon took the bottle and pulled the cork. He took a drink and nodded his head. "Much better."

With bottle in hand he left the saloon, heading for his room. Entering his room, he closed the door, noticing that there was no lock on the door. He placed the bottle on the table and took the chair and jammed it under the door knob to secure the door. He picked up the bottle and sitting on the bed he took a long drink. Returned the bottle to the table and lay back on the bed. He was asleep in a matter of seconds.

Chapter 54

When Deacon awoke, it was dark. He lit the oil lamp and poured water into the basin. After washing his face and hands, he walked into the adjoining room. The young Mexican girl was stirring something on the stove. She smiled at him. "Señor, you have slept a long time. Would you like to eat now?"

"Yes, if it's not too much trouble."

"It is no trouble. I have made for you Hot Tamales and beans. Is that okay, yes?"

"Yes, that will be fine."

She poured a glass of water from a picture and set it on a table. "The water is fresh from the well; it is still cool. Please sit."

He drank the glass empty. The water was cool and refreshing. He started to get up to get the pitcher when she stopped him. "Please, I will serve you." He sat back down as she brought the pitcher and poured the glass full again.

"Thank you. Do you own this place?"

"Oh no Señor; I only work here. It belongs to Señor Stone. He owns most of the town. He has a big ranch not far from here to the north. He raises many cattle and horses."

She turned and walked to the stove. Shortly, she returned with a plate of food. "I hope you do enjoy."

"Thank you." He picked up his fork and took a bite. The food was good. "Señorita, this is good."

She smiled. "Thank you."

After he had finished his meal, he started out the door.

"Señor."

He stopped and turned to her. "Yes."

"Be very careful tonight."

He put his hat on as he walked out the door. That was twice he had been warned to be careful since he got here.

The night air was cool; there was a dog barking somewhere in the distance. The little town had come to life. Horses were tied at hitching rails, and men were standing around talking and drinking. He went to the livery to check on Dusty. As he entered, the lantern lit stable, Dusty raised his head. There was a bucket next to the wall; he picked it up and started outside to get water for Dusty.

He heard a voice from the shadows. "I did that already."

He turned to see Billy walking toward him with a short-barreled shotgun under his arm.

"Thanks, Billy. What's with the shotgun?"

"Can't be too careful these days."

"You, expecting trouble?"

"I always expect trouble when this bunch hits town. I figure it's only a matter of time before the word gets around about that horse and that hi-dollar saddle of yours being in here."

"I see."

"There is a couple of fellers ridin' with this outfit that would steal the pennies off'en their own momma's dead eyes. And they just soon shoot a man in the back to do it too."

"What about them two I saw earlier? I know they came to see you after I left."

"Yeah, they came, nos'en around, trying to find out what I knew about you. I told em' nothen' and sent them no-accounts packing. Worthless pieces of dog shit, if you ask me. Ain't near one of them done a days' worth of work in their whole lives."

"Where did all these cowboys come from?"

"Local ranches. Some from both sides of the river. It's Saturday night, you know, and the end of the month. They'll get liquored up and start fighting. It won't be safe on the streets. A man could catch a stray bullet."

Deacon walked over to the feed box, opened it, and took out the bottle. He looked at the contents. "I don't think there is enough in here to last us both all night. I'll go back to the room and get my bottle."

"Give me that one; I'll be working on it till you get back. While you're at it, see if that pretty young señorita has anything to eat. I ain't had nothing to eat since this morning. My gut thinks my throat has been cut."

Deacon handed him the bottle. "Go easy on that till I get back. Wouldn't want you to fall into the watering trough."

Billy snatched the bottle from his hand. "You're a funny man. But I ain't laughing. Now get and come back with the bottle and something for me to eat. Go on, get."

Deacon smiled at him, turned and walked away."

Billy pulled the cork from the bottle and took a drink. "Hey mister."

Deacon stopped and tuned to look at him. "Name's Deacon."

Billy pointed the bottle at him. "Watch your back."

As Deacon entered the house he saw the young girl over by the stove. She had a concerned look about her. Then he noticed the oil lamp was lit in his room and could hear someone in there. He pulled his pistol as he walked toward the room.

When he entered, he did so quietly. A man was standing by his bed; he had removed everything from his saddle bags and was going through it.

"You finding anything that interest you?"

The man slowly turned and looked at Deacon. He had a wad of money in his hand that Deacon had taken from Crabtree. "You want to tell me where you got this?"

"Not till you tell me who you are and why you are going through my belongings."

"Fair enough. My name is Edward Stone, and I like to know who is coming and going in my town."

"You may own this town, but you don't own me, and you got no right going through my stuff. Now put the money down on the bed before someone you own has to bury you in the cemetery that you own."

The man cocked his head to one side and laid the money on the bed. "Mister, you are treading on thin ice; one word from me and you'll be dead by morning."

Deacon smiled and holstered his pistol. He stepped closer to the man. "I think we got off on the wrong foot. Now that you have put my money down, and I have put my gun away, let's talk like gentlemen."

"Something I said?"

"Nope, you don't scare me, because you don't own me."

"I see."

"I don't think you do, Mister Stone. If you owned me, then you could possibly say when and if I live or die. But you don't own me."

The man smiled. "I could still have you killed."

"You can try. But know this if you do try, I will kill you." He smiled at him and stuck out his hand. "They call me Deacon; can we be friends, or do you want to continue this out in the street?"

The man took his hand in a strong grip and smiled. "I think we can."

"Good."

"You the man that killed Taza?"

"I am."

"And that low life in Mexico that was running guns and enslaving children."

"I did."

"Come, I want to buy you a drink."

Deacon picked up the bottle on the table. "Got my own thank you, and someone to share it with. You care to join us?"

"I'd like that. I want to hear about all of it from the source, not these rumors that have been flying around."

The two men walked out of the room, closing the door behind them. The girl looked at them as they entered the front room. "Señor, can I get you anything?"

Mister Stone smiled at her. "No, Victoria, we are fine, thank you. Tell anyone who may try to go into Mister Deacon's room that I said to stay out."

"Yes, Señor."

Deacon cleared his throat. "Actually, Victoria, I need something to eat, please."

"All I have is cold beans and tamales."

"That will do fine, thank you."

She fixed the plate and handed it to him.

"Thank you, I'll return the plate."

Chapter 55

There was a lot of noise coming from the saloon as the two men walked toward the livery stable. Mister Stone entered first, and when Billy saw him he pointed the shotgun at him. "What do you want?"

Mister Stone held is hands out. "Easy with that mare's leg, Billy."

Deacon stepped past him into the light. "It's okay Billy, he's with me. Here, I brought you something to eat."

Lowering the shotgun, he took the plate of food. "Why did you bring him in here?"

Deacon looked from Billy to Mister Stone. "You two have a problem?"

Billy propped the shotgun against a nearby support timber and sat down in a rickety straight back chair. "You could say that." He peeled the corn shucks back and took a bite from one of the tamales. "She makes the best tamales for a hundred miles."

Mister Stone frowned at him. "How would you know, you haven't been a hundred miles from here in at least thirty years."

"You go to hell, Ed."

"You first. Hell, I knew it was a mistake coming in here."

Deacon raised his voice. "Hey you two. I don't know what your beef is but give it a rest."

Stone took the bottle from Deacon and took a drink. "I tell you what our beef is, at least what his is. Billy is my older brother by two years. He is still mad at me because a girl picked me over him."

Billy choked down a mouth full of beans. "You stole her from me, but you couldn't make her happy and she ran off with a Tinker. Give me that bottle. Hey, and let's not forget that you swindled me out of my share of the ranch after dad died."

"Get real Billy, I did no such thing, that was your doings."

Deacon stepped between the two of them. "Enough already. Sounds like this squabble between the two of you runs pretty deep. I don't know either of you and I don't know who may have wronged who. But if I may, I would like to say something to both of you. You're brothers, you're blood, nothing and I mean nothing should come between that. Work it out, forgive and forget. Get on with your lives before one of you does something that you will regret for the rest of your lives."

Ed got a chair and sat down beside Billy. "He's right you know."

Swallowing a mouth full of beans, Billy glanced over at him. "I know."

Deacon pulled up a chair and the three sat looking out the doors of the stable at two men fighting in the street. Both were so drunk that they could hardly stand.

Deacon took a drink from the bottle and handed it to Billy. "Reckon we should stop them before one of them gets hurt?"

Billy took a drink from the bottle and handed it to Ed. "Nah, they're so drunk they want feel anything till morn'en."

They sat in silence for a long time and the bottle kept making it's rounds.

Ed leaned up and looked over at Deacon. "Tell me about Taza."

"You want the whole story or just the part when I killed him?"

Billy looked first at Ed and then at Deacon. "You killed

Taza?"

"I did."

"I got to hear this, but first I got to go see a man about a horse." He got up and went to a nearby empty stall and relieved himself. He came back and sat down. "When did you kill that no count savage?"

"A couple days ago. By the way Ed, how did you know about Taza's death?"

"A young man that works for me off and on, was riding by and saw the whole thing. He lives on a neighbor ranch. He came racing in to the ranch all excited. Said, after you killed Taza them other four Indians just sat their horses. Like they were too afraid to move."

"Why didn't he come help me. Them other four could have come at me after I killed Taza."

"Deacon, he's just a boy. Didn't even have a gun on him. Now tell me about it."

Deacon spent the next several minutes reliving the experience, all of it, from St. Louis to the killing of Taza, for Billy and Ed.

Ed took a long drink from the bottle. "That's quite a story. Those men that helped, say they were from Texas?"

"Yeah."

"What part?"

"Not sure, they didn't say."

"This Charlie fellow was he a big man?"

"Yeah, pretty good size. Why?"

"I think I know him. Met him in San Antonio several years back. He's got a mean right cross and a fist like a tree stump."

Deacon laughed. "Sounds like the same guy. Never heard his last name but I heard him talk about his wife. Her name was Nettie."

Ed nodded his head. "It's the same man, she's meaner than he is, and he's as afraid of her as I would be a bear. He was in the saloon one night raising hell. The town marshal sent for her and when she walked in the door of that saloon it got deathly quiet. Charlie set his drink on the bar and walked out of there like a whipped pup with his tail between his legs." He laughed. "Funniest thing I ever saw."

Deacon turned the bottle up and drank what was left. "Looks like we need another bottle. I'll go get us one."

Ed pulled money from his pocket and handed it to Deacon. "This one is on me."

Deacon took the money and walked to the saloon. When he returned he could hear Billy and Ed talking. He stood out side for a few minutes to give the two brothers some time alone before going in.

As he walked in the door he could see the two shaking hands. "Everything good?"

Both men looked at him. "Yeah."

Ed turned to Deacon. "It has been a pleasure meeting you. I hope you will come back through this way again."

"You leaving?"

"Yeah, I need to round my boys up while they can still sit a saddle and get back to the ranch."

"Before you leave I want to ask you something."

"What's that?"

"Have you ever heard of a man called Rat Dobbs?"

"He ain't no man, he's an animal from what I hear."

"So, you know him?"

"I know of him. I've never had the pleasure of meeting him."

"Do you know where I can find him?"

"You got a death wish or something?"

"Or something. Do you know where he is?"

"No. Last I heard he was in New Mexico somewhere, and I hope he stays there. He's more trouble than a sack full of rattlers."

Billy spoke up. "Yeah, I've heard of him too. Usually has several sidewinders riding with him. They've been known to ride into a small town and when they leave there ain't nothing left but ashes. You going after him?"

Deacon smiled. "Let's just say that he and I have some unfinished business."

Edward Stone walked toward the saloon shaking his head. "Deacon, if you live long enough, come back and see us."

"I'll do that."

Billy went to the lantern and blew it out. "I'm going to bed. I've had too much to drink."

Deacon helped him close up the livery and walked back to his room.

He cleaned off the bed and laid down. His head was spinning from the whiskey. As he drifted off to sleep, his thoughts were on Rat Dobbs.

Chapter 56

Deacon hung around the small town of Eagle Pass for another day enjoying Victoria's cooking and playing cards with some of the locals.

The next morning, he ate breakfast with Victoria and gave her twenty dollars extra. "Thanks, Victoria for feeding me so well."

"Thank you, Señor Deacon. You come back and see me again sometime, yes?"

"Maybe someday." He gathered up his stuff and walked to Billy's Livery Stable. When he walked in, Billy was bringing Dusty out of the stall. "Saw you coming with your stuff, figured you was leaving."

Deacon laid his saddle bags down and took his saddle off the rack. "Yeah, I need to get on down the trail."

"You going after this Dobbs feller, are you?"

"We'll see where the trail leads."

"Why don't you forget about that feller and go on back home?"

Deacon tightened the cinch and turned to Billy. "I got nowhere to be, Billy. I have no home anymore."

"I don't believe that. You're a likable enough feller, from what I've seen. Surely there's someone who cares fer you. Ain't you got family somewhere?"

Deacon smiled at him. "Billy, you ask to many questions. What about you and your brother, you two going to patch things up?"

"Yeah, maybe. This thing between us has been going on a long time. Truth be known we never was real close anyway. I guess the girl gave us something fight over."

Deacon shook his head as he placed the saddle bags on his horse. "Fighting over a girl that dumped both of you. Now that don't make any sense at all Billy, and you know it."

"Hey, how'd you do that? We was talking about you, not me."

Deacon placed his foot in the stirrup and swung his leg over the horse. He took a hundred dollars from his pocket and with it in his hand he reached down to shake hands with Billy. "See you around Billy."

With the hundred dollars in his hand he watched as Deacon rode out of the barn. "Hey, mister."

Deacon stopped and turned in the saddle. "They call me Deacon." He smiled, tipped his hat and heeled Dusty into a lope.

Billy watched as Deacon rode down the street, headed out of town. He looked down at the money in his hand for the first time. When he saw how much it was, he started to call out, but the man was gone. He stood staring at the empty street for a few seconds. "Was he ever really here?" He said to himself. He placed the money in his pocket as he continued to look down the street. He smiled. "Yeah, he was here."

Chapter 57

As Deacon traveled up the border, stopping in every town he came to, asking about Rat Dobbs. He kept getting the same answers. No one knew where the man was. Or if they knew they weren't saying. So, he continued to ride. He had been on the trail for over three weeks and nothing. He was tired, his back hurt from sleeping on the ground or bad beds in cheap hotels.

He hadn't had a hot bath in days, he needed a hair cut and a shave. He topped over a hill as the last rays of sun were fading and saw a town ahead. "I sure hope they got a bathtub in that town someplace."

It was dark by the time he passed a sign that read "Welcome to Dublin." He watered Dusty at the first water trough he came to, then rode to the hotel. Painted on the side of the building in big letters, which were now faded, were the words "Hotel Lavern." The place wasn't much to look at but hopefully they'd have a tub. He dismounted, removed his saddle bags and rifle and went inside.

As he walked to the counter he looked around. The lobby was clean and well furnished, not what he expected from looking at the outside of the two-story building. When he reached the counter there was no one around. He noticed a bell setting on the counter, so he rang it. A well dressed, balding, middle-aged man came from an adjoining room and walked behind the counter. "Yes sir. Can I help you?"

"I hope so. I need a room, a hot bath, a hair cut and shave, a hot meal and a bottle of good rye whiskey."

"Oooookay. We can take care of all that for you." He looked Deacon over. "Would you like to have your clothes laundered?"

Deacon looked down at his dust covered clothes. "Oh, hell yes, I forgot about them."

"My name is Howard. If I can be of an assistance while you stay at our hotel, please let me know. Now if you would please sign our registry." He pushed the book toward Deacon and handed him a pencil.

Deacon signed the book and slid it back across the counter to Howard.

Howard turned the book and looked at the name. "Okay Mister Deacon Reeves…" There was a pause as the man looked up at him with his mouth open. "Deacon Reeves?"

"Yeah."

"The Deacon that killed that savage Indian, Taza?"

"Yeah."

"Oh my God, I can't believe you are staying in my hotel. I have to tell everybody."

"I wish you wouldn't do that. It weren't no big deal."

"No big deal you say." He smiled and shook his head. "That savage has been killing folks and stealing livestock all the way to New Mexico for years. And you really killed him?"

"Yep, he's dead, I stuck his own lance through his heart."

"I got to tell everybody that you are here."

"Please don't. Right now, I want a hot bath and a warm meal."

Howard handed Deacon the keys to a room. "Top of the stairs to the left. Bath house is around back, and I will see to it that your horse is taken care of as well."

"Thank you very much." He picked up his belongings and went up the steps. When he reached the top step, he turned around, Howard was watching him. "When will my bath be ready?"

Howard came around the counter looking up at Deacon. "Fifteen minutes, sir."

"I think I'll eat first."

"Mable's Cafe is right down the street, they have good food."

"Okay, thanks."

He went to his room to put his stuff away. When he came back down Howard was talking to a young man. They both looked at him as he descended the stairs. Howard spoke up. "Mister Deacon, this is Jody, he will see to your horse."

"Thank you, but I will see to my horse."

"He'll take good care of him for you."

"I'm sure he will, but all same, I'll tend to him."

"Yes sir, whatever you say, sir."

Deacon took his horse to the livery stable. The owner met him as he rode up. "I'm about to close up for the night, you need something?"

Deacon dismounted. "Yes sir. I would like to put my horse up for the night."

"No problem. Put him in that stall yonder."

"Can you put new shoes on him tomorrow?"

"I can probably handle that, no problem. I'm going home, wife's got supper on the table. Feed is in the feed box over there and there's hay if you want it. Blow out the lantern and close the door when you leave."

"Okay, thanks." Deacon took care of his horse and closed the barn door. He could hear someone banging on a piano at the saloon as he crossed the street to Mable's Cafe. There were a few people milling about in the street, but they didn't concern him. He was on a mission, and that was to get a good hot meal under his belt.

After a meal of fried chicken, mashed potatoes and

gravy with beans and cornbread he went to the saloon. The saloon was busy; the man at the piano was still banging away. He made his way to the bar and ordered a shot of rye.

The bartender poured his drink and as Deacon reached for the glass the bartender placed his hand over the glass. "That'll be two-bits, stranger."

Deacon placed the money on the bar, picked up the glass and drank it down. "This will do. Now, I want a bottle of the same."

He paid for the bottle and left the saloon. When he got back to the hotel, Howard was at the counter. "Mister Deacon your bath is ready."

"Thanks." He went to his room and got his extra set of clothes, which were dirty, that he kept rolled up in his bed roll. He gave them to Howard when he came back down. "Can you have these cleaned for me?"

"Yes sir."

After he finished his bath he went to his room. He took several drinks from the bottle and laid down on the feather bed and slept.

Chapter 58

Deacon awoke the next morning with the sun shining through the window. He washed the sleep from his eyes from a basin and ran his fingers through his hair. Looking at himself in the mirror, he thought how haggard he looked.

He finished getting dressed and walked to the cafe for breakfast. The little town of Dublin was busy. There were wagons, buckboards and men on horseback making their way through the streets. The town was growing, new buildings were being built at the far end of town and even a church was being erected.

He was eating his breakfast when a man walked up to his table. "Sir, may I have a word with you?"

Deacon set his coffee cup down and gave the man a once over. He was a man in his forties, wearing a white shirt and vest with garters on the arms, just above his elbows. "And you are?"

"My name is Olin Housten and I am the owner of the Dublin Tribute, which is the only newspaper for miles around. I was wondering if I could write your story?"

"And what story is that?"

"You are Mister Deacon Reeves, aren't you?"

"Yes."

The man pulled out a chair and sat down across from Deacon. "I want to..."

Deacon interrupted him. "You're being a little presumptious, aren't you? I didn't ask you to join me and I don't have anything to say to you. So, if you don't mind, I would like to finish my breakfast."

"But sir."

Deacon gave the man a cold stare. "Leave, now."

The man stood and pushed the chair back to the

table. "If you insist, but the people need to hear your story."

"Not interested." Deacon watched as the man walked away and thought to himself. "That's all I need, my name on the front page of a newspaper."

After his meal he got a haircut and a shave. As he was leaving the barber shop he noticed the newspaper man following him. He walked to the marshal's office, opened the door and looked inside. The town marshal was sitting at his desk. He looked up as Deacon entered the door. "What's on your mind this morning besides your hat?"

"I'm passing through and was wondering if you knew the where abouts of a man that goes by Rat Dobbs?"

"You some kinda lawman or a bounty hunter, maybe?"

"Neither one."

"A friend of his, then?"

"Not that either. You might say he and I have some unfinished business."

"You that Deacon feller I been hearing about?"

"You're full of questions, aren't you?"

"Just like to know who I'm talken' to. You him or no?"

"Yeah, they call me Deacon, now how about it, do you know where he is?"

"Nope. Don't want to know, as long as he stays away from here."

"Thanks anyway." Deacon turned to leave.

"Where you going? I'd like a sit down with you, if'n you got a minute."

"What about?"

"I think you know. Did you really kill Taza?"

"Yeah."

"That's the best news I've heard in a long time. That crazy Indian has been killing folks and stealing stock on both sides of the border for the last five years."

"Well, he won't be doing it anymore, but I doubt it stops. One of the other braves will step up and continue in his footsteps. Mostly, they're killing for food."

"You're probably right."

"I know I'm right. I've been to their village. They're eating their horses to stay alive."

"You've been to their village? Did you see his father Mangas?"

"Yep."

"Could you lead a troop of men in there to wipe them out?"

"First off, they are in Mexico, and I don't care if I ever go back. No, I won't lead a troop of men in there to slaughter women and children, and that is what would happen. Besides, it's some long way from here and I'm headed in the other direction."

Deacon left the marshal's office and went to the hotel. When he came through the door, Howard called to him. "Mister Deacon, I have your clothes."

He went to the counter and Howard handed him his freshly washed and ironed clothes.

"Thank you, Howard. I'll go change and give you the ones I have on, so they can be washed, also."

When he came back out of the hotel, Olin, the newspaper man walked up beside him. "Let me buy you a drink."

Deacon never looked at the man. "No thanks."

"Mister Deacon, I am going to write a story and I would prefer it to be the truth and not some rumor."

Deacon stopped and faced the man. "Look Olin, it is Olin, isn't it?"

The man nodded his head. "Yes."

"I thought so. Look, Olin, I don't want my name in

your paper or in anybody's paper. I'm asking you not to print this story, but if you do, leave my name out of it. All the people need to know is, Taza is dead. It don't matter how or by who."

"A story isn't a story without a name."

"No story then." He walked away.

After checking on Dusty, he went to the "Two Aces Saloon." He ordered a beer and went to a corner table and sat with his back against the wall.

Two hours and three beers later, he got up to leave and met Olin coming in. "Mister Deacon let me buy you a drink."

"Mister Olin, I have nothing to say to you."

"All I want to do is buy you a drink."

"I don't want a drink, and I don't want to talk to you; have a good day."

Deacon rode out of Dublin a day later. Staying with the main trail even though it was leading away from the river. His thoughts were constantly on Rat Dobbs. Every town he rode through, he only stayed long enough to ask about Dobbs.

He was getting closer to the New Mexico Territory. In the last town, he had found out that Dobbs was seen in a little town called Casey, on the Texas side of the New Mexico southern border.

Chapter 59

Deacon was two days ride from Casey when he noticed that someone was watching him from a distance hill. He saw the rider that morning when he was saddling his horse.

As he started to mount up, he realized his water canteen was missing. He looked all around, it was no where to be found. He gave up looking and decided he must have lost it the day before.

As he rode during the day, he kept watching for the rider that he saw that morning. By late afternoon he had seen the rider three times, always in the distance.

He camped near a creek that night. He made a fire and put coffee on. As he ate beans and jerky, he sat staring into the fire. His thoughts were on who the mysterious rider might be.

After his meal, he checked on his horse and then stretched out in his bed roll to sleep. During the early hours of the morning, he woke with a start. He lay in his bedroll not moving. His hand was gripping his pistol. Had he heard something or was it a dream? He was laying facing the fire, which was now only a few embers. The moon was in its last quarter and was giving very little light. What was it that woke him?

He sat up, looking around, he got to his feet. The air was cool; he could see his breath even in the dim light. He reached for the poncho which was by his saddle when he saw it. His canteen was laying on the poncho. "What the hell?"

He picked up the canteen and shook it. It was full of water. He tossed it on the ground as he reached for the poncho. He slipped the poncho on and kicked up the fire by adding wood. Whoever took his canteen the night before, brought it back tonight, and they were still out there. There would be no more sleeping tonight.

When day broke, it found him saddled and ready to ride. Deacon looked to the hills in the distance and could see the man on horseback watching him. He took the canteen and walked out so the man could see him clearly and poured the contents on the ground. He wasn't taking a chance that there was something in it besides water.

He mounted up and rode toward Casey. By the time he reached the small town, it was midafternoon. The town wasn't much to look at. There were only a few small buildings, and they were in poor condition. He stopped at the make shift saloon and went in. The room was dimly lit, and it took a few seconds for his eyes to adjust.

He made his way to the so-called bar, which was nothing more than a couple boards laid across two whiskey barrels.

The man behind the bar was a short fat man with a full beard and dirty stringy hair. He set a glass on the bar and picked up a bottle while looking at Deacon. "Whiskey?"

"You have anything else?"

"Nope."

"Then whiskey it is."

He poured whiskey in the glass. "You a stranger in these parts, ain't you? Least ways I ain't never seen you before and I know about everybody for miles around."

"Yeah, just passing through." Deacon set the glass down. "Another."

As the man refilled his glass, Deacon asked. "Seen Rat Dobbs lately?"

The man's arm jerked at the mention of Rat's name

causing him to spill some of the whiskey. "Never heard of him." He turned his back on Deacon and acted like he was cleaning some glasses.

With the drink in his hand, Deacon turned around and looked at three men playing cards. He walked over to the table. "How about you gents, any of you seen Rat Dobbs lately?"

All three looked up at him and shook their heads. One of the men folded his hand of cards and laid them on the table. "Never heard of him. I got to get to the house, boys; got things to do."

All three men slid their chairs back, got up and walked out.

Deacon watched as they walked to the door. "Was it something I said?"

One of the men turned around. "Mister, best thing you can do is get on your horse and high tail it out of here. You'll live longer." At that he walked away.

Deacon walked back to the bar and set his empty glass down. "How about another?"

Staring at Deacon, the man picked up the bottle. When he shifted his eyes to the glass Deacon reached over the bar and grabbed him by the back of the neck pulling him closer to him. "Mister, you and your friends have been lying to me. Now I'm going to ask you again, and I want the truth this time. Have you seen Dobbs lately?"

"Okay, mister, turn me loose, you're hurting my neck."

Deacon turned him loose and the man backed up, rubbing the back of his neck.

"What about him?"

"Yeah, he has been here, but he left."

"Where did he go?"

"Hell, man, I don't know. He comes and goes as he pleases, I ain't his daddy."

"Where does he hang his hat mostly?"

"I don't know that either. Like I said, he comes and goes."

"When was he here last?"

"Three days ago; no, it was four."

"How many men does he have riding with him?"

"Four, I think. Could have been five, not sure."

Deacon picked up the glass and drank it down, then tossed money on the bar. "Now that wasn't so hard was it?"

"Look mister, Rat ain't somebody you want pissed at you. He don't bother me and I don't him. He comes in here from time to time, and I serve him drinks, that's all I know. It ain't like me and him send letters to each other; hell, we barely speak to one another."

"Okay, I get it. Do you have any idea where I can find him?"

"You won't find him till he's ready to be found. Odds are, he'll find you. But you might try El Paso."

After watering his horse and refilling his canteen at a well, Deacon left the little town of Casey and headed toward El Paso. He decided he would rather sleep on the ground out on the trail than stay in Casey.

That night he camped in a shallow ravine. He didn't see the mysterious man on horseback after he left Casey, but he had a feeling he was still out there. "Who is this man, and why is he following me." He wondered if it was Rat; and if so, "Why didn't he kill him in his sleep when he had the opportunity? If it is Rat, he knows I'm after him and that I will kill him if I can."

He lay back on his bedroll, wrapped in his wool poncho to ward off the chill of the night, and he tried to sleep. But his sleep was restless. He woke to the least little sound, listening, ever listening for that tell-tale sound that someone was out there in the dark.

Chapter 60

The next morning as Deacon was saddling his horse, he got to thinking. "Why would Rat go to El Paso?" He mounted his horse; and instead of going south, he rode back to Casey.

When he walked into the little make shift saloon, the greasy-headed barkeep looked surprised. "What'd you come back for?"

Deacon walked up and reached over the two-plank bar and took the man by the front of his dirty shirt, pulling him closer. "Why did you want me to go to El Paso? You know Dobbs isn't there, so, where is he?"

"Mister, I don't know where he is. I told you that already."

Deacon pulled his pistol and pushed the barrel against the man's face. "But you knew he wasn't in El Paso, didn't you?"

"Yes. But... but I was only trying to keep you alive, mister. Honest I was. When he finds out you are looking for him, he's likely to kill you, and if he thinks I put you on his trail, he may kill me."

Deacon released his hold on the man and holstered his pistol. "Why don't you let me worry about that."

The bartender poured a shot of whiskey into a glass and handed it to Deacon. "Here, have one on me."

Deacon took the glass and drank it down, handing the glass back. "Thanks."

"Are you a lawman?"

"Nope. And my business with Rat is of no concern of yours."

The man held his hands up and backed away. "Okay, I won't ask anything else. You're right. It's none of my concern."

Freedom Rides
R. D. Gregory

Deacon laid money on the bar. "Give me a bottle." He took the bottle and mounted his horse and headed east. He was close to finding Dobbs. To catch him he would have to think like him. As he rode he drank from the bottle. "Dusty, what do you think; what's he up to? I'll tell you what I think. I think he is looking to replace the men he lost. In order to do that, he is going to have to go where that kind of men can be found. I think he's headed to Odessa or Abilene. Or what if I've missed him, and he went south into Mexico."

Dusty blew his nose.

"Yeah, I agree, I can't see him going into Mexico to recruit men. But then again, he might if he was desperate to get a gang together."

He reined his horse to a stop and looked around. He took another drink, then turned his horse in a circle. As far as he could see in every direction, nothing, not a soul, a cow, nothing except the prairie.

A cold wind was picking up out of the northwest and it looked like it was going to rain. He slipped the poncho on and pulled the collar up on his coat. "Come on, Dusty, we need to find some shelter." He kicked Dusty into a trot and dodged the tumbleweeds as they came rolling by.

A slow rain was falling when he saw the rooftops of a town in the distance. "Lookie' there Dusty. You may get to sleep in the dry tonight."

As he rode down the street of the small town of Dunlap he could see no hotel. He stopped at the one and only saloon and went in. Though it was late afternoon there was only four people there, not counting the barkeep.

He went to the bar and ordered a beer. As he paid for the drink he asked. "Do you have someplace where a man can rent a room for the night in this town?"

"Yeah, down the street, last house on the left. A woman rents rooms; but I warn you, she won't put up with no swearing or drinking. She can put your horse up too; got a barn behind her house."

"Thanks, what did you say her name was?"

"Rose, Rose Doyle."

"Thanks, I'll go see her."

"Might as well have another beer, cause she ain't going talk to you for another hour or two."

"Why not?"

"Cause they're fixing to have a prayer meeting in her parlor, and she plays the piano."

"Maybe I can get there before the meeting gets started."

It was almost dark as he rode in the rain toward Rose Doyle's house. When he arrived at the house, he could hear her playing the piano. He knocked on the door and waited. When the door opened, he was surprised. He was expecting an older woman with gray hair and wrinkles. What was standing before him was a beautiful woman in her mid-thirties.

He realized she was saying something to him.

"What do you want?"

He took his hat off. "Ma'am, I'm sorry to bother you, but I understand you rent rooms."

"Yes, I do."

"I also need to put my horse in the barn."

She looked past him to his horse. "You'll have to tend to him yourself. I don't do that. Besides, I'm busy. Put him in the barn. You'll find grain and hay out there. Come through the back door and wipe your feet before you come in. There's chicken and dumplings on the stove, help yourself. I can smell alcohol on you, I don't allow the devils brew in my home. Don't bring it in. Understand?"

"Yes ma'am."

She turned and walked away leaving him standing on the front porch with his hat in his hand.

The cold rain mixed with sleet was coming down harder now. Deacon led Dusty around the house to the barn. He opened the barn door and led his horse inside. He was welcomed by a nicker from a horse standing in one of the stalls.

As he unsaddled and rubbed Dusty down, he could hear the piano from the house. From the corner of his eye; he saw someone come through the barn door. He placed his hand on the butt of his pistol as he turned. It was a young man about fourteen or fifteen years old. He took his hand from his pistol and continued to brush Dusty.

The boy walked to the other side of Dusty and looked over his back at Deacon. "Ma ask me to come out here to make sure you found everything."

"Thanks, I haven't looked for the grain as yet, but I'm sure I can find it."

"We keep it in that feedbox over yonder, so's the mice and other critters don't get in it."

Deacon looked at the feedbox setting in the corner. "That's a good idea. What's your name, son?"

"Zach, and I ain't your son."

"Okay Zach, I didn't intend to offend you."

"What's yours?"

"They call me Deacon... Deacon Reeves."

Zach watched as Deacon led his horse into a stall. "You a lawman?"

"Nope."

"Where you from?"

Deacon smiled. "Got no place I call home, I guess you

could say I'm from all over."

"That don't make no sense. You got to be from somewhere."

Deacon chuckled to himself. "Yeah, I guess you're right. A long time ago I lived up in the panhandle. Last few years I've been hanging my hat in Denver. You want to fetch me a scoop of grain from that box?"

The boy walked toward the feedbox. "What'cha you doing down this way?"

"You ask too many questions."

Zach poured the grain into the trough. As he turned around to step past Deacon, he felt of the poncho that Deacon was wearing. "You get this in Mexico?"

"Yep."

"What was you doing in Mexico?"

"Like I said, you ask too many questions."

"Mister, my ma don't need no trouble. So, if the law is after you, I wish you would just ride away."

Deacon smiled at him. "Rest easy Zach, I'm not wanted by the law, I don't mean you or your mother any harm. All I want is a dry place to sleep and something to eat. If you would feel better about things, I'll sleep here in the barn."

"No, I guess you're okay. It's just that I worry about ma now that my pa got killed." He started toward the barn door. "Close up the barn and come on to the house when you're done."

"I'll be right in." Deacon watched as the boy trotted the short distance to the house through the cold rain. His thoughts turned to his dead wife and son. "His son would be about that age now if he was still alive."

Chapter 61

As Deacon entered the back door of the house, he could hear several people singing a church hymn in the parlor. He wiped his feet, removed the poncho, and hung it on a peg by the door along with his hat. He looked toward the stove at a pot of chicken and dumplings. There was a plate along with silverware, a glass of water, and a loaf of fresh sourdough bread setting on the table.

Zach came through the door with a large pot of water and set it on the stove. "Heating up some water for your bath. Ma ain't going to let you sleep on her fresh clean sheets the way you smell."

"Can't say I blame her for that. I am kinda' rank. Not a lot of places to bathe where I've been."

"And where was that?"

"There you go with the questions again."

"You brought it up."

Deacon glanced at the boy and smiled as he dished himself an ample portion of the chicken and dumplings into a plate and sat down to eat. The singing in the parlor had stopped by the time he had finished eating.

Rose Doyle entered the kitchen followed by a man. Deacon stood. "Mrs. Doyle, I appreciate you allowing me to rent a room, and I really enjoyed the food. I haven't had chicken and dumplings that good in a long time."

She put her hand out to shake hands and smiled. "Please call me Rose, and you are?"

He took her hand in his, it was warm and soft yet strong. "Deacon Reeves, ma'am."

"How long do you plan on staying, Mister Reeves?"

"Please call me Deacon. Not sure, a couple days maybe. As soon as this weather lets up I'll be moving on."

"Very well. Can I have my hand back now, or do you

plan on taking it with you when you leave?"

He released her hand. "Yes, of course, sorry."

The man behind her cleared his throat. Both Deacon and Rose looked toward him. Rose said. "Forgive my manners. This is our pastor, Reverend Bell."

Deacon shook hands with the man. "Reverend, pleased to meet you."

"Likewise, I'm sure. I must be going. Rose, will you walk me to the door, please?"

The two of them walked out of the kitchen. Deacon could hear them talking as they reached the front door.

"Rose, you must stop bringing strangers into your home."

"What else am I to do? I have a boy to raise and no other way of making money."

"You have another option."

"I've told you I'm not ready for that. So please, don't ask again."

"Very well, but I wish you would reconsider."

The door opened and closed.

Rose came back into the kitchen. She looked Deacon over from head to feet. "Deacon, you are a mess."

"Ma'am?"

"Well, look at you, how long you been on the trail?"

"Ma'am, I don't know, why?"

"Your clothes are filthy."

"Yes, ma'am, I know. I had them cleaned a couple weeks ago."

"When that water gets hot, you get out of them clothes and take a bath. I'll clean them for you, but it will cost you two dollars."

Deacon looked from her to her son, who was trying to hold back a laugh with his hand over his mouth. "Yes, ma'am, I got a change of clothes out in the barn. I'll go fetch them."

"You'll do no such thing. It's pouring down rain and you have already tracked up my kitchen enough. You're about the size of my late husband, I'll get you something of his to put on."

"Yes, ma'am."

As she walked to the stove, she asked. "Would you like a cup of coffee while you wait for the water to heat?"

"That would be nice."

She poured the coffee and they sat at the table.

As Deacon sipped his coffee he felt uncomfortable. It had been a long time since he had been in this kind of environment, and he didn't know how to deal with it. He was more accustom to hotel rooms and saloons.

Rose smiled at him. "Mister Deacon, are you alright? You seem edgy about something."

He looked down at his coffee cup then up at her and smiled. "Yes, ma'am, I guess I am. I'm on the trail a lot and I'm not used to sitting down in someone's home. I feel out of place, like I'm intruding."

"What kind of work do you do, Mister Reeves?"

"Please call me Deacon. I find people."

"Are you a bounty hunter?"

"No, at least not now. I was once, but now I work for a detective agency. It's a long story, and I would rather not talk about it. What happened to Mister Doyle, if I may ask?"

She frowned as she stared into her coffee cup. When she looked up there was a tear in the corner of her eye. She brushed it away with the back of her hand. "He was the town marshal. A group of men came to town and were causing trouble. He tried to arrest them, and they killed him along with several other people."

"I'm sorry, I didn't mean to bring up bad memories."

She stood and walked to the stove. "The water is hot. You can take a bath now. You will find soap and towels near the tub in the room down the hall to the left. Your bedroom is the room on the right."

She reached for the pot of water, Deacon stood and went to the stove. "Let me do that."

He was standing close to her as she turned to hand him the folded hand towels she was going to use to pick up the hot pan of water. He took them from her, and his fingers brushed the back of her hands. She smelled of fresh bread, soap and lilacs. She looked into his eyes and blushed. Dropping her head, she turned away and walked out of the room.

Deacon was sitting in the bathtub when he heard a knock on the door. "Deacon, I have you some clean clothes. Can I come in?"

"Ma'am, I'm in the tub."

"Very well. Stay there; I'm coming in."

He grabbed a towel that was nearby. "But... ma'am."

The door opened, and she came in, laid the clothes on a table, and started gathering his dirty ones. "I will have these ready for you by tomorrow afternoon." She turned to walk out of the room; and as she reached the door, she turned back. "I assume you will be staying that long?"

"Yes, ma'am, I guess I will." As the door closed, he mumbled to himself. "Since you have my clothes, I guess I'll have to."

After his bath he put on Rose's late husband's clothes. He went to his room and laid on the bed. He wanted a drik of whiskey to take the edge off, so he could fall asleep but found out he didn't need it. He was asleep in a matter of minutes.

Chapter 62

The next morning Deacon was up at first light. He started a fire in the stove and put a pot of coffee on. He slipped on his poncho and hat and went to the barn. He fed both horses in the barn and collected his change of clothes. As he was doing that he noticed that someone had been snooping around in his saddle bags. As far as he could tell, everything was there. "Probably the kid."

He went back inside. As he was hanging his poncho and hat, Rose came into the kitchen. He looked at her and smiled. "The rain has stopped."

"Yeah, I noticed. I guess you will be leaving now?"

"Can't, you have my clothes."

She took a long look at him and smiled. "My husband's clothes fit you well."

"They're okay. I made coffee, I hope you didn't mind?"

She ran her fingers through her hair realizing she hadn't brushed it. She was still in her night gown with a robe on over it. "I apologize, I must look a mess. Most of the time, it's just me and my boy here... I'm sorry, let me go get dressed."

"Rose, it's not necessary. If I could be so bold to say, I think you are beautiful."

She smiled and took two cups from the cupboard. She set them on the table and sat down as he poured the coffee. "Who are you?"

He looked at her. "I told you. Deacon Reeves."

"Yeah, that's your name, maybe. But who are you, and why are you here in my house?"

"I'm only passing through, Rose."

She sipped her coffee and looked into his eyes. "I have a confession. I went to the barn last night while you slept. You're not a cowboy; that's for sure. Most men don't ride a horse as nice as yours, and they sure don't have a saddle that cost as much as that one you ride. Is that real silver?"

"Yes."

"And what about all that money in your saddle bags. Did you rob a bank or something? You're an outlaw, aren't you? Oh, dear God, why did you have to stop here? I want you out of my house." She stood and walked to the window with her back to him.

"Rose, I'm not an outlaw. I haven't robbed a bank, and the law is not after me. But I will leave. I'll leave right now if you wish."

She turned from the window and pointed toward the door. "Good, get out."

He stood and walked to the door. He took his poncho and folded it across his arm. Taking his hat from the peg on the wall he opened the door. He stood there for a few seconds looking at the floor. "Rose, can I have my clothes back?"

She put her hands on her hips. "Come back this afternoon. I'll have them ready for you."

He went to the barn and saddled Dusty. Zach came out the door as he was getting on his horse. "You leaving Mister Deacon?"

"Yeah."

"But ma is fixing breakfast. Ain't you staying for breakfast?"

"I'm not hungry." He heeled Dusty and rode around the side of the house. He could see her watching him out the window. He tilted his hat to her and rode down the street.

He rode to the saloon and went in. The bartender was sweeping the floor. Most of the chairs were turned upside down on top of the tables. He stopped what he was doing when he saw Deacon come in. "It's a little early for drinking, so I'm guessin' you want some coffee?"

Deacon took a chair from a nearby table and sat down. "Got anything to eat to go with that cup of coffee?"

"Figured you was staying at Rose Doyle's house. She always feeds her renters."

"Do you have anything to eat or not?"

"Sure, I'll whip you something up."

The bartender returned with a cup of coffee. "I'll have you something to eat shortly."

"Thanks."

After eating he went to the mercantile and bought some supplies. He returned to the saloon and sat with his back to the wall. There were more people coming in, even though it was still mid-morning. There was a low stakes poker game going on at one table, and a couple cowboys were leaned against the bar.

Zach slid through the door and came to Deacon's table. "Zach, what are you doing in here?"

"I wanted to talk to you."

"If your ma catches you in here, she will skin you alive."

"Yes sir, I know. How come you to leave?"

"It was the right thing to do. Your ma didn't trust me to be there."

"How come?"

"It's hard to explain Zach, but it was right thing to do. Maybe she thought I would harm you or her. So, you go on back home and take care of her. Come on, I'll walk with you."

When they were outside Zach looked at Dusty. "He's

a pretty horse."

"You want to ride him?"

"Could I?"

"Sure."

Zach untied him and climbed into the saddle.

"He's not a buggy horse. You ride him with only one hand."

"Yes sir. I know about neck reining."

"Okay. Take him down the street and bring him back."

Zach rode Dusty down the street in a trot. When he got almost to the end of the street, he turned around and brought him back in a short lope.

Pastor Bell walked up beside Deacon. "What do you think you are doing?"

Deacon glanced toward him and then back at Zach. "Nothing."

"You stay away from Mrs. Doyle and her son."

Deacon turned to face him. "Pastor Bell, good morning to you, too. Let's get something straight; first I know your name is not Bell. I can't put a name on the face, yet, but I will. I saw a poster on you in Colorado. Seems you are wanted for running off with the church's bank account. And second, I think you need to leave town before I remember what your name is and report you to the marshal." He smiled at the man.

"You are mistaken. It wasn't me."

"Mister, I don't forget a face. And it was you. I advise you to get now. In fact, you should leave Texas and soon."

The man turned on his heels and walked away as Zach rode up and stopped. "What did he want?"

Deacon watched as the man walked away. "I think he came by to tell me he was leaving town."

Zach stepped down off Dusty, glanced at Pastor Bell

and handed Deacon the reins. "Good riddance. He was constantly bugg'en ma to marry him."

"Well, I'm pretty sure he's gone. So, go home."

"Thanks for letting me ride your horse. I hope to have one like him someday."

"Maybe you will." He tied Dusty to the hitching rail as Zach walked back toward his house. He went back into the saloon, ordered a beer, and sat in a chair against the wall.

He finished his beer and started to leave when four men came in. They ordered whiskey, drank them down and ordered another. He watched as they walked away from the bar, each going in different sections of the room. Something was going on but what?

All four men pulled their pistols at the same time and pointed them at Deacon. He sat with his hands on the table. If they wanted him dead, he would be dead already. One of the men walked toward him and stopped in front of his table. "If you want to keep living, keep both hands on the table. There is someone who wants to talk to you."

Chapter 63

The batwing doors opened, and Rat Dobbs came in. He walked up to the table and sat down across from Deacon. He smiled at Deacon as he leaned back in the chair. "Barkeep, two whiskeys. How you been, Deacon?"

The bartender brought two glasses and set them on the table. His hand was shaking as he poured the glasses full.

Deacon leaned toward the table. "What do you want, Rat?"

"Just a little chat among friends."

Deacon picked up his glass and poured it into the floor and set the glass on the table upside down. "We're not friends, never have been, never will be."

"Now, now Deacon, I had hopes that we could get along."

Deacon leaned up. "You are a murdering bastard. You almost killed my brother, and let's not forget you was going to drygulch me."

"Deacon, Deacon, can't we let bygones be bygones.

"No."

"Look, I don't why, but I like you. I want you to ride with me."

Deacon leaned back in his chair and laughed. "You have lost your mind."

"Think about it, me and you riding together, we could be rich."

"I don't like sleeping with snakes; besides I thought you was rich. What happened to all that money you took from that rancher up in Greenbrier?"

"Funny thing about that. Remember when I shot that cowboy and took his horse. Well, due to all the pain I was experiencing with that bullet in my shoulder, I forgot to take the money when I changed horses."

Deacon laughed so hard he could hardly talk. "Now that was some horse trade. That cowboy rode out of Greenbrier the next day and never said a word about finding any money in those saddlebags."

Rat frowned. "It's not funny."

"Oh, yes it is."

"Deacon, I'm serious here. I want us to ride together."

"It's not going to happen."

"I could kill you right now; in fact, I could have killed you back on the trail."

"So, that was you?"

Rat smiled.

"Rat, I realize that you could have me killed right now and that you also could have killed me out on the trail. You should have, because I am going to kill you. So, if your plan is to kill me, make your play. But, are you willing to bet your life that I can't put a bullet in you before I die. Now you either make your play or get out of my face. This conversation is over."

Rat stood, his hand hovering over his pistol. "I want to ask you one more question."

"What?"

"Did you kill Taza?"

"Yep."

Rat turned and walked away. When he reached the door, he stopped. "I wished we could have been friends."

"I'll be coming for you Rat."

His men were backing toward the door, still holding their guns on Deacon.

One of his men called over his shoulder to Rat as he reached the door. "Can I kill him now?"

He heard Rat answer no.

When the last man went through the door, Deacon

jumped up. "You got a back door to this place?"

"Yeah." Came the reply from the bartender.

Deacon sprinted around the bar and to the back of the building. With his gun in his hand, he ran out the door and around to the alley that led to the street. When he reached the street, he saw Rat and his men loping their horses toward the end of town.

He holstered his gun and ran to get his horse, but his horse was gone. In fact, there wasn't a horse on the street anywhere. "Rat, you, sonofabitch."

He went to the marshal's office. When he walked in he saw the marshal putting something in a set of saddlebags. "Marshal, I need a horse."

"And you're telling me this, because?"

"Because you are the marshal. Rat Dobbs was just in town. He took my horse and I need one so I can go after him."

"I know, I saw them taking the horses."

"You saw them and didn't do anything?"

The marshal slung the saddle bags over his shoulder and looked at Deacon. "That was Rat Dobbs, I ain't going up against him. I don't get paid enough to go against the likes of him."

"What kind of marshal are you?"

"A live one, and I intend to stay that way."

"You aren't fit to be a lawman."

"You want the job?" He took the badge off his shirt and handed it to Deacon. "Here you can have it. Me, I'm getting the hell out of here. He's done killed one marshal in this town, and I don't plan on being the next." He opened the door and looked around outside before walking out.

Deacon placed the badge on the desk. "You run now, and you'll be running for the rest of your life."

He stopped and turned to look at Deacon. "That may be true, but I'll be alive to do so."

Deacon walked out in the street. He could see men and women all up and down the street in small groups talking.

Deacon thought about what the marshal said. "Dobbs has already killed one marshal in this town. I bet my hat that it was Rose Doyle's late husband." He looked down at the shirt he was wearing. That explains the small holes on the left side of the chest, it's where a badge had hung.

He walked up the street to Rose's house and knocked on the door. When she opened the door and saw who it was she turned around. "Come in, I have your clothes ready."

"Rose, you and Zach need to get out of town."

She turned around. "Why, what has happened?"

"Rat Dobbs has come back."

She put her hand to her mouth. "No, not again. He killed my husband."

"I figured as much. He was the marshal, wasn't he?"

"Yes. They shot him down in cold blood then dragged his body through the streets."

He took her by the arms. "Rose, take Zach and get out of town now. Dobbs is gone for now, but he will be back."

"I have nowhere to go."

"It don't matter where you go. Get in the buggy and leave, go to the next town and stay till this is over."

She took a deep breath. "No, I won't let that dreadful man control my life."

"I can't make you leave, but I wish you would reconsider. If he's not stopped, he will burn this town to the ground before he leaves."

"How do you know this?"

"I know him, and I know what he does. Now please leave."

She clenched her teeth. "I'm not leaving. This is all I have, and I have nowhere to go."

Chapter 64

Deacon looked at Rose. "You have got to be one of the most stubborn women that I have ever met."

She smiled a fake smile. "I'll take that as a compliment, considering the source."

He shook his head at her. "Do you have a gun?"

"Yes."

"Do you know how to use it?"

"Yes."

"Good. Get it and make sure it's loaded. Lock the doors and don't come out. If anybody tries to come in, shoot them. You got that?"

"Yes."

"Where's Zach?"

"I don't know, but I'll find him."

"Both of you, in this house and don't come out."

"Deacon, what are you going to do?"

"I'm going to kill him."

"You can't do this alone. Get the marshal to help."

"The marshal has left town."

"That coward."

"Not exactly what I would call him." He started to leave, when he reached the door, she called to him. "Deacon."

He stopped and turned around. "Yes."

She was walking toward him. As she got close, she put her hands on his chest and tiptoed, kissing him on the lips. After a moment, she pulled back, looking into his eyes. "Please be careful."

He placed his hand on her face and brushed her flowing hair back, allowing it to entwine between his fingers, as he gazed into her green eyes.

"Rose, this is what I do, I take down bad men." He

walked out the door and down the street. He entered the saloon and walked to the bar. The place was empty except for the bartender.

He laid money on the bar. "Give me a bottle of rye."

The bartender set the bottle on the bar. "Mister, you best be hightailing it out of here."

Deacon looked at him. "What's your name?"

"Most folks call me Vern."

"Well Vern, Dobbs took my horse and almost every other horse in this town."

"He's coming back ain't he?"

"Yep."

Vern started putting bottles of whiskey in crates.

Deacon uncorked his bottle and took a glass from the bar. While watching Vern, he poured the glass full. "What are you doing?"

"I'm going to hide my good whiskey before they come back."

Deacon took a drink. "Good idea, except it's not going to matter."

Vern stopped what he was doing and looked at Deacon. "Why do you say that?"

"Because, if Dobbs isn't stopped, he will burn this town down and kill everybody in it."

Vern placed his hands on the bar. "What are we going to do?"

"Don't ask me, I don't live here." Deacon took another drink as he watched Vern's reaction.

Vern walked around the bar toward the door. "I got to go talk to the marshal."

"Good luck with that. He's left town. You're on your own and you're wasting time."

"What do you mean?"

"Vern, there is no one to save you and this town

except the people who live here. Now if I lived here, I would be getting all the able body men together and when that bunch rides back into town I would gun them down."

Vern walked closer to Deacon. "Mister, we tried fighting back three years ago when he came to town. He killed six people, including the marshal. Dragged him through the streets, they did, and then hung him on the porch of the bank and burned him."

"Yep, that sounds like the Rat Dobbs I know. So, what are you going to do, let him have the town?"

"Look mister, I don't know who you are, but the people who live in this town ain't gunfighters."

"You must have some gumption about you or you wouldn't be living out here. Now grow a backbone and fight for what's yours; or tuck your tail between your legs and run."

Vern stood staring at Deacon. "Why ain't you leaving?"

"I told you, Dobbs has my horse."

"Nah, that ain't the reason. You got a score to settle with him. I heard you talking to him. You two have history."

"We do, and I aim to kill him."

Vern took his apron off and tossed it on the bar. "What can we do to help?"

Deacon smiled. "Now we're talking. Gather everybody that can use a gun and meet me back here."

Chapter 65

Deacon left the saloon and went to the marshal's office. There were a couple shotguns and three rifles on a locked rack behind the desk. He started going through the desk drawers looking for a key. He found a set of keys and went through them one by one till he found the one that fit.

He laid the guns on the desk and checked them to be loaded. He picked up two and went outside and looked around for the best place to put them. He walked down the street to the mercantile and went down the alley, setting one against the back wall. Then he walked two buildings down and placed another. He had scattered the guns around town in different places. All except for one Henry and a short double-barreled shotgun, which he kept with him.

By the time he went back to the saloon there were several men there drinking.

Deacon looked at the group. "Vern, no more drinks."

A murmur went across the group. One of the men spoke up. "Why not?"

Deacon walked in among the seven men who were staring at him. "If you are here to fight for what's yours, then you need to be sober. The men that are about to come into this town are some of the meanest and toughest men you have ever seen. They will kill you for the fun of it and laugh at you when you beg for your life. Then they will shoot you. These aren't your ordinary run of the mill cowboys out for a good time on Saturday night."

One of the men spoke up. "How come you know so much about them? Do you know them?"

"Not personally, but I know their type. I must warn

you. If you go against these men, it must be to the end. If you give up, they will torture you and kill you. So, if you don't have what it takes, leave now. I don't want you in my way."

"Who are you? I ain't seen you around here. For all we know you could be one of them."

"I'm called Deacon, and no I'm not from around here."

"How do we know you won't run out?"

"Mister, I don't run. I am either going to kill Rat Dobbs or he's going to kill me before this is over. And I'm going to do it with or without your help. So, make up your minds if you're in this. If not, go crawl under a rock somewhere."

The men started talking among themselves. One of them stepped up. "I... I can't do this. I got..."

Deacon interrupted him. "I don't want to hear your excuses, just leave." The man kept standing there looking at Deacon and the rest of the men. "Go, go now!"

The man walked toward the door with his head down. Deacon looked around at the rest. "Anybody else?"

Two more men walked out, leaving four and Deacon.

Deacon looked over the four men, shopkeepers and a blacksmith. "I want each of you to get yourself a pistol and a rifle or a shotgun. Have plenty of shells and don't be afraid to shoot. If you hesitate, you will be dead. Find a good place to hide and wait. And please do not shoot my horse. I think Dobbs will be riding him so leave him to me."

"How many men does he have?"

"I don't know. I've seen four, but he has to have more. My guess eight to twelve."

"We don't stand a chance against that many."

"I've gone up against bigger odds than that and came

out of it. We can too if we do this right. He made a mistake by coming in and leaving. Now we know he's coming, we'll be ready for him. Now go, he could ride back in at any time."

Everyone left the saloon and Deacon went to the marshal's office. When Dobbs took his horse he also took his poncho and his extra shells. He found what he needed plus a heavy duster coat. He put several shotgun shells and a box of rifle shells in the pocket of his coat. Picking up the Henry and the scatter gun he went to the back of the building.

Leaning the scatter gun against the side of the building. He took the Henry and climbed to the top of the marshal's office, using a ladder he found lying next to the building. The front of the building had a wall that extended above the roof line which would provide him with some protection. He sat down to wait.

He looked at his pocket watch; it was going on four o'clock. The wind was coming out of the north, and the air had a chill in it. He looked at the gray sky. "Great, it's going to rain. I should have picked a dryer spot to hold up."

A slow drizzling rain started to fall shortly after dark. Deacon pulled his coat collar up and buttoned the top button to keep as dry as he could. "I wish I'd brought that bottle with me."

An hour later he heard someone screaming at the far end of town. A woman was running down the street screaming that her house was on fire. Deacon stood and watched as people started coming out of their houses and ran toward the burning house. "I can't believe it. Stupid, stupid people, you are doing exactly what he wants you to do."

As a crowd of people gathered in front of the burning

house four men stepped out of the dark. One of the men shot his pistol in the air to get everyone's attention. "Everybody, unless you want to die, go to the saloon."

Deacon watched as the group of town people were herded into the saloon, among them was three of the men that were going to help him with Dobbs. "This gets better and better. I need a drink."

He climbed down off the roof and went through the back door of the marshal's office. "I think I saw a bottle in one of those desk drawers." He stumbled around in the dark and rummaged through the drawers till he found the bottle.

He sat down in the chair and pulled the cork. "What the hell am I going to do now?" He was looking out the window as Dobbs rode down the street on his horse with four more men. They got off and went into the saloon. "They are all in there, I could lock the doors and burn the place down, but then I would also kill half of the town people. That won't work." He took another drink.

He got up and went out the back door. Picking up the scatter gun, he walked to the street. He sprinted across the street and went to the window of the saloon and looked in. Dobbs and his men were drinking and harassing a couple men. There was one man standing by the door, but he was more interested in what was going on inside than watching outside.

Deacon checked the shotgun, cocked both hammers and eased toward the door. He could see the man at the door; he was looking inside and drinking from a bottle. Deacon hunkered down and eased closer to the door.

When he reached the door, he stood up. "Hey, dummy."

The man still had the bottle to his lips when he turned to look down the barrels on the scatter gun. Deacon pulled both triggers and ran across the street.

When he reached the other side, he kicked the door open to a building and went inside. He reloaded the shotgun and waited.

"Deacon, is that you?"

"Yep."

"We don't have to do this."

"No, we don't. Get on your horse and ride out."

Dobbs laughed. "It's raining. I don't like rain."

Deacon watched as two men came from the alley beside the saloon and ran across the street two buildings down. He also saw two men running across the street in the other direction. He thought to himself. "They are boxing me in. I got to move."

Chapter 66

Deacon dashed out the door and ran down the boardwalk. A hail of bullets started hitting all around him as he darted into alley and ran to the back of the buildings. He stopped at the edge of the building and looked around the corner. He could see two men creeping toward him with their pistols in their hands. He took a deep breath and stepped out with the shotgun at ready. The men were less than ten feet away as he pulled the triggers. Both men went down but weren't dead.

Deacon pulled his pistol and shot them again. He heard a shot from behind him. He spun around to see one of Dobbs men's legs give away and he fell into the mud, face down.

Behind him was the marshal, his gun smoking. "I thought about what you said. I ain't no coward, I ain't never run from a fight before and I ain't going to start now."

Deacon stepped over the dead man and walked up to the marshal. "Glad you decided to come back."

"You got a name, mister?"

"They call me Deacon. And you are?"

"Robert Ford."

"There's another one out here somewhere."

"I saw him going back toward the saloon."

"Let's go back to the street."

They went to the corner of the building and looked across the street toward the saloon. Deacon reloaded his pistol and the shotgun. "He's down four men; he's not going to be happy."

"What do we do now?"

"Next move is his. Unless we can draw more of them out."

"How can we do that?"

"I don't know, what I do know is I want a drink."

The marshal started back down the alley. "Come on, let's go to my office."

The two men went to the back of the marshal's office and as Deacon walked past the Henry rifle propped against the wall he picked it up. They entered through the back door and Deacon went to the front window. He was looking out across the street at the saloon when the marshal struck a match to light an oil lantern.

"Put that out. We'd be sitting ducks in the light from that lantern. The bottle is on your desk."

"You been in here?"

Deacon smiled. "Yeah, I got cold sitting on the roof. I needed something to get the blood flowing again."

The marshal handed Deacon the bottle. "You wearing my coat?"

"Yeah. I hope you don't mind." He turned the bottle up and took a drink, then handed it back to the marshal.

He took the bottle. "Don't get any holes in it."

"You're funny. But I'll try not to."

"Have you got a plan on how the hell we are going to get out of this alive."

"I had one, but it went to hell in a handbasket. Rat is smarter than I gave him credit for."

"What do you think he'll do next?"

"I'm not sure. He has all them folks in there, I hope he don't start killing them."

"Yeah, me, too."

"Right now, I figure they are getting liquored up, except for Rat. He won't get drunk; he may drink a little, but he won't get drunk."

"Sounds like you know him."

"Yeah, our paths have crossed. And I aim to kill him

this time."

The marshal took another drink and sat down in his chair. Deacon continued to watch the saloon from the window. After a bit, he looked back at the marshal and realized he was asleep.

Deacon took the bottle of whiskey from the desk and went to a chair setting in the corner. He sat down with the shotgun in his lap and took a drink from the bottle. "I sure wish I knew what was going on in that saloon right now."

From his position in the corner, he could see the street through the window; although he couldn't see the saloon.

As the night passed and in the early hours of the morning Deacon heard a board squeak on the boardwalk. He cocked the hammers on the shotgun and waited. He could see the doorlatch moving. He raised the shotgun as the door slowly opened.

One of Dobbs' men crept in slowly and could see the marshal sitting in the chair. He started to aim his pistol at the marshal when Deacon opened up with both barrels of the 12-gauge scatter gun. The man was blown back out the door and landed on the boardwalk jerking before he died.

The marshal jumped up from his chair drawing his pistol. He looked at the bloody mess lying halfway in the door. He turned to look at Deacon. "You could have warned me."

Deacon reloaded the shotgun, snapping the barrels closed; he grinned. "Didn't have time." He walked to the door and looked out. He could see someone looking over the batwing doors of the saloon. "Hand me that rifle."

Deacon took the rifle and took aim at the face.

The marshal was looking out the window. "Don't

shoot! That's Vern from the saloon."

Deacon lowered the rifle and handed it to the marshal. "Here take this and keep me covered." He reached down, taking hold of the dead man, he dragged him to the street. He stepped back on the boardwalk. "Rat is using Vern to keep watch. That's not very smart. You keep me covered; I'm going across the street. I want to see what's going on in that saloon if I can."

The marshal stood in the door as Deacon ran across the muddy street. When he reached the corner of the saloon he hunkered down and eased to the window. Deacon could see Rat sitting in a chair talking to one of his men, and neither man was being pleasant toward the other.

"Looks like we have a little discontent among the men." Deacon looked around the room and could only see Rat and two of his men. The town's people were all sitting against one wall except for Vern who was standing at the door. Deacon thought to himself. "Is there another; if so, where is he?"

A shot rang out from the marshal's office. Deacon turned to see the marshal fall onto the board walk. He jumped up and started running across the street when one of Rat's men stepped into the doorway of the marshal's office. Deacon fired two quick shots at the man as he ran toward the marshal.

The man ducked back into the office firing a shot at Deacon as he did. With his pistol in his hand, Deacon took a quick look at the marshal; he was still alive. He grabbed him under his arms and began dragging him toward the alley beside the marshal's office. When he was almost there a bullet tore through his right thigh muscle.

He managed to get the marshal into the alley. He

looked at the wound in his leg, it was bleeding badly. He took off his bandana and tied it tight around his leg, slowing the bleeding.

Rat called out to him. "Hey Deacon, I bet that hurts like hell." He laughed.

Chapter 67

Bending over, Deacon checked the marshal's wound. The marshal tried to get up. "Lie still, I need to stop this bleeding."

"How bad is it?"

"Best I can tell you got a bullet in your back. Now, how bad could that be? Lie still!"

"Anybody ever tell you that you've got bad bedside manners?"

Deacon took the marshal's bandana from his neck. Folding it he placed it over the wound. "I need to get you somewhere safe."

"Help me up."

Deacon helped him to his feet. "Now what?"

"Let's go to the back of the mercantile. The Cruzes' live above the store; hopefully, they're not in the saloon with everybody else."

Deacon placed the marshal's arm over his shoulder. Leaning on each other they made their way to the back door of the mercantile. Deacon beat on the door. "Open up."

He tried the door, it was locked. He beat on the door again. "Come on, open up."

"Mister Cruzes, open up. It's me, the marshal."

The door opened a crack and then opened all the way. "Marshal, you're hurt."

"Yeah, me and him need some help. We both been shot."

"Come in, I'll do what I can, but I'm no doctor."

Deacon limped in. "I just need this bleeding stopped before I bleed to death." He sat down in a nearby chair. "Him, he needs a doctor. He's got bullet in his back; but right now, see if you can stop his bleeding."

Mister Cruzes and his wife helped the marshal up on a counter. She tore his shirt open and started cleaning the wound.

Deacon took his knife and split his pant leg away from his bullet wound. "Mister Cruzes, do you have something I can pack these holes with."

Cruzes grabbed some clean towels and knelt down to look at the wound. "You're lucky, the bullet didn't hit the bone. It passed through the muscle." He cut the towel in half and covered each hole. Using Deacon's bloody neckerchief, he tied it around his leg. "That should stop the bleeding, but it needs to be properly tended to."

Deacon stood. "Thanks, but I got things to do. Take care of him. He's a good man."

Checking his pistol, he started toward the back door. Looking both directions, he slipped out the back door and around the corner of the building toward the street. Glancing in both directions he started across the street. When he reached the other side, he leaned against the wall.

The sun was coming up as he started toward the saloon with pistol in hand. He heard someone screaming, "Zach." He looked down the street and saw Zach coming down the street with a pistol in his hand. He limped out in the street and blocked Zach's passage. "Where do you think you are going?"

"Get out of my way. He killed my pa."

"I know he did, and I am going to take care of him. Now go back home before he kills you. Your mother needs you. Now go, I'll handle Dobbs."

Rose Doyle came running up and took hold of her son. "Zach, come with me."

At that moment a bullet hit Deacon in the back of his left shoulder. He spun around and saw the shooter on the boardwalk. Deacon raised his gun he squeezed the trigger. The man went down as Deacon fell to his knees, his gun slipping from his fingers.

Rose bent over him, helping him back to his feet with tears in her eyes. "Deacon, Deacon, let me help you."

He took a deep breath. "Get Zach out of here before the two of you get hurt."

"Deacon come with me. You're hurt."

Deacon looked toward the saloon, Rat was coming through the door, heading their way. "I can't Rose; I have to finish this. Now go!"

Rose took Zach by the arm and led him away.

Deacon turned back toward Rat who was coming at him with his gun in his hand.

Deacon started to make a step when his legs gave way and he fell to his knees. He tried to get up and fell back to one knee.

Rat walked up to him. "Deacon, Deacon, Deacon, I do tell you are in bad shape. Look at you wallowing here in the mud like a pig."

Deacon looked up at him. "Go to hell, Rat."

Rat laughed. "If you had only done as I asked you wouldn't be in this shape right now. I gave you a chance and you turned me down. I had such hopes of us being friends. That's gone now, but what amazes me is that twice now you have managed to kill all my men. This is a set back for me. So now I going to put a bullet in your head. I'm tired of you interfering with my plans."

Deacon's pistol was lying in the muddy street at his left foot. He tried to pick it up, but his arm and hand would not do as he asked them, due to the slug in his left shoulder. He reached for his shoulder gun with his right hand when he remembered that he never got it back from the Indians.

Rat grinned. "Here let me help you up. I want you standing on your feet when I kill you." He leaned over, and with his left hand he took hold of Deacon's coat. His right hand was still holding his gun and he placed it on Deacon's left shoulder.

As Deacon stood he pulled his knife with his right hand and shoved it under Rat's ribs and into his heart. He looked into Rat's eyes as he twisted the knife and grinned. Rat's face had a look of pain, surprise and disbelieve.

Deacon spoke thru clenched teeth in Rats good ear "I've wondered many times, as probably you have, which of us was the faster. Now we will never know." Rat blinked his eyes twice and tried to speak but couldn't.

He let Rat slide down into the muddy street. He turned to walk off, but instead he fell unconscious.

Chapter 68

When Deacon came to, he was weak, he tried to sit up but didn't make it. The soft warm hand of Rose Doyle pushed him back to the bed. "Lie still, you've lost a lot of blood."

He cleared the fog from his eyes by closing them and opening them again. He looked at Rose. "I need a drink."

She poured a glass of water and holding the back of his head, she put the glass to his mouth. He took a drink and coughed. "That's water."

"Yes, Mister Deacon, it's water."

"How long have I been out?"

"A few hours. You lost a lot of blood."

He tried to move his left arm and it hurt so bad he moaned. "Who took the bullet out of my shoulder?"

"I did."

He raised the sheet to look at his leg; that's when he realized he didn't have on any clothes. He jerked the sheet back down. "Who took my clothes?"

She smiled. "I did. And if you remember, they weren't yours anyway."

"Yeah, sorry about getting them in such a mess. And I suppose you gave me a bath after you took your late husband's clothes off me?"

"Oh, I couldn't do it by myself, I had help. You were a muddy, bloody mess. You should have seen my kitchen. It took us hours to clean up the mess after we got you in bed."

Deacon took a deep breath and closed his eyes. "I'm afraid to ask who helped you."

She smiled and cocked her head to one side. "It was the ladies from my prayer group."

"Oh God. Why didn't you just let me die?"

She laughed and patted his arm. "You rest, I'll go prepare you something to eat."

"I need a drink."

She smiled as she walked out of the room.

"Rose."

She stopped at the door. "Yes."

"Dobbs, is he dead?"

"Yes, you killed him."

"What about Marshal Ford?"

"He's going to be okay. Like you, it is going to be a few weeks before he gets around."

He nodded his head and closed his eyes. "Good."

Rose came back into his room and had to wake him to feed him. She spoon fed him chicken soup and made small talk as he ate.

After he finished the soup, she got up to leave.

"I need a drink."

She smiled. "Go to sleep, you need your rest."

The next morning, he managed to get to the sitting position. He was propped against the head board when she brought him his breakfast. "What are you doing up?"

"Sitting here, I can't go anywhere, you have my clothes. Not that it matters if I walk around without any clothes on because half the ladies in town have seen me naked. Thanks to you."

She smiled and set the tray of food across his legs. He flinched when the tray touched his injured leg.

She picked it back up. "I'm sorry."

"It's okay, I'll be alright."

She set the tray on a table. "Let me look at it."

"I don't think so. It's okay, honest."

"Stop being foolish. I've already seen everything you have. Let me look at that leg."

"Maybe you did, but I wasn't awake when you and

your friends had your way with me."

She laughed. "Men! You all are silly." She raised the cover to look at the bandage.

He was watching her expression's as her face went red and she raised her eyebrows. She put the cover back down. "Well, it looks like you are getting your strength back, and that bandage needs to be changed. We will do that after breakfast." She walked toward the door.

"Where are you going. I can't reach my coffee."

"I'll be back in a minute."

When she returned she picked up the tray and sat in a chair next to his bed. Holding the tray in her lap, without a word, she handed him his coffee.

He took the coffee cup and sipped the coffee. "You make good coffee."

"Thanks. Are you ready to eat?"

"Yeah. I think I can feed myself with one hand."

"You can't and hold that cup."

He smiled. "True, but I can set it down."

She picked up a fork full of eggs and smiled. "Open your mouth and shut up."

After breakfast she took the tray and left the room. When she came back she had a pan of warm water, towels, and clean bandages.

She pulled the covers back and looked at the bandage on his leg. With a pair of scissors, she carefully cut the bandage away. "Deacon, we have to raise that leg to remove the bandage. It may hurt."

"I know, do it, I'll help if I can."

Deacon gritted his teeth and between the two they were able to get his leg high enough to remove the bandage.

"Keep it there if you can while I clean it. Deacon, if this gets infected you will lose your leg."

"Don't let it get infected."

She looked at him. "I'm no doctor, but I will do the best I can."

"That's all I'm asking for."

After she was finished she looked at him. "You got to get out of that bed, so I can change those bloody sheets."

She started out of the room when he stopped her.

"Rose, I really could use a drink."

She smiled and walked out.

"Blasted woman. She's got my clothes and won't let me have a drink."

She came back in and laid fresh linen on the table. "Deacon, I don't have anything that you can put on. You can't wear any of my gowns or robes and I've cut up my husband's night shirts."

He stared at her and shook his head. "What? You want me to stand on one leg naked while you change these sheets?"

"Yeah, something like that. I'll wrap a sheet around you."

"Okay, get the sheet."

She unfolded a sheet and wrapped it around him as he sat in bed. With her help he was able to get both feet on the floor. "Put your arm around my neck and try to stand on your good leg."

With his right arm over her shoulder, she held to his wrist with one hand and her other arm was around his waist.

With her help, he was able to slide out of bed and stand on his good leg. She looked up at him. "Now let's get you to the chair."

As they moved he could feel the sheet slipping off his shoulders. "Rose, the sheet is falling."

She reached for the sheet and he started to fall. She

let the sheet go and grabbed him around the waist with both arms holding him to her. His right arm was on her shoulder for added support. She looked up at him. "Are you okay?"

"No, Rose I'm not. I feel like I'm going to pass out."

"Don't you dare. Don't do that."

She heard a gasp and looked toward the door. One of the ladies from town was standing in the doorway. "Mrs. Jones, come here quick."

The elderly lady pointed her finger at Rose. "I told you that this was a bad idea."

"Mrs. Jones, get over here and help me. He's going to fall, and I can't hold him."

She ran around the bed. "What do you want me to do?"

"Help me get him in the chair."

She looked at Deacon. "Oh my." She walked up behind him and put her arms around his waist.

"Ruth, I need you around here."

Mrs. Jones eased around Deacon without removing her hand from his body. "Where do you want me?"

Rose took his arm and placed it around Ruth's neck. "Hold his wrist and put your other arm around his waist. Ruth, he can't use that right leg; so, hold him tight."

As Ruth put her arm around his waist, she looked down so as not to step on his foot. "Oh my!" She pulled him close to her, so she could support his weight. "Oh, my, my."

Rose carefully raised his left arm and placed it on her shoulder. He gritted his teeth to keep from cussing, it hurt so bad.

The two of them were able to get him to the chair. When he sat down he screamed out in pain.

He gritted his teeth together and growled at them as

they stood looking at him. "Will you cover me now, please."

Ruth Jones turned around. "Oh, Lord Jesus, forgive me."

Rose picked up the sheet and with a fake smile put the sheet around his shoulder. "I'm sorry."

With his good hand Deacon tried to pull the opening of the sheet together. "Can I have that drink now?"

Ruth turned her head to look at him. "You want some water?"

Rose was shaking her head at Ruth.

Deacon glared at Ruth. "Hell no, I don't want any water."

Chapter 69

Two weeks later Deacon was sitting in a chair on Rose's front porch. Rose came out with a pitcher of lemonade and two glasses. She poured the lemonade and handed him a glass, he took it and smiled at her. "Thanks."

The sun was shining and there was a slight breeze blowing from the south. Rose went back into the house and came out with her knitting bag. She reached in the bag and took out a bottle of rye whiskey and smiled at Deacon.

He looked at the bottle and poured the lemonade out. As she was pouring from the bottle he looked at her. "Thought you didn't allow the devils brew in your house."

"Normally, I don't."

"What changed?"

"You."

"What do you mean?"

"You've been here for two weeks. At first, you were constantly asking for a drink."

"Yeah, so?"

"You quit asking."

He lifted the glass to his nose, smelled it, smiled, and took a drink.

"You thought I was a drunk, didn't you?"

She smiled as she poured some in her lemonade. "The thought did cross my mind."

They sat there sipping their drinks. A lady walked by looking toward them, she smiled and waved. "Rose, Mister Deacon, nice day for a walk, don't you think?"

Rose smiled and waved back. "Yes, it is."

"She was one of them, wasn't she?"

Rose smiled and took a drink. "Yep."

A few minutes later, two more women walked by and waved.

Deacon took a sip from his glass. "What about them?"

"Only the one on the right."

"I got to get out of this town." He drank the glass empty and handed it to her to refill.

She looked at him. "Are you sure?"

"Yep. I need it to hide my shame."

She poured the glass half full. "You got nothing to be ashamed of."

He looked at her and took another drink. "Now I know I have to get out of this town."

She laughed.

Another lady walked by and waved. Deacon looked at Rose and she nodded her head.

"I got to get off this porch." He stood and reached for his crutch. She handed it to him. "Where are you going?"

"For a walk, a short walk."

"Do you care if I join you?"

"Not at all."

She helped him off the porch, and they started around the house toward the barn.

"Deacon can I ask you something?"

"Sure."

"Did you have anything to do with the preacher leaving town?"

"Maybe."

"Why?"

"Because he was a crook."

"It wasn't because you found out that he asked me to marry him?"

"That may have been part of it. Rose, he was no good. He's wanted in Colorado for running off with the church's bank account."

"So, you were trying to protect me."

"Yes, and the church."

She smiled. "Thank you."

When they reached the barn, Zach came out leading Dusty. "Hey Mister Deacon, I've been riding him every day. You know to give him exercise."

Deacon smiled at him and rubbed Dusty between the eyes. "Good. Keep him in shape for me, and I'll pay you for doing it."

"Oh, Mister Deacon, you don't have to pay me. I like riding him."

"Well let's see you do it."

Zach climbed on Dusty and rode down the street as Deacon and Rose watched.

Rose looked up at him. "You're good with him. Thank you."

"If my boy had lived, he would be about that age."

She looked at him and could see the sadness in his eyes.

"You want to tell me about it?"

"Not much to tell, he and my wife were killed during the war."

"Was her name Clara?"

Deacon turned and looked at her. "How... why do you ask?"

"I'm sorry, you kept calling her name when you were out. I just thought she might be your wife."

"No, she was a lady I knew. Let's go back to the house, I'm getting tired."

"Yes, let's do. We don't want you falling out here."

Deacon kept getting stronger as the days passed. He was able to walk now without using the crutch and was moving his left arm some, but it was still stiff and sore in the shoulder.

Rose watched out the back window as he was practicing his draw with his left hand. She had a gnawing in her stomach, and she couldn't make it go away. A tear ran down her face. She wiped it away and turned from the window.

Zach walked into the room and could also see Deacon out back. "He's getting stronger every day, ain't he, Ma?"

She ducked her head and walked past him. "Yes son, he is."

He turned and looked at his mother. "What's wrong, Ma?"

She ignored him and went to her bedroom and laid across the bed crying.

That night after Zach had gone to bed, Rose and Deacon were sitting in the kitchen drinking coffee. She got up and went to the cupboard and took down the bottle of rye.

Deacon smiled. "Now we are talking."

She waved the bottle back and forth in his face. "One glass only."

"Well, make it a large glass."

They both laughed. After pouring drinks for the both of them, she sat looking at him.

He took a sip from his glass and looked at her. "Rose, the other day you asked me about Clara."

"Yes, I'm sorry, you don't have to tell me."

"No, I want to. She was a lady that I knew in a town in north Texas. She was killed by Rat and his gang."

"Oh, Deacon, I'm so sorry. Did you love her?"

"Yeah, I guess I did. I didn't want to admit it at the time, but now that I look back I think I did."

Tears swelled up in her eyes. "It's hard to lose someone you love."

He drank down his glass of rye and stood, turning his back to her.

She stood and placed her hand on his back. "Deacon, will you hold me?"

"I would love to, but I shouldn't."

"Please, it's been so long since a man held me. Please hold me."

He turned around and put his arms around her as she buried her face into his chest. After a few moments, she looked up at him, and he kissed her forehead. "You are one fine looking woman. And you feel good in my arms. But this can't go any further."

"I know. You're leaving, aren't you?"

"Yes."

"When?"

"Tomorrow morning, I was going to stay another week, but I can't, not now. Zach told me about you crying this afternoon."

"Stay, please. You're not strong enough to ride."

"No, if I stay I may never leave."

"Would that be so bad?"

He smiled at her. "No. Problem is I've made too many enemies in my years and they will catch up to me some day, if I don't stay on the move."

"Take us with you."

"Rose, you know I can't do that. Every time I care for someone, something happens to them. I don't want anything to happen to you, or Zack."

"I'm willing to take that chance."

"I'm not."

She tiptoed and kissed him on the lips. He pulled her close and returned the kiss.

The next morning Deacon kissed Rose on the cheek as

he slipped out of bed. He quietly got dressed and went to the barn. He was saddling Dusty when she walked in.

"Were you going to leave without saying goodbye?"

"Rose, last night should have never happened."

She shook her head. "Maybe not. No regrets here. I know what you are, and I know what you do, and I don't care. I know you don't want to hear it, but I love you Deacon Reeves. I guess I will till the day I die."

He took her in his arms, inhaling the aroma of her. He lifted her chin with his finger and gave her a long passionate kiss as he slipped both arms around her and pulled her close to him. He released her, and she placed her head against his chest.

"Deacon."

"Yes."

She looked up at him. "Don't leave without saying goodbye to Zack. It would break his heart."

"I wouldn't do him that way. I'm only getting things ready." He smiled at her. "I was hoping for one more plate of eggs, and gravy, with some of them cathead biscuits of yours."

She smiled. "I think I can take care of that. You finish up here and come on back to the house. I'll go put some coffee on and get breakfast started."

He watched her as she walked back to the house.

After they had eaten, Deacon pushed his plate to one side and picked up his coffee cup. He took a sip and looked at Zack and then to Rose. "Do you have pencil and paper?"

She got up and went to the other room, when she returned she handed him the writing material.

He took it and wrote something down, then handed it back to her. "This is where you can reach me, if you ever need anything."

She took it from him and held it to her. Tears swelled in her eyes.

He stood and took her in his arms as Zack watched. He looked over her shoulder at Zack. "Come here."

As Zack walked up, he took both of them in his arms. "I'm not very good with goodbyes so please don't make this any harder than it already is."

Rose pulled away. "I'll fix you some things to take with you. So, you can eat on the trail."

Zack looked up at him. "Why do you have to leave?"

"I explained all this to your mother. She can fill you in after I leave."

"Ok, but I wish you would stay."

"Zack, you are a fine young man. You take care of your mother. She needs your help."

"Yes sir, I will."

The three walked to the barn. Deacon reached in his pocket and handed Rose four thousand dollars as Zack was placing the bridle on Dusty. "This is for taking care of me. Use part of it to buy Zack a good riding horse. A boy needs a good horse."

She looked at the money. "This is too much."

"Keep the money, I'm sure you can use it."

She put the money in the pocket of her apron. "Thank you."

He mounted Dusty and she walked up placing her hand on his bad leg. "Be careful."

"Yes ma'am, always."

He tilted his hat and heeled Dusty.

Tears ran down her face as she watched him ride away. "Goodbye, Deacon Reeves."

Zack put his arm around his mother's waist as he watched Deacon ride down the street. "Do you think he will come back?"

She smiled at him. "I don't know. Maybe."

Chapter 70

Deacon walked into the office of the Balancer Detective Agency. He removed his hat and smiled at the receptionist, the pretty Mrs. Smith. "Is the boss in?"

She looked up from her desk. "Deacon Reeves, I began to wonder if you were alive or not. We haven't heard from you in ages."

"Yes ma'am, I'm still alive and kicking, with one leg anyway."

"You want some coffee?"

"No, thanks, already drunk a pot."

The door to Mister Balancer's office swung open. "Deacon get in here."

Deacon entered the office and shut the door.

Mister Balancer looked him over and smiled. "My God, son, it's good to see you."

He sat behind his desk and took out two glasses and a bottle of Scotch. "I know it's early, but this calls for a celebration. Sit down and tell me what you've been up to."

Deacon took the glass of Scotch not really wanting it but not wanting to offend his boss either.

Deacon started talking and caught him up on everything. There were only a few minor interruptions when his boss would ask him questions for clarity.

When he finished with his story, Mister Balancer got up and walked to the window and looked out.

He turned around to face Deacon. "That's quite a story. You have been busy. You will be glad to know that officials here in the States are working with the Mexican government to locate other children."

"That's good. It's time someone did something."

"And Rat Dobbs is dead?"

"Yes sir."

"Did you collect the reward?"

"Sort of. I had it sent to the lady that took care of me while I was incapacitated."

He smiled at Deacon. "Son, you have a heart as big as Texas."

"Sir, I didn't need that money. I have my horse, saddle, and a bed roll. That's all I need."

"How's the arm and leg?"

"They're a lot better. I still walk with a bit of a limp. In time, I think, that will go away. And if you're asking if I can draw my shooter, the answer is yes."

"Are you ready to go back to work for me now?"

"Yes sir."

"Good, I got a job for you."

The End

Freedom Rides
R. D. Gregory

Freedom Rides
R. D. Gregory